BLOOD & STONE

A RADAZAN MYSTERY

Tamara M Bailey

Clan Destine
PRESS

First published by Clan Destine Press in 2024

PO Box 121,
Bittern Victoria 3918
Australia

National Library of Australia Cataloguing-In-Publication data:

BLOOD & STONE

ISBNs: 9781922904805 (paperback)
         9781922904812 (eBook)

Cover design by Willsin Rowe

Cover illustration by 'altocello' (Andrea L Farley)

Design & Typesetting by Clan Destine Press

Clan Destine
P R E S S

www.clandestinepress.net

To Chris

One

It was the brutality of the murder that struck Tomi Cardozo the most. She pulled on leather gloves and, sweeping her coattails away from the splayed entrails, crouched by the mutilated corpse. 'What have you got so far?'

From the other side of the body, Payana pointed her examining rod at the slash that opened the torso from heart to groin. 'The murder weapon appears to be a blade, probably a knife or dagger. The way the intestines and organs are protruding makes me think someone reached their hand in–' she mimicked the action in the air '–and yanked. It's not neat or professional.'

'No,' Tomi said. 'It's angry.' She studied the mess of innards. 'Any organs missing?'

'Not that I can see, but I'll know for sure when I do the autopsy.'

Tomi noticed a slight tremor in Payana's voice and lifted her gaze to her friend. 'Are you well?'

It wasn't like Payana to be unsettled by a crime scene. They'd worked messy cases before. Payana never flinched; other medica mavens called her Frost Queen behind her back.

Payana didn't quite look at the victim's face. 'Did you know him?'

'Of course not.' Payana scanned the apartment. Tomi turned to see what she was searching for. Sweepers wandered in and out, cloth masks over their nose and mouth to dull the reek as they catalogued items on long sheets of parchment. One was bent over a satchel on the floor with parchment pages spilled out.

'What's the matter?' Tomi said.

'Nothing.' Payana pointed her examining rod at the stained rug. Her work voice returned, professional and detached. 'The blood spatter suggests the victim was already lying on the floor when he was attacked.'

'Held down?' Tomi said, swatting flies from her face.

'There doesn't seem to be bruising to suggest it, and there isn't any sign of a struggle.'

'Huh.'

'He could've been sedated.' Payana nodded at two goblets and a bottle of rhee sitting on a drum table by one of the leather sofas. 'We'll check his stomach contents.'

The victim's expression showed no sign of the horror of his death. His eyeglasses were still on, albeit slightly askew. Tomi picked up his hand to inspect his ragged nails. Indents and tan lines on the base of his fingers suggested missing rings. But surely this wasn't just a robbery. It was too personal, too violent.

Which was why it didn't make sense for him to have been sedated. Why would the killer have a drink with the victim if they were in a murderous rage?

The sound of retching and a splatter came from the bedroom. Tomi gave Payana a questioning look.

'The artist,' Payana said. 'Finished sketching the body then ran to find the chamber pot.'

'Ah.' Tomi hesitated. Something felt... off. She couldn't put her finger on it. Payana was impeccable as always in expensive black pants and a matching waistcoat. There was purple paint on her lips and hints of shimmer-dust on her plump brown cheeks. Her long, dark braid was wrapped and pinned at the back of her head in the same style as Tomi's. Payana had got up and dressed as usual this morning, suggesting everything was fine at home.

Which meant something about the crime scene was troubling her.

'Are you sure you're well?'

'Of course I am.' Payana sounded irritated now, but that was nothing unusual. 'Are you still coming to dinner tonight?'

'I can't now.' Tomi gestured to the body. 'I just got put on a case.'

'That doesn't mean you have to stop eating. Besides, you've cancelled on us the last three times, and Mia's been desperate to tell you – well, you'll have to come around to find out.'

Tomi suspected she knew the reason for the persistent invitations, and, despite Payana's promising tone, Tomi wasn't sure she was ready to hear what Mia had to say. She doubted she'd ever be ready.

'You should come,' Payana said, as if that was the end of it. 'It'll be good to take your mind off... you know. Tomorrow.'

It felt like someone had filled Tomi's stomach with stones.

'Hey there, Cardozo.'

Sleazy Shadwell started over, his bright blue sweeper uniform reminding Tomi of a species of toxic frog she'd seen once at the menagerie. The colour screamed: *WARNING – DANGEROUS CREATURE.*

She wished her ex had been bright blue.

Sleazy Shadwell gave her the once-over as he sauntered towards them, but Payana pointed her bloodied examining rod at him and said, 'No.'

He held up his hands in surrender, backing away as casual as ever. On his way he passed Damian, who strode through the front door with a scroll under his arm. Damian was fresh off the academy baking tray, a complete cookie. He caught sight of the body and said, 'Did you know there's a dead guy on the floor?'

Tomi fought a laugh. 'The smell didn't give it away?'

'No different to the ablution blocks in my atrium.'

Payana gave Tomi a *who is this jester?* look.

'Damian, this is my medica maven, Payana Thraseep,' Tomi said. 'Payana, my new attending officer, Damian Kamara.'

'Since when did you get an apprentice?' Payana said.

'Since yesterday. Surprise.'

Payana eyed Damian, taking in the kid's cloud of black curls, wide nose and rich, dark eyes. He gave a hopeful smile when he realised he was being examined.

'Nope,' Payana said at last. 'I don't approve.'

Damian's smile widened. 'You'll learn to love me.'

'Payana doesn't love anyone,' Tomi said. 'She only tolerates them.' She nodded to the parchment under Damian's arm. 'Is that the victim's residential scroll?'

'Sure is.' He unrolled the parchment to skim through it. 'Professor Ivan

Jupel. Forty-one. Immigrated here about 20 years ago. No known relatives in the country. They're all still in Elumina, according to this.'

Tomi stood. She'd done a brief survey of the room as she'd entered, but it was only now she realised what was wrong. 'That's peculiar.'

'What?' Damian said.

She quirked an eyebrow at him. 'You tell me.'

He scanned the apartment. The balcony doors were open, but that wasn't unusual in this season. A pipe sat on the balcony table, next to a box herb garden. Inside the doors was the drum table with the goblets and open bottle. The goblets were mostly full, although their sticky sides meant at least one sip had been taken from each.

'The victim knew his killer,' Damian said.

'Though not well,' Tomi said, 'since there's no offering of smallfruits. That's essential when entertaining in high society. It says something interesting about their relationship – civil, but not friendly, perhaps.' She did a slow walk of the room, the heels of her boots clicking on the blackstone floor. 'But that's not the peculiar thing I noticed. Think about what's missing.'

She had Damian's full attention now. He ignored the stench, stalking the place with a keen eye. It was a single-occupant apartment, like Tomi's, only much more spacious. It had various plants in decorated pots and a heatherwood study desk. An ornamental box half-full of triller herb sat on an accent table, its lid askew, its potent smell layered beneath the corpse's. There was a kitchen sink, which marked the professor's social status more than anything else in the room. Cooking utensils hung from the granite wall. The carving knife gleamed especially bright.

Damian examined the bookshelves lining the walls. They held volumes of various topics and in several languages, as well as delicate trinkets and bronze ewers.

'There are spaces in the dust here,' he said. 'The professor's been robbed.'

'Good observation,' Tomi said, letting her tone suggest there was something else.

She didn't expect the cookie to pick up the intricacies of the job immediately – what would be the point of mentoring him if he already knew everything? Still, she'd hoped for a hint of brilliance. He was supposed to be one of the best cadets in the city.

'I don't know–' he said, turning slowly in his spot, and she found herself surprisingly disappointed '–unless you're talking about the missing blood?'

He shot her a grin, and she realised he'd been baiting her. 'The killer made a mess with Jupel's body. There should be blood everywhere. Smears on the door handle. Splatters on the floor. Drops in the sink, assuming the killer would've tried to wash themselves afterwards. But the only blood I can see is on the rug.'

Tomi suppressed a smile of her own. 'Well done.'

'The killer could've mopped afterwards,' Payana said. She sounded less impressed.

'No.' Tomi crouched to run her gloved finger across the stone. It came back streaked with red dust. She held it up for Damian and Payana to see.

'What is it?' Damian said.

'I'm not sure, but I noticed it when I picked up this.'

Damian leaned in to examine the small brass key she held out. 'Where did you find that?'

'Here, between the body and the door.'

'Do you think the killer dropped it? Or was it there before?'

'I think the killer was holding it during the murder. There's a splash of blood on it.'

Damian plucked the key from her hand and tucked it in his fist while miming a stabbing. 'Like this, right? So how would the blood have gotten on it? The key is completely covered.'

'Except,' Tomi said, taking the key back and pointing to the loop at the top, 'it was on a keyring or the ribbon of a pouch. It was dangling out of their hand.'

Damian moved to take the key back from her, but it slipped between them and landed on the ground, tinking noisily. His curls quivered as he swooped to get it. Maybe he was more nervous than he was letting on.

Tomi turned to the sweeper cataloguing the contents of the professor's work satchel. 'Get a sample of this dust, would you?'

The sweeper headed over with a pouch of vials and a brush.

'Anything interesting in the professor's bag?' Tomi said.

'Nothing but a few books and what I think are lecture notes. Can't read a word of them – the handwriting's atrocious.'

'Take them anyway, just in case.' She handed the sweeper the key. 'More evidence. There's blood on it. Bring that carving knife on the kitchen wall to Particulars as well.'

'You think it's the murder weapon?'

'Won't know until we check it.'

'Cardozo!' Sleazy Shadwell strode out from the bedroom. 'You need to see this.'

From her spot by the corpse, Payana whipped her examining rod towards him and said, 'If you're about to make some innuendo, I will cram this so far up your nose it'll hit your brain.'

'No,' Sleazy Shadwell said. Tomi saw the way his nostrils flared and his eyes stretched a little too wide. Her curiosity was piqued. It took a lot to unnerve a sweeper. 'Just come here.'

She followed him into the bedroom, Damian at her heels. The room was decked out with more shelves and trinkets and several hanging pot plants. The sketch artist was curled in the corner of the bedroom, weakly hugging the chamber pot to his chest as he stared, ashen faced, towards the floor where the bed had been pushed away.

A false stone had been lifted to reveal a cavern of treasures – coloured cloth, jars of oils and dried flowers, pouches of powders and bones, a silver chalice, a ceremonial knife.

'I think we've found ourselves a witch,' said Sleazy Shadwell, breathless.

'Ah,' said Tomi softly. '*Shit.*'

Two

'Is this bad for you?' Damian said as they walked down the
curl of the atrium's interior balcony. Apartments lined the perimeter of the
cylindrical building to leave a communal space in the middle. A skylight
arched five storeys over their heads, allowing morning sunshine to flood in
to the central enclosure, which was different to the one in Tomi's atrium.
Rather than grass and plants, it was aquatic-based, with waterfalls and river
reeds. Minnisks played inside, their large, furry bodies loping across the
rocks before diving gracefully into the water. One lifted its brown face
to look at Tomi. A fish hung from its sharp teeth. Its round ear twitched
before it turned away to rip into its meal.

'You know...' Damian prompted when Tomi didn't answer, 'because of
tomorrow?'

Tomi was unsurprised he'd found out about the hearing. With the way
things currently were at the station, it was to be expected that someone
would have warned her cookie about his law-breaking, witch-loving
superior.

'I'll be fine,' she said.

They reached the ground floor. Only a few residents still lingered, most
having left for work. A teenage girl with frizzy brown hair stood at the

calling booth by the entrance, her hand cupped over her mouth so she could she whisper into the receiver. A child played alone in the playground. Two men sat, talking and smoking, by the oven fires. Blue clouds unfurled from their pipes as their attention flicked up to Professor Ivan Jupel's open door, where sweepers hurried in and out.

Tomi headed to the apartment with a gold number three nailed onto the wood. After a sharp rap, a man opened up. He had thin, owl-eyed glasses and a moustache that curled up at the ends. He couldn't have seen more than 25 frosts, but there was a heaviness to his eyes that spoke of deep shock.

'*Seno* Georgio Herliz?' Tomi said.

'That's me.' His voice was laden with resignation.

Tomi pointed to the brass badge clipped to the right side of her belt next to her pistol holster. 'I'm Officer Tomi Cardozo. This is my AO, Damian Kamara. Would you mind if we asked you a few questions?'

The man moved aside. 'Of course. I didn't go to work in case you needed to talk to me.'

'Thank you.' Tomi stepped across the threshold. 'You were the one who called the Justice Department, correct?'

Herliz twirled his moustache. It seemed to be more of a gesture of stress than a grooming one. 'I went to check on Ivan this morning before work, and I found him – I found him–' He choked off.

'That must have been awful,' Tomi said gently. 'I'm so sorry for your loss.' She guided him to a sofa. His apartment was larger than the professor's, as was usual in atriums. Lower floors tended to be larger, space enough for families. Even so, a quick scan of the room told her that he likely lived alone. The place was brimming with even more curios than the professor's, although these were less delicate and more on the bizarre side. Like the stuffed woodland creature crouched in the corner with a green hat hanging from one of its long ears. Or rocks cracked like eggs to reveal shimmering crystals inside. Heat flooded the place from the chimney pipe – the ground-floor apartments backed directly onto the oven fires – and a musty smell lingered in the air. What did this young man do to afford a place so big?

While Tomi sat on the couch across from Herliz, Damian shut the door and remained beside it, the professor's residential scroll tucked under his arm. He took out a department-issued parchment book and jotted something down with his scratch stick.

Herliz pulled a handkerchief from the pocket of his embroidered blue waistcoat to dab at his forehead. His black curls were damp with sweat. Grief? Or was he nervous about something?

'Did you know Professor Jupel well?' Tomi said.

'We would often share a pot of tea in the communal parlour. Incredibly clever man. So much insight, so much passion.'

'Were you aware that he was a witch?'

There was a beat, then Herliz exhaled with an 'Ahhh' and dropped his forehead to his fist. 'I suspected,' he said, his eyes closed. 'But I never knew for sure.'

The scrapes of the scratch stick stopped.

'*Seno* Herliz, any activity suggesting the presence of a witch must be reported to the Justice Department by order of the Supreme Court,' Tomi said.

She felt Damian's weighted stare and knew she sounded like a hypocrite.

Herliz lifted his head, mouth tight with defiance. 'Ivan was a good man. He never hurt anyone. He was here to pass on his wisdom.'

'I understand, but it's not up to us to pick and choose which laws to follow.'

The correct thing to do now was charge Herliz for breaking the Metropolitan Civics Agreement. Proper procedure had to be followed – Damian was right behind her, scribing the entire conversation.

Instead, she said, 'When did you last see the professor alive?'

'Yesterday evening, around nine bells.' Herliz showed no indication he knew how narrowly he'd avoided trouble. 'We had a drink together after supper in the communal dining area–' He moved the handkerchief over his mouth, failing to suppress a choking sob. 'I'm sorry,' he said when he regained himself. 'I'm not handling this very well.'

'I understand. I promise we won't be long. I just want to clarify some de–'

'I think I saw the killer.'

Tomi stopped. 'You *saw* the killer?'

'No, well, I can't be sure. I was coming back from the communal ablutions last night and I saw *someone* hurrying down the balcony from the top floor. I didn't get a good look at them; the lanterns were dimmed.'

'What time was this?'

'Just after 11 bells. The rest of the place was quiet. We don't normally have visitors so late. Actually, Ivan doesn't normally have visitors at all. He's not the social type. The only time he leaves the atrium is to go to work, as far as I know. But the frost doors are locked at 10 bells, so if the person was a visitor, someone would've had to let them in.'

'This person wasn't a resident?'

'I don't think so.'

'What did they look like?'

'They had a coat on.' Herliz squeezed his eyes shut. There was a stretch of silence, except for the ticking gearwheels of the timekeeper on the wall and Damian's scratch stick. 'It was tan. Armiene suede, by the look of it. The hood was raised so I couldn't see their face.'

'Did you see them leave the atrium?'

'No. I'd returned to my apartment before they reached the ground floor.'

'Did you come out again before morning?'

'I'm afraid not. And I didn't hear anything else. I'm a very heavy sleeper.'

Tomi watched a bead of sweat trickle down Herliz's cheek. 'Was Professor Jupel acting differently over the past few days? Like he might've known he was in danger?'

'No, I... I don't think so.'

'Can you think of anyone who might have wanted to hurt Professor Jupel?'

There was a brief beat before Herliz answered. 'Not really. He was the quiet sort.'

'No one knew he was a witch?'

'I couldn't say.'

'What about other areas of his life? You can't think of anything amiss? The smallest detail could help.'

Herliz mopped at his neck. 'Yesterday he complained about a staff member at the University. He didn't mention a name.'

'What was the complaint?'

'Something about them being untrustworthy. But he didn't go into details. He normally doesn't speak ill of any of his colleagues, so it was a surprise when he let it slip. He was quick to change the subject.'

Tomi checked to make sure Damian was keeping up before continuing. 'Tell me more about this person you saw last night. What sort of frame did they have? Tall, short?'

'Medium height. A bit stocky, although maybe not – the coat was bulky, like it had something in the pockets.'

'Could've been the trinkets,' Damian said.

'Do you know if Professor Jupel had anything worth stealing in his apartment?' Tomi asked Herliz.

He gave a surprised chuckle. 'Everything in his apartment is valuable.

14

He's a collector of cultural artefacts. It's what we talk about the most. Even I'm impressed with his finds, and I see all sorts of precious items in my line of work.'

Tomi surveyed the strange things in the apartment again. 'What do you do?'

'I'm the junior overseer at Eversea Shipping.'

'That's an impressive job for someone your age.'

'My grandfather is part-owner of the company. We trade in rare and curious items from across the continent. That's why I had a drink with the professor yesterday. He has triller herb shipped in specially from Elumina; insists it's better than the stuff here. I drop a pouch off to him on the second-last day of every month. It's enough to fill that lovely ornamental box of his.'

The sentence had started fondly, but his gaze lowered as he finished it. It had probably just hit him that he would never be dropping triller herb to the professor again.

'It was brutal,' he whispered, 'what happened to him.'

'We'll do everything we can to catch this person, *Seno* Herliz.' Tomi stood, then paused. 'If you can't be sure the person you saw last night was the killer, does that mean you didn't see any bloodstains on their coat?'

Herliz frowned thoughtfully. 'No, I don't think so.'

'Nothing at all?'

'No.' He tilted his head. 'Wait. Surely blood would have been all over them? Considering how Ivan…' He curled his fingers around his handkerchief.

'What about the stranger's hands?' Tomi said.

'I don't know. They were in their pockets.'

Tomi nodded. 'Thank you, *Seno* Herliz.'

Herliz walked them out of the apartment and closed the door after them.

'You think the killer cleaned their clothes the same way they cleaned the room?' Damian said as he and Tomi headed to the next apartment. The child who had been in the playground was watching the minnisks now. The two smokers and the teenage girl were gone.

It was so quiet – a striking difference to her own atrium. The Clinker District was filled with artisans who haunted the common areas, moaning about their *art* and their *angst*. Rest days were for whenever and night-time didn't necessarily mean bedtime.

Afflaris doesn't care what time it is, Tom-eee, her elderly neighbour, Lyrica, proclaimed when Tomi pounded on the wall at two in the morning to stop her from singing operetta tunes out the window.

Tomi was sure the Tassela of Inspiration had better sleep etiquette than that.

'I suspect,' she murmured, 'the cleanliness has something to do with the red dust.'

'How do you figure?' Damian said.

'The dust was everywhere there should've been blood, which makes me think it *was* the blood.'

'But blood doesn't dry as powder,' Damian said. 'Unless – oh.' He lowered his voice to a hush. 'You think the murderer was a witch too?'

The nod she gave was barely perceptible.

He whistled lowly. 'The other JOs are going to be so jealous.'

This time she couldn't appreciate his humour. A killer witch on the loose didn't just complicate the case.

It destroyed her chance of being acquitted tomorrow.

Three

A KILLER WITCH AS DAMIAN'S FIRST CASE. WHAT A LEGENDARY beginning to his career. Sure, a man had been murdered. Mutilated, potentially by a witch, and the rancid stench alone almost had Damian losing his breakfast. He'd seen bodies in the morgue, preserved and cold and empty. It wasn't the same as the wet, visceral experience of the recently deceased Professor Ivan Jupel.

But even his heaving stomach couldn't mar the fact that he was here. This was real. He'd been scribing for *Tomi Cardozo* all morning.

He still couldn't believe his application to be mentored by Tomi Cardozo had been accepted. At 31, just 10 years older than Damian, Officer Cardozo had the highest closure rate for murder cases in the whole of Radaza. She'd stopped a massacre, led a task force to take down a major human trafficking ring, and caught the man who'd assassinated a city councillor. Criminals whispered about Tomi Cardozo the way children whispered about monsters in the dark.

Everyone at the academy had told Damian not to bother putting in a request to be her attending officer. They said that even if he managed to graduate in the ninety-ninth percentile (which he had), allowing him to skip the mandatory five years in general duties (which he could), Tomi Cardozo never took on apprentices.

Damian was glad he hadn't listened. He'd only wanted to work with the best, and his determination had paid off.

Now, not only was he working a potential witch murder, but Tomi had tasked him with taking this last interview alone. While she checked the resident registry for anyone missing from the atrium, he was sitting with a resident in the communal dining area, entrusted to ask the right questions and watch for signs of a lie.

Not that the guy Damian was interviewing seemed likely to lie. *Seno* Bontly was plenty happy to say exactly what he thought about Jupel and witches and Elumenese in general.

'This witch business has gotten out of hand,' Bontly was saying, his war medals glinting in the sunlight. Damian had a feeling he'd put them on specifically for the interview. 'Do you know people are selling candles and amulets down at the Traders' Market like it's some sort of jest? No one's taking it seriously anymore. Now look what's happened.'

'Uh huh.' Damian wrote down Bontly's complaints and added a note questioning why old men were always grouchy. Behind them, the minnisks splashed about in their water enclosure. 'Do you know of anyone who might've wanted to hurt Professor Jupel?'

'How should I know? He barely socialised. The last time I saw him talk to a person besides Georgio Herliz was his frost lover, Serillia something. But that was a year ago. She hasn't come by since – probably realised what a nasty piece of work he was. I tell you what, that professor's tainted our home. It's not hard to guess he was killed by another witch, too. Violent, sneaky cratters, the lot of them. You need to flush 'em out and shoot 'em all.'

'By myself?'

'It's the Elumenese that's the problem,' Bontly said, ignoring him. 'They're strolling into Agriterra whenever they like. Those dally folk in Immigration need to do their damned job. There should be rigorous checks at the borders.'

'Not every Elumenese person is a witch, *Seno* Bontly.'

'But every witch is Elumenese.' Bontly gave Damian a sneering once-over. 'They shouldn't be giving you people positions of power. We can't tell whether you've got magic or not just by looking. Ministers, judges, justice officials – any one of you could be a witch hiding in plain sight. The only way to be sure we're free of the plant fuckers is to kick out the lot of you.'

'How do you fuck a plant?'

'Think you're smart, do you, boy?' Bontly grabbed his cane and hauled himself out of his chair. 'On your feet. Go on. Get up.'

'Er, why?'

'Get up, you coward, and face me like a soldier.'

'Is this a fight?'

'Get up!'

'*Seno*, I'm not going to fight you. You're, like, a million years old.'

'Stand up!' Bontly's neck tendons were bulging. Residents walking along the curved balcony or crossing the communal area had stopped to look.

Damian stood with a sigh. His biceps were about three times the size of Bontly's. Working at the docks since he was 14 had its (few) upsides.

Bontly faltered slightly when he realised Damian was almost two lengths tall.

'Let me make sure I'm understanding you,' Damian said. 'You're insulting an officer of the law and threatening lethal violence against witches?'

Bontly shifted his weight. 'I have the right to voice my concerns.'

'Oh, I know. I was just checking there were no miscommunications. Because I have a few opinions too. For example, *I* believe Perlians should've stayed away after you got chased out in the Rebellion.'

'Don't speak of the Rebellion to me, you ignorant blassard,' Bontly snarled. 'I fought for Radaza's freedom before your shit-eating parents were even born.'

'You're making a lot of assumptions, *Seno* Bontly. Shall I do the same? You hate Elumenese people. You live in the same building as the murder victim. You just told me you believe witches should be killed. Now, if we were hunting an anti-witch acquaintance of Jupel, who do you think we'd suspect?'

'That – you – I didn't even know Jupel was a witch until today!'

'So you say.'

'How *dare* you accuse me of lying!' Bontly lifted his cane and Damian caught it mid-swing.

'What in the name of the Tassela is going on?'

Tomi strode up, her coattails whipping behind her. Her brown, freckle-strewn face was a thunderstorm.

'Your attendant here is a menace.' Bontly changed the trajectory of his cane to jab it towards Damian. 'I thought soffs were supposed to look after the citizens of Radaza, not threaten them.'

Tomi threw a knife-like glare at Damian before saying to Bontly, 'I apologise profusely for Officer Kamara's behaviour. Be assured he'll receive a reprimand.'

'Good!'

'Thank you for your assistance. We'll do everything we can to get the perpetrator off the streets. If you think of anything else or have any further questions, please call the station and ask for me directly.'

Bontly harrumphed. He glowered at Damian but was appeased enough to limp away.

'He could very well be the murderer,' Damian said as Tomi took his parchment book from him. 'He hates Elumenese people and thinks witches should be shot.'

'But he has an alibi.' She pointed to Damian's notes from the interview. 'You've got here that he was playing cards with five other residents until two bells.'

Damian had forgotten about that.

'People can be despicable without being murderers,' Tomi said, slapping the book against his chest. 'We can't arrest them for that.'

'Unfortunately.'

Tomi didn't smile. She headed out the frost doors. Damian followed meekly behind. This wasn't how his first day in the field was supposed to go.

Their grousdu were waiting at a tethering post in the shadow of a skybridge. Tomi's was ripping the branches off a perfectly manicured hedge.

'Fin,' she said, sighing.

Finley turned a beady black eye to her and rasped crankily. She stroked his long neck, making shushing noises until his bristled butterhoney feathers relaxed. Damian had the feeling she was keeping her back to him on purpose.

'Hello, Brix,' he murmured as he untied his own grousdu.

She clacked her beak beneath her leather mask in greeting. He climbed onto her saddle and glanced at Tomi. Her bronze skin and curly hair – braided and intricately pinned on her head – marked her as Elumenese too, though from a more southern region. Did people like Bontly single her out as well?

'The thing is,' she said, mounting Finley, 'when you're wearing the badge – and a pistol – *you're* the one in the position of power.'

'Bontly–'

'Was an 80-year-old man. You're a young, fit officer. Do you know how it looked with you looming over him like that? Don't get arrogant. Just because you're an AO now doesn't mean it has to stay that way. If you get busted down to general duties, you'll have to complete your mandatory five years before you can reapply for a position as a justice official.' She flicked Finley's reins. 'Trust me. I know from experience.'

Damian decided against making a joke and flicked Brix's reins to follow.

You're the best cadet to come through in years, kid, his training officer had said at graduation. *But if you don't stop being so headstrong, they'll boot you straight out again.*

'Sorry,' Damian said as their grousdu broke into a trot.

Tomi didn't reply. Theirs were the only birds on the street. People didn't live in the Shores if they couldn't afford a minnisk. The long-bodied steeds galloped over the smooth eggstone roads, their owners strapped behind their shoulders. There were even a few minnisk-drawn carriages, which must've come from the Black Ivory District.

After dodging a shaggy heartbeast hauling a cart of supplies, Tomi said, 'There were a few residents missing from the atrium today.' Her voice was still cool but less unfriendly than before. 'It's a rest day tomorrow; we'll come back for more interviews then.'

Without giving Damian a chance to respond, she spurred Finley into a run. Damian followed. It would take at least an hour to reach the University. Herliz had mentioned there may have been an issue with one of the staff, so they were planning a thorough interrogation of Jupel's colleagues.

They left the Shores and the grousdu were able to pick up the pace as the eggstone pavement gave way to rougher common rockslate.

'Let's grab a bite,' Tomi said as they passed a food strip in the Commerce District.

Damian was relieved. He was starving but hadn't wanted to be the one to suggest it.

Stalls offered pots of bubbling stews, stuffed meese intestines, cauldrons of juice, and fire ovens of pastries, breads and flatcakes. After leaving their grousdu at a tethering post, Tomi treated Damian to seared fish in orka sauce and a harshnut loaf. They sat at a communal bench among the woodsmoke, listening to people in fancy suits talk about pre-frost overtime and import tax. The buildings were tall enough to shade them from the sun.

'Listen,' Damian said, picking at his bread. He kept his voice below the rabble. 'As much as I never want to talk about Bontly again, you should know he suspects the killer of being a witch.'

'Mm.' Tomi sipped her spiced vegetable soup. 'He's not the only neighbour to come to that conclusion.'

Across from them, a group of traders broke into raucous laughter over an article in a newscloth.

'We could be wrong,' Damian murmured. 'Right?'

Tomi's tight smile wasn't reassuring. 'It might not be our problem for much longer, depending on tomorrow.'

'Right, your hearing. What happened, anyway?'

'Too much wine, a frosty night, and a spiteful ex.'

'I don't mean who dobbed you in. What happened with the *witch*?' He mouthed the word.

'It was years ago. A cookie blunder. Not something I'd do again.'

'Was it why you got demoted from your AO position?'

'No, that was a separate mistake.' She tore apart her fried bread. 'You'll make a lot of them as an officer. Trust me.'

'Oh, I know,' Damian said, thinking of Bontly. 'If it helps, I didn't write down the thing Georgio Herliz said.'

'What thing?'

'About how he suspected Jupel of being a... you know.'

Tomi dropped the bread onto her plate.

'You didn't charge him for failing to report it,' Damian said, wondering why she looked so shocked. 'I figured if I wrote it down, you'd get into trouble. Especially considering tomorrow.'

'You can't lie in official documents.'

'It was the *tiniest* omission. And I did it to protect you.'

'I appreciate your loyalty, but don't do it again. Each deceit is a step towards full-blown corruption. You should–dammit.'

Damian followed Tomi's line of sight to a woman wearing a red corset and multi-layered skirts. She sauntered up the street, calling silkily for people to buy sweet rolls from her tray.

Damian grinned. 'Got a problem with the Honeybun Girl?'

But when he turned back, Tomi had already abandoned her food and was heading for the grousdu.

Four

Tomi's heart was still unsettled when they reached the University grounds. She'd known Umbrine worked in the Commerce District but hadn't expected such a cruel sense of humour from the heavens. What were the chances the Honeybun Girl would be in *that* section at *that* hour?

An omen for tomorrow?

She tried to push it from her mind as she slowed Finley to an amble. The University covered an entire peninsula extending into the Madeira River. Its five main buildings, set out like a star, were as grand as any in the Church District – towering greystone walls, soaring spires and gleaming stained-glass windows. Tunnels connected them to each other and smaller buildings within the fort-style layout.

Tomi scanned the students milling at the main entrance, where the motto *Love of Wisdom* was carved into the arched stone. They were smoking, eating or studying on the steps in the sun. The day was warm but the leaves were brown and crunchy underfoot, and the northern hills glittered ominously. It was the last day of Harvest. Moonrise would mark the start of Harrow, and sometime during the month the wild season would end abruptly with the settling of the frost. Sometimes the wandering frost was early, sometimes it was late, but always it came during Harrow.

She noticed many of the students had armiene coats draped over their satchels.

She and Damian dismounted. Her black-and-green-striped pants flexed and stretched with her movements. Costly, considering they were imported all the way from Perlia, but worth it. They had ruffles instead of cuffs to match her frilly, high-collared shirt. Mia delighted in the fact that she had instilled a sense of fashion into Tomi, who had only ever cared for practicality at first. It was one of Mia's self-proclaimed highest achievements, and that included graduating with a law degree.

After Tomi and Damian tethered their grousdu, they headed inside. The lobby was magnificent. The greystone glowed amber from countless oil lanterns positioned across columns, railings and archways. The high ceilings were painted in a style popular at the time of the Perlian Invasion, and the mouldings and trimmings boasted extraordinary craftswork. Tomi knew enough about architecture to appreciate what she was seeing.

Damian stared, mouth open like a gapper fish. 'And here I thought the Shores had glimmer.'

'Haven't you been inside a church?'

'We go to a local parish. It's small, but it's close to home.'

Something snagged in Tomi's mind. It was the same sensation as a piece of clothing getting caught and tugging her backwards, except it was a tug on her thoughts, and it always happened whenever an interviewee gave her information that conflicted with what she already knew. What had Damian just said to spark it?

An older woman in a blue suit smiled from the greeting desk. Tomi dismissed the snag, at least for now. Damian was hardly her main concern, and besides, she owed him. Despite her scolding, she had to admit he'd done her a huge service by not writing down that Herliz suspected Jupel had been a witch. Ordinarily, she would've made him add it to his notes. But the non-chronological order might raise questions and get him into trouble, and Tomi didn't want to risk it.

They headed towards the woman in the blue suit. She was standing next to a lanky youth who had a strong chin and the careless air of someone who got whatever he wanted. His hair reminded Tomi of grousdu feathers.

'Good day,' Tomi said. 'I'm Justice Official Tomi Cardozo, and this is my attending officer, Damian Kamara.'

'Welcome,' said the woman. 'I'm Chancellor Gloudling.' She pressed her right hand over her heart.

Tomi returned the formal greeting as Gloudling gestured to the young man. 'This is Nomik, Professor Jupel's AP.'

'Attending... professor?' Damian said, taking notes.

'Assistant to the professor.' Nomik had the clipped, formal accent of the Perlian elite. There was no mockery in his tone for Damian's mistake, though he gave a wry smile as he said, 'I'd say it was a pleasure if it weren't for the circumstances.'

'You've heard, then?' Tomi said.

Gloudling started to speak, but Nomik answered for her. 'Yes, I called the professor's atrium this morning to find out why he was late. One of his neighbours informed me of the death. We've been waiting for someone from the Justice Department to arrive.'

'I'm sorry for your loss.'

Gloudling cupped a palm to her forehead. Her nails sparkled with ochre paint, and chunky rings adorned her fingers. 'I couldn't believe it. Poor man.'

'You were close?' Tomi said.

'Unfortunately, no. I oversee a great deal of staff here.'

'And you?' Tomi asked Nomik. 'As his AP, you must've had a lot to do with him.'

'He was difficult to befriend. I have a feeling he didn't let any of us see past the surface.'

Tomi wondered if the same could be said for Nomik. He exuded geniality, as if he could make conversation with a bunch of sea rocks, but something about him felt *too* casual. His sleeves were rolled up to his elbows, revealing strong, tanned arms. The black boots over his soft-fur trousers may have been mistaken for an everyday outfit if not for the brown embroidered waistcoat that would've cost as much as Tomi's annual salary. His coin pouch hung freely on his belt, unlike hers, which was tucked into the inner pocket of her tailcoat next to her dagger of emboldened steel. He wanted to appear approachable yet couldn't help touting his wealth.

'You should know,' Gloudling said, drawing Tomi's attention away from the AP, 'that I signed off on an incident report about Professor Jupel last monsoon season.'

'What happened?'

'A tussle between him and another staff member. When I asked him about it, he dismissed it as a disagreement that had gotten out of hand. He claimed they'd been drinking at the time.'

'Do you know the identity of the other staff member?'

'It's slipped my mind – as you can imagine, a lot happens around here. I've sent a messenger to fetch the report from the South River Archives. They'll have it at your station by sunset.'

Tomi turned to Nomik. 'You don't know who it was?'

'I'm afraid not. It happened before I became his AP.'

'Did he have any other problems with his colleagues that you were aware of?' she said. 'Disagreements, personal or professional?'

'He had some issues with professors in the Religion Department, but they cause problems for everyone.' Nomik glanced at Gloudling. Her only response was a slight crease in the brow. Tomi couldn't tell whether she disapproved of the religion professors' controversies or Nomik's statement.

'You should ask Professor Quaide,' Nomik continued. 'He shares an office with Professor Jupel. Maybe he'll know more.'

'Yes, well, we'd like to go through Professor Jupel's belongings and speak to any staff members or students who were close to him.'

Gloudling nodded, her grey-streaked bob swinging. 'Of course. Whatever we can do to help. Nomik can take you to his office. Please come and see me if you have any further questions.'

Tomi and Damian thanked her, then left the lobby to follow Nomik through a passage to the next building. Brass signs on the archway, blackened from smoky oil lanterns, listed the locations of lecture theatres. The place was surprisingly quiet. Tomi saw more caretakers doing pre-frost structural checks than she did students. No one was wearing a coat inside.

'What did Professor Jupel teach?' she asked Nomik.

'Three languages, ethics and philosophy.'

Damian fell slightly behind, writing and walking at the same time. 'Nomik, what was your full name?'

There was a beat before the answer was forthcoming. 'Nomik Noritof.'

'And your major?' Tomi said.

'Philosophy.'

'Are you going to subsume?'

'Most APs commit to the University.'

'What about you? Are you planning to become a lifelong learner?'

Nomik's lips quirked. 'I doubt it.'

Tomi couldn't figure out what was funny. Maybe it was a University thing. An inside joke. Still, there was something about Nomik that bothered her. Was it the lack of grief over the death of his mentor? The feeling that his amicability felt like a façade? Or was this the normal way Perlian elite acted, and she'd just forgotten?

The more she puzzled over it, the more she wondered whether she should've taken longer to interview each resident in Jupel's atrium. What if she'd missed something? She certainly felt there was more to Georgio Herliz's story, just from the small pauses and shifts in his countenance. But what if she was looking for something that wasn't there?

The Tassela damn it. She was second-guessing herself, and she knew exactly who to blame. The same thing had happened a month ago when everything had first fallen apart. Seeing the Honeybun Girl was a reminder of her grievous error in judgement. Tomi might very well be kissing her job goodbye because she'd trusted someone she shouldn't have.

She had to snap out of it. There was a murder to solve, and Jupel deserved a competent justice official on his case.

She decided to switch songs with Nomik. 'Do you own an armiene coat?'

He glanced at her, eyebrows high. 'Why's that?'

'Yes or no?'

'Yes,' he said, 'of course I do. Everyone has one this season.'

'Everyone with coin,' Damian corrected under his breath.

They reached the next building, which had a bronze plaque over the archway that said *Whistcliffe*.

'This is our section,' Nomik said. 'I hope you're ready to meet Professor Quaide.' Before Tomi could ask what he meant by that, he knocked on a door.

'Yes?' came a gruff voice from inside. 'What?'

Nomik opened up.

'Oh, it's you,' said the voice. 'What do you want?'

Tomi and Damian stepped through the arched doorway after Nomik. The interior looked more like a room in a library. Bookshelves lined the walls, as crammed as those in Ivan Jupel's apartment. A double staircase curved behind the twin desks, leading to a small mezzanine where maps and wooden chests glowed beneath a star lamp.

The angriest looking man Tomi had ever seen sat at the left desk. He was a stocky, squat fellow with a broad-bridged nose and scars down his left cheek. The peak of his head was completely bald, though long hair flowed from the sides, and he had a white bushy beard.

'Who're you?' he asked.

Tomi formally identified herself and Damian. She'd barely gotten the words out before Quaide launched to his feet. 'What are you doing, boy?'

Nomik almost dropped the parchment pages he'd been emptying from the drawers on the vacant desk. 'Clemency help me, old man, you're going to make my threads jump right from my skin one day.'

'We asked him to look through Professor Ivan Jupel's things,' Tomi said. 'You're aware of his death?'

'Of course I'm aware. Despicable business.'

'Were you and Professor Jupel close?'

Quaide snorted. 'No one gets "close" to Ivan Jupel. He's a mystery masked amid mysteries. And I should know. I'm the Head Professor of Enigmatics.'

Damian frowned as he scribed.

'Enigmatics?' Tomi said.

'A branch of philosophy dealing in the unknown.' Quaide said the last few words with relish, as if his area of study was the most intriguing possible topic.

Nomik rolled his eyes.

'I suppose we're in the same landscape, then,' Tomi said. 'Are you aware of anyone who may have wanted to harm Professor Jupel, or did he have any issues with other staff members? There was an incident last monsoon season – a tussle between him and another staff member – but Chancellor Gloudling can't remember who it was.'

Quaide tugged his beard thoughtfully. 'A tussle? That doesn't sound like Ivan.' His attention shifted to Nomik, who had finished emptying the study desk and was now selecting books from the shelves. 'What did he tell you about it?'

'About as much as you'd expect: nothing.'

'Nomik mentioned there might have been some issues with professors in the Religious Department,' Tomi said.

'Ah, yes,' Quaide said with a furrowed brow. 'The Way of the Weavers.'

Tomi suppressed a sigh. She'd suspected as much.

'Professor Jupel's philosophy branch specialised in intercultural communications,' Quaide continued. 'He consulted with officials on how to establish relationships with settlements across the Freelands of Elumina on behalf of Agriterra.'

'This was a problem?'

'Absolutely. The Weavers can't stand the thought that we might be talking to witches.'

Tomi and Damian exchanged a glance.

'Speaking of,' she said, 'were you aware Ivan Jupel was a witch?'

'What?' Quaide bellowed, then gave a roar of laughter. 'That rascal! He should've said.'

'You jest,' Nomik said.

Quaide leaned forward as if conspiring. 'You know, my grandmother was a witch. Got outed in '62. The whole family was banished, but I was allowed to stay because I didn't have a lick of magic. Too much Perlian in the blood.'

'They let you stay?' Tomi said in disbelief.

'Oh yes,' Quaide said cheerfully. 'TADOW were horrifically invasive. They watched me for over three years, raiding my home every few months to keep me on my toes. But they didn't find anything, so I could remain in Radaza and continue my studies.'

'I thought every child of a witch had magic,' Damian said.

'Not necessarily.' Quaide's enthusiasm was palpable.

Tomi realised his thick, furrowed eyebrows and scarred cheek were misleading; besides his initial gruffness, he seemed perfectly cordial.

He pulled out a few books from the shelf and opened them to various pages. 'There are all sorts of theories as to why, but the common one among witches is—'

'Professor Quaide,' Tomi said. 'I'm sorry, we're not here to ask about magical bloodline theories unless it has something to do with Ivan Jupel's murder.'

Quaide snapped shut the book he was holding. 'If someone knew Ivan was a witch, that's all the motive you need. The nonsense Weavers spout about witches being an abomination. An abomination! Imagine. Clemency blessed those folk with magic, and humans snarl like jealous children. Then you've got your anti-witch groups, accusing people left and right, burning stalls at the Traders' Market because they sell a couple of herbs, attacking citizens in the dark.'

This wasn't helping. While she couldn't go announcing it without proof, Tomi was sure Jupel had been killed by another witch. Quaide's assumption for the motive was wrong; she needed to direct his thoughts elsewhere. 'Let's say, for now, that Professor Jupel was able to keep his secret. Can you think of anyone else who might want to hurt him?'

'It's hard to imagine, isn't it?' Quaide said, putting the books away. 'Someone you know being capable of murder.'

Nomik had climbed the steps to the mezzanine and was collecting rolled maps. Quaide kept glancing at him, as if expecting the AP to take the wrong thing.

'Did you notice any recent changes in Professor Jupel's behaviour?' Tomi said. 'Fear, shiftiness, paranoia?'

'Not recently, but things changed for him after the last frost. Struck me as odd, actually.'

'What did?'

'Ivan used to be a studious, reliable employee,' Quaide said. 'His lectures were profound. It was common for other professors to sit in and hear what he had to say. I suppose his experience in Elumina had given him broader horizons than the rest of us. But the past year...' He wrinkled his wide nose. 'I don't know what happened last frost, but he was constantly scatterbrained. Bumbling, repeating himself – sometimes he wouldn't even show up to his own lectures. It was like, well, like his mind was degrading.'

Tomi glanced up at Nomik. 'Do you agree?'

'Unfortunately, yes,' Nomik said, coming down the stairs with the maps. 'Professor Jupel's classes were more cohesive before. This year, I got the impression he was always thinking about something else.'

'And he started leaving the grounds at lunch times,' Quaide said. 'Don't have a clue where he went, but he got browner, as if he'd been out in the sun. Of course, he might've just been going out for a walk. For his health, you know?'

'Did you have any reason to believe he was sick?' Tomi said.

Quaide stroked his beard. 'Maybe. It was nothing specific, it was more...'

'A feeling,' Nomik said. 'He felt wrong.'

The two men looked at each other, and for the first time since the interview started, Tomi had the impression they were in accord. She wished their agreement was for something more solid.

The professor *felt* wrong?

What, in the name of the Tassela, was that supposed to mean?

Five

Familiar panic clawed at Tomi's insides before she recognised the cause. She braced herself for the shaking, the breathlessness, the bile that burned her throat.

Bitter pinjora, a blossom native to the mountains, produced a distinctive scent and was commonly used in cleaning products. Over the past 23 years she'd yet to find a way to control her reaction to the smell.

She slowed Finley to a walk and sucked in deep, steadying breaths. It was pouring now, grey and cold, looking much closer to sunset than it was. Clouds of steam billowed from her gasps. She hadn't even seen the rain roll in, but that was the trouble with the wild season. While the hilkskin hood of her tailcoat was waterproof, it did little to protect her face from the rain. At least it hid her watering eyes.

Damian slowed Brix too. 'Are you well?'

They were right outside the station, near the black ivory statue of the first principal officer to be installed after the Resurgence. The pool at its feet sloshed with raindrops and spray from the fountain.

'I'm fine,' she said. 'Just missed a sneeze.'

The source of the smell was obvious – a cleaner was scrubbing graffiti from the smooth eggstone wall of the station.

A timekeeper atop the station rang five bells.

Damian dismounted and led Brix around the side of the rectangular building, its upper levels adorned with columns and balconies, to the grousdu enclosure.

Tomi curled her fingers in front of her stomach, forcing her mind to focus on something else. She mentally listed all the staff and students they had interviewed at the University. The religion professors stuck out particularly. Those who lectured on behalf of the Followers of Light had been gracious and charming, especially when they discovered Tomi was part of their church. The professors representing the Way of the Weavers had been similarly amicable – until they found out Ivan Jupel was a witch.

When Tomi's breathing had settled and the panic had subsided, she took Finley to the enclosure and then squelched into the station. The ground floor was for general officers. Normally, she received a few greetings or at least a smile. But the past month she'd been met with cold silence, even a hissed 'traitor' as she passed. Today was no different. She climbed the stairs towards her office and wondered whether it would be the last time she'd have to worry about that. Tomorrow, she might be turning in her badge.

'Join the minnisks for a dip, did you?' Minwell Warrick said as she entered the JO quarters on the second floor. 'That's what you get for taking a case in a glimmer district. Did you at least get me a fish?'

Tomi peeled off her tailcoat and hung it on the rack. 'What's the matter, Warrick, not enough bonus coins to buy your own dinner?'

'As a matter of fact, I closed another case today.' He gave her a dimpled smile. 'I'm catching up to you, Cardozo.'

'You wish.' She sighed at the sight of her desk, which was piled high with rolls of parchment. 'I see inventory's in.'

'Either your sweepers were very specific, or your victim owned too many things.'

'I think it's a little of both. Where's Damian?'

'Iloura called him into her office. She wanted a briefing on your case.'

Tomi glanced at her superior officer's room. The blinds were closed.

Why did Iloura want to speak to Damian in private?

'The boss is on your side, Cardozo,' Warrick said, softer, so the other JOs didn't hear.

Tomi hoped so. Iloura had issued the formal complaint against her, but only because she'd had to. Hopefully, she'd argue on Tomi's behalf tomorrow.

There was no point agonising over it. Initial inventory was an ocean of work. She sifted through the rolls of parchment to find Jupel's vault ledger that had been sent over from the treasury. One of the first things she did was check the victim's incomings and outgoings to see if there were any irregularities.

Her thigh bumped her desk and it rocked strangely. Before Tomi could figure out what was wrong, her entire desk leaned backward and landed with a heavy thunk on the floorboards. Parchments tumbled, books slid, ink bottles smashed.

A group of JOs in the corner burst into laughter.

'Well done, Officer,' one of them said. 'Good luck for tomorrow, eh?'

Tomi exhaled slowly. She'd endured a full month of this nonsense. There had been a gleeful spark in her colleagues since they'd learnt of her mistake. It didn't matter that the incident had happened 10 years ago. They were clinging to it like khar birds snatching at scraps. Those who had previously praised Tomi, vied for her attention and congratulated her with each new achievement, were now basking in the knowledge of her public failure.

Maybe they would've felt better if they knew how deeply she'd failed on the one case that mattered.

Iloura burst through her office door. 'What in the Umbra is going on?' Her gaze landed on the mess. 'Cardozo, what is this?'

Tomi crouched by the desk to find its back two legs had been sawn off. The top had been sitting precariously on them. All it had taken was a knock to unbalance them.

Iloura realised without needing an explanation. She rounded on the other JOs. 'Right. Who's responsible?'

'Maybe a witch did it,' Jerry Lorenze said. His mates sniggered.

Iloura stormed towards them as Warrick bent down to help Tomi pick up her things.

'They shouldn't let Weavers into the Justice Department,' he muttered.

Tomi sighed. She hated to admit it, but, 'Not all of them are Weavers.'

It wasn't just witch haters or Perlians who had targeted Tomi this month. People seemed to have all sorts of reasons for taking personal offence to Tomi's actions.

Damian came over to help as well.

'Take your items to my office,' Iloura called over, still in the middle of reprimanding the JOs in the corner. 'You can work in there for the rest of the evening.'

Tomi, Warrick and Damian carried everything into the office. Iloura assured them the other JOs would be cleaning up the ink and broken table.

'Thanks,' Tomi said to Warrick as he dumped the last of the inventory lists on Iloura's desk.

'Of course,' Warrick said. 'How am I supposed to feel good about beating your record if you're not at your prime?' He gave Damian a wink before leaving, closing the door behind him.

Tomi turned to Damian. 'I'm sorry about this. It probably wasn't a good time for me to be taking on an AO.'

He punched a fist into his palm. 'Want me to hold those blassards down while you beat them up?'

'No, but I appreciate the offer.'

Damian's grin faltered. 'Oh, by the way.'

'What?'

'I sort of didn't mention to Iloura that we suspect the murderer is a witch. It's not an omission,' he added quickly. 'But we don't have any proof yet. There's no point alarming people until we know for sure. Right?'

Against her better judgement, Tomi said, 'I suppose that's true.'

It would help for tomorrow, at least. If the hearing committee didn't have the idea of a killer witch fresh in their minds, they might consider Tomi's past conduct as the compassionate action it was meant to be rather than an unforgivable decision.

And it meant one less day she would have to deal with TADOW. She – and most of Radaza – hated the officers working in the Tracking and Deporting of Witches Authority.

Damian surveyed the intimidating pile of work. 'So, where do we start?'

'See if there's anything unusual in here,' Tomi said, handing him the vault ledger. 'And the insurance list of Jupel's possessions should've been sent over, too. We'll compare it to the inventory list to check what's missing.'

She found the insurance list and got to work. Damian sat in the visitor's chair, leaving Tomi to take the boss's seat.

Iloura's office wasn't big, but it was private and had a view of the station's entrance. Her medals and awards hung from the walls. A clay doll, made and painted by little hands, sat on a shelf beside a pile of parchments. Tomi had stared at that doll in painstaking detail when, exactly a month ago, Iloura had brought her into this office and explained that Tomi had been accused of dereliction of duty.

May the Tassela damn her ex straight to the Umbra.

Initial inventory was a monumental task, but at least it was absorbing. The rest of the world faded away as Tomi read, made notes and compared lists. The itemised list from Jupel's secret witch's nook was filled with curious items. Some of them were everyday knick-knacks, like crystals, seashells, feathers, rocks and twigs. Others were less common: rodent bones, patches of animal skin, crooner scales, trat teeth, coolu beaks and horns. She read with interest. She'd had little to do with witches and knew only the basics. Where had Jupel got these things? And what had he used them for?

She knew witches could sense and manipulate energy. They used nature to change things to their will. Tomi's history classes had focussed on the horrors witches had unleashed upon their enemies during past wars, but she'd also heard they healed and protected and assisted with crops. She'd been exposed to plenty of folklore that weaved a much kinder tapestry of witches than what the official textbooks said.

Tomi imagined the truth was somewhere in between. Witches could be good or bad, just like humans. They seemed to have no problem living among humans in Elumina, but they weren't allowed into Agriterra. That was the law, and no one was above the law, no matter how good their intentions were.

After failing to find any strange activity in Jupel's vault ledger, Damian brewed a pot of tea. They drank under the warm glow of the oil lamps while rain battered at the window. The other JOs went home, replaced by the night crew.

When her eyes grew tired, Tomi rolled a freshly cleaned board into Iloura's office to pin up the artist's sketch of the body. She drew a timeline of events, chalked in the professor's general details and wrote *robbery gone wrong?* underneath. Then she added *armiene coat, medium height, stocky (maybe), probably known by the victim*, noting that Georgio Herliz had provided the description.

Damian left his seat to join her.

'Your first murder board,' Tomi said. 'How does it feel?'

'It's like a grisly version of school. Chalkboards, problems to solve, obscene pictures shared between classmates... it's all here.'

'Well, I'm glad you can find comfort in the familiar.'

He shook his head, staring at the sketch. 'My *bamki* always said no good comes of receiving visitors after nine.'

'I don't think this was what she was talking about.'

'Oh, this is exactly what she was talking about. Our district has questionable residents.'

Tomi's lips twitched. She wasn't used to joking in front of a murder board. In fact, she wasn't used to sharing her cases at all. Most JOs didn't take on partners. It meant splitting the bonus and few of her colleagues were prepared to do that.

'Do you think Jupel deserves justice?' she said. 'Even though he was a witch living here illegally?'

'Everyone deserves justice. That's, like, the very definition of the word.'

She smiled. Maybe her judgement wasn't so terrible after all.

She returned to the desk and sorted through the rolls of parchment. They'd written down the objects missing from Jupel's apartment according to his itemised list of possessions. The stolen objects were all trinkets small enough to fit inside coat pockets. Tomi had included the absent rings from the body.

'Something here is bothering me, and I can't figure out what it is,' she said, scanning various words from different lists.

- *1x potted carris fern, green, several leaves recently torn off*
- *1x sml jar eggshell pieces*
- *1x snow bear rug, bloodstained*
- *4x incense sticks, composition unknown*
- *1x gold-inlaid ornamental box ½-full of triller herb*
- *Satchel contents: 1x penswann quill*

'Did you read the transcript of Jupel's notes in the satchel?'

Damian found the parchment and passed it to her. It had a lot of question marks. The scriber appeared to have had difficulty translating the professor's scrawl.

Tomi frowned at the words. *Difficulty comm. with new stlmnts – qora readers, watch for prblms during talks = good, BUT not good if anti-human? What can humans do to ensure fairness?*

'What are qora readers?' she said.

Damian shrugged. 'Must be a witch thing, if they can be anti-human.'

'Jupel was exploring the possibility of Radaza opening communication with witch settlements.'

'A motive for murder?'

'Maybe.' Tomi set the transcription down again and massaged her forehead as the timekeeper on top of the building chimed nine bells.

There was a knock on the door, and Iloura stuck her head in. Her short black hair was flecked with raindrops, as was her tailcoat. She had a sealed envelope in her hand. 'This was waiting for you downstairs.'

'Good,' said Tomi, catching sight of the stamp identifying it as university property. 'That'll be the incident report. Let's find out who Professor Jupel was fighting with last season.'

Iloura and Damian waited as she broke the wax seal. She skimmed through it and pursed her lips, satisfied.

'Can I guess?' Damian said. 'Was it one of the Weavers?'

'Good call. Tailor Happershift, religion professor representing the Way of the Weavers.' Tomi set the report on top of the other pages on the desk. 'We'll send a general officer to pick her up for questioning in the morning.'

Iloura cleared her throat. 'It'll have to be in the afternoon, Cardozo.'

Tomi's breath caught. For a precious chunk of time, she'd forgotten about the hearing.

'Ah,' she said. 'Right.'

It was possible that she wouldn't even be the JO questioning Tailor Happershift. Maybe Warrick would take over. He was due a bonus and a few rest days, but if it meant beating Tomi's record, he might accept Jupel's case anyway.

'You need to be at your best tomorrow,' Iloura said. 'Get a solid night's rest, all right?'

Tomi nodded, though she was sure everyone in the room knew she wouldn't be sleeping tonight.

Six

ALL DAMIAN WANTED TO DO WAS GET INTO HIS APARTMENT. He wasn't physically tired, but his hand ached from trying to keep up with the millions – surely *millions* – of interviews they'd done today, and his mind felt like it had been run through a mill. It was exhausting keeping track of every clue, every comment, every twitch that seemed out of place. He'd been flooded with information and just wanted to flop on the couch.

But Imni had caught him on the spiralling interior balcony, and she wouldn't let him go. She twisted her yellow hair around her fingers, asking about his day, touching his tailcoat. She seemed to like the tailcoat.

Damian had always appreciated Imni's attentions – she'd seen two frosts more than him, and he'd always been slightly infatuated by her – but he was desperate to escape. The central grousdu enclosure was particularly stinky tonight, and adding to that were whiffs suggesting someone had pissed on the wall of the common ablutions block on the ground floor. Again.

Why was it so hard to walk the extra 10 steps and use the flow-ways?

Imni either didn't notice or didn't care about the smell. She leaned against the balcony railing, jutting back her shoulders as she spoke. Peeled paint from the balcony flecked onto the skirts of her dress. Damian stared at the tiny red pieces, studying the shape and colour, bright against the soft green fabric. Red flecks. Red entrails. Red dust. Red, red, red. It was everywhere today.

'Oi. Marsh-brain.' Imni clicked her fingers in his face. 'You there?'

Damian blinked, returning to the present. 'Sorry,' he said, moving past her. 'I have to go.'

'But—'

'I have to clean the intestine stains off my clothes.'

She jumped back with a squeal. At last, he was free to trudge the rest of the way to his apartment. He tried not to feel too guilty. He probably didn't have intestine stains on his clothes, but it wasn't impossible.

'Well, well. If it isn't Radaza's finest officer.' Pa was at the round, rickety table when Damian walked in. He peered at Damian over the frames of his square eyeglasses. 'Was beginning to think you'd gotten yourself in trouble on the first day in the field.'

'I did, but I talked my way out of it.' Damian walked forward and fell facedown on the threadbare couch.

'Tough day?' Pa sounded as though he was smiling.

Damian grunted.

'Did you get all inspired, seeing the great Tomi Cardozo in action?'

Damian grunted again.

Pa laughed. 'I'll fetch your dinner.'

There was the *step-thump* of Pa's lopsided gait across the darkwood floor. Damian took in a few more breaths before he had the energy to lift his head. Despite the cold rain, the window was open to let out smoke from the fire pit. Their atrium, like most, had a common cooking area, but only a few residents used it. Often it was graffitied or the doors to the fire ovens were broken off. Oli Glen swore he'd once found the remains of a roasted trat inside one of the ovens. Whether the rodent had got into the logs or someone had put it there, no one knew.

Pa ladled thin stew from the pot into Damian's bowl. 'Up. You can't eat where you sleep.'

Damian looked pointedly at the table. It was covered in pouches that Pa was filling with vials of worm paste and gizzard stones for the atrium's grousdu.

'Take a chair and sit by the fire.'

Damian did as he was told while Pa continued with his job.

'Wait until my first bonus, *Ap'pa*,' Damian said between slurps of stew. 'I'm going to buy the best meat in the Traders' Market. We'll be having pingee steak next time.'

'You think you're going to solve a case soon?'

'Better believe it. All I need is a good night's sleep, and I'll be able to tell you who the killer is.'

The door to the adjoining apartment swung open. *Bamki* Rivers hobbled inside, still in her pink heels. 'May the *faronye* protect you, Damian Kamara; you swore you'd knock as soon as you got home.'

'He's only just arrived, *Bamki*,' Pa said. 'Would you like some stew?'

Bamki Rivers took one look at the contents of the pot and snorted. 'Is that what you're giving the *rabbal* after a hard day's work?'

'I imagine being an officer is a pleasant breeze compared to the hurricane of the docks,' Pa said.

Damian wasn't so sure. While physical labour took its toll, this mental work drained every part of him. All those late nights he'd spent studying law at the academy were nothing compared to the actual job.

And the pressure. He had been practically bounding when he got the call this morning, but the realisation had walloped him during the day – if he failed, a killer walked free.

'So,' said *Bamki* Rivers, spooning stew into Pa's used bowl, 'tell us about this case you're on.'

'You know I can't do that.'

'Cah! We're family. It doesn't count.'

Bamki Rivers wasn't his real grandmother, though he called her *bamki*. She was from Khvu, like them, and had been a great friend of Damian's real grandparents when they'd first arrived in Radaza. She'd looked after Damian since he was a toddler while Pa worked at the docks. Even after Pa couldn't work anymore, she still acted as if their two apartments were combined. Pa had built the door in the adjoining wall years ago for her to come in and out as she pleased.

She sat on the couch to eat. Pa didn't say anything. There weren't any chairs left, and besides, he wouldn't have dared.

Damian was tempted to tell them about witches being involved. *Bamki* Rivers was always looking for opportunities to regale him with stories of the witches she'd fought beside in the Rebellion. And she'd been born in Elumina, living there long enough to lament the lack of witches in Radaza.

'They were just so useful,' *Bamki* Rivers had said. 'If you were sick or wanted to attract a potential partner, or even if you just had snowlows eating your plants, a witch would sort you out. Radazans don't know what they're missing.'

When Damian had come home one day, about seven years old, happily proclaiming a family of witches in the atrium next door had been arrested by TADOW, *Bamki* Rivers had pointed a knobbly finger and said, 'Those're people you're laughing about. Living, breathing people, with an *Am'ma* and *Ap'pa* and maybe even a pet poffin.'

Damian had owned a poffin then (its name was Smoky), and he had hugged the fluffy creature to his chest. 'Will the poffin be all right?'

'Forget the poffin,' *Bamki* Rivers said. 'Never forget, *rabbal*. People are people, no matter what they call themselves. And no person deserves this treatment. Witches were living here long before the Perlians invaded.'

She'd aged dramatically since that day, time dragging at her brown face and neck, flooding her pinned-back hair with grey. But every morning she still painted her lips pink (wobblier than before), clasped her string of duskpearls around her neck and dressed in her finest clothes. Her steadfast presence had been a gift from the Tassela, especially through Damian's teenage years.

Damian had just decided to discuss the case with them when there was a heavy pounding at the front door.

Pa dropped a handful of gizzard stones. They scattered across the floor.

'Take Erika back home,' he said softly, easing the wooden stump of his leg down so he could pick up the stones. The fact that he'd used *Bamki* Rivers' first name was a sign of how frightened he was.

The pounding came again.

Damian couldn't move. His insides had iced over, as if they'd been exposed to the frost.

He hadn't heard that knock in three years.

'Damian!' Pa whispered.

Damian's inner frost splintered. He set his bowl down and helped the shaking *Bamki* Rivers to her feet.

'The nerve of them, coming here when people're trying to eat dinner.' Her mutterings would've sounded brave if he hadn't heard the tremor in her voice. He took her bowl and escorted her to the adjoining door.

'Don't you lock me out, *rabbal*,' she said as she went through.

He flipped the lock across anyway. They'd only installed it when Damian was 14, and it had nothing to do with keeping her out.

He lurched forward as a third, faster round of knocks hit the front door. Making them wait would only send the situation spiralling.

As soon as he opened up, Yaverly and Winsor muscled through like a couple of snarfles. Yaverly grinned a gold-toothed smile at Damian. There was always a sadistic delight to the bald man whenever they met, probably to do with the fact that he had knocked Damian out cold when Damian was 16.

Both knuckles stepped aside to let Bunter Vittam stroll through.

'Apologies for the late visit,' Vittam said pleasantly. 'Hope we're not interrupting.'

Sometime in the past three years, Damian had stopped waking from night terrors. That would change – he knew it as soon as the smoke-rasped accent chilled the apartment and the smell of hartmint drifted in.

Vittam gave Damian the once-over with the same sort of relish Imni had. 'Nice tailcoat.'

Pa staggered to his chair. He set the stones quietly on the table and tucked his wooden leg out of the way. 'Vittam–'

Vittam silenced him with a lift of his ring-laden hand, never taking his gaze from Damian. 'Congratulations on the new job.' He circled Damian to get the full view. 'How was your day?'

'I haven't gotten paid yet.'

'Your pay pouch comes every quarter moon. I'm aware.' Vittam returned to stand in front of Damian and nodded as if he liked what he saw. 'Congratulations on wriggling your way into Tomi Cardozo's pocket. No one's managed to do that before.'

'I'm bendier than others.'

Vittam's smile faded. 'Ah, Damian. I can't say I've missed that mouth of yours.'

Yaverly and Winsor shifted, their fingers flexing.

Pa shot Damian a frightened look as Vittam spoke again, this time all friendliness gone. 'Do you think I put a pause on your repayments to be kind, sapling? Do you think I relinquished my fastest night messenger for fun?'

'You knew I'd get more coin in the Justice Department than I ever did at the docks or being your runner.' Damian kept his voice light. 'You'll get a cut of my salary and every bonus pouch, just like we agreed.'

'You're denser than I thought. I left you in peace while you studied so you'd be my most loyal informant in the Justice Department.' One side of Vittam's mouth quirked up in a grin, and he pulled a sprig of hartmint from the inner pocket of his gold-thread suit. 'Never in my wildest dreams did I expect you to score Tomi Cardozo for a mentor. Tell me, what has she been up to?'

'The usual. Painting, dancing, street performing. She does a whole comedy routine on the Grand Stage at sundown. You should check it out.'

Vittam popped the hartmint leaf on his tongue. 'I know she has that hearing tomorrow. Did you find anything to get her discharged?'

'Besides the comedy routine?'

Pa pleaded softly to Damian in their native language.

'Forget it,' Damian said to Vittam. 'You won't be getting information from me.'

Vittam crooked a finger at his men. Yaverly's eyes gleamed as he stalked forward. Damian didn't have a chance to brace himself before a meaty fist slammed beneath his right ribs. He doubled over, wheezing.

'Wait,' Pa said, switching languages. 'Wait, Vittam. Please. I'm sure we can come to an arrangement.' He tried to stand, but Winsor shoved him back in his chair.

'Sorry, Kamara,' Vittam said, admiring his multitude of sparkling rings under the light, 'your grousdu minder coin doesn't quite cut it.'

Yaverly grabbed Damian's hair and yanked him upright to punch him in the ribs again. The blow was hard enough to send Damian to his knees.

'You're playing with the big boys now, Damian,' Vittam said.

Damian couldn't answer – the air had been knocked from his lungs. He lifted his gaze, his vision blurred by tears of pain.

'We were lenient before because you were a kid, and you were useful,' Vittam continued. 'I'd like to think Yaverly taught you some respect during those mouthy years, but perhaps not.' He sauntered up to Damian, his soft-leather shoes reflecting the dying glow of the firepit. When he leaned down, all Damian could see were thick black eyebrows in a white, square face. 'You were the one who offered to repay your father's debt. You owe me.'

'I... owe you... *coin*, not treason,' Damian said through gasps.

'Wrong.' Vittam's face was so close, the smell of hartmint almost had Damian gagging. 'As long as your contract is ongoing, you owe me whatever I please.'

'I'm not... telling you... anything.'

Vittam straightened and turned to Winsor, who was still standing by Pa. 'Stab him.'

Damian had barely comprehended the words before Winsor unsheathed a dagger and slammed it into the table. It was only from Pa's screams that Damian realised the blade had pierced his hand.

'No.' Damian struggled to his feet. Yaverly shoved him back.

'Tell me something useful about Tomi Cardozo,' Vittam said over the noise.

The blade was still through Pa's hand, pinning it to the table.

'No.' Damian pushed against Yaverly. 'No. No–'

'Damian,' Vittam said with a sigh.

From the adjoining door came a sharp rapping. It was ignored.

'No. No, no, no–'

The word was a cloud in Damian's mouth, billowing and curling. Pa tugged in vain at the dagger's handle, his face wet with tears. Damian rammed against Yaverly, but it was like trying to move a mountain.

'Just tell me something useful, and we'll let you get on with your evening,' Vittam said.

'No.' The sobs were wet in Damian's aching lungs. Blood slicked the shining steel of the blade.

Vittam shook his head, as if he was disappointed. He turned to Winsor. 'Do the other one.'

Winsor ripped the dagger from Pa and forced his other hand on the table.

'Wait!' The scream scraped Damian's throat like a razor.

Winsor paused, red-stained blade in the air. The rapping at the adjoining door stopped.

It took Damian several tries to coax his raw voice to work. 'I'll tell you.'

Vittam gave a nod. Yaverly released Damian, and Winsor released Pa. Pa clutched his injured hand to his chest, rocking in his spot. Damian could see the effort he put into stifling sounds of pain.

'We're investigating the murder of Ivan Jupel,' Damian said. The words were as cracked as the concrete outside his atrium. 'It looks like his killer was a witch.'

It was a jewel of information, dooming Tomi's chances for tomorrow. But Vittam curled his lip and said, 'I already knew that.'

Damian didn't have the energy to question it. Vittam knew everything.

'We didn't tell our superior officer,' he said tiredly. 'There's no proof yet, and we thought it might hurt Tomi's statement at the hearing.'

'Hm.' Vittam chewed his hartmint thoughtfully. 'Sounds like wilful omission to me.' He stepped forward and clapped Damian on the shoulder. 'There. That wasn't so hard, was it?'

Pa choked back a sob. Damian glimpsed bone through the blood. They needed to get to the hospital.

'This was enlightening for all of us, I think.' Vittam gestured for his men. 'I look forward to a long and prosperous relationship, Officer Kamara.'

Then they walked out, leaving the door open in their wake.

Seven

IT HADN'T OCCURRED TO TOMI UNTIL SHE REACHED THE SUPREME Court that there would be protesters. Perlians carrying picket signs and chanting something about witches thronged the steps between the tall greystone columns. Iloura had promised it would be a quiet affair, but considering the behaviour of the other JOs, it didn't surprise Tomi that one of them had spread the word.

She squinted across the sunny plaza, uncertain how to proceed. It wouldn't be smart to walk through that crowd. They sounded hungry for blood.

While she was still deciding, a newscloth blew off the alfresco table of a restaurant and swept past her. A familiar sketch marked the cover. She picked up the fabric and studied the illustration. It was a portrait of Jupel, done before his death. The headline read: *Witch Gutted in Own Apartment*.

It was only then Tomi realised what the people at the courthouse were protesting about. They were angry that Jupel had slipped past the borders. That he had spent years shaping students' minds at the University.

Better borders, safer schools! one sign read.

Ban Elumenese immigrants!

He should never have been allowed in!

Tomi slipped through the protesters, unnoticed except for one man who shoved a pamphlet in her hand. She let it fall before she reached the doors. Their jeers and shouts disappeared once the doors closed behind her. Silence settled like frost.

She'd been here many times before but as an arresting officer, not a defendant. The interior had reefstone columns and flagstone tiles and a ceiling that, today, seemed much too high. Reporters scurried by with rolled parchments, obvious among the red-coated servants of the court. Judges were easy to spot – their faces were coated with paint ground from silver ore. The paint shimmered in the muted sunlight that streamed through the tall windows.

Tomi found her way down the hall to the smaller rooms near the back. She felt unkempt. Her hair was pinned unevenly, which was ridiculous. She'd pinned up her hair for the past 13 years, yet today was the day it refused to sit right. And, despite having been hung near the exposed chimney pipe in her apartment overnight, her freshly washed tailcoat still had wet patches. The Tassela must've been having a laugh with her today.

Iloura was waiting outside the doors. 'Ready?'

Tomi gave a nod. This hearing had been looming for a month. The sooner it was over, the better.

Iloura opened the doors and they walked inside. It wasn't an impressive room: a few tapestries, a green rug, two chairs facing a long heatherwood table. A portrait of the city's founders hung on the back wall.

Two women and a man, all Perlian, were chatting casually at the table. Their informal manner reminded Tomi that this was just another hearing for them, one of many they would have today. Their reputation didn't hang in the balance. Their jobs weren't in danger.

When they saw Tomi and Iloura, their discussion faded, and the woman in the middle, with silver on her face, drew her pile of parchments closer.

'Please, take a seat,' she said, gesturing to the chairs.

Tomi and Iloura sat side by side.

'Do you have any questions before we begin?'

Tomi shook her head.

'All right, here we go.' The judge nodded to the man, who picked up a scratch stick and began writing. 'First day of Harrow, 1092. Hearing JO459BD11 for Officer Tomi Cardozo, presenting her oral response to complaint 74113695, stating dereliction of duty. Hearing committee consists of Radazan Commander Dawn Parsons, Justice Misconduct

Officer Wendyn Gracer, and myself, Judge Syelda Stock. Also present, the defendant's superior officer, Prudence Iloura, who issued the complaint. Wendyn Gracer will be scribing.'

The man's scratch stick flew across the parchment, reminding Tomi of Damian's diligent hand yesterday.

'Do you understand why you are here today?' Judge Stock said.

Tomi could feel a wet patch on her tailcoat. It seeped its chill through her pants into the back of her thigh. 'Yes,' she said.

'Is the accusation in the named complaint accurate?'

'Yes.'

'You admit to allowing a witch to go free?'

'Yes.'

The Radazan commander, Parsons, made a note on the parchment before her.

Judge Stock continued. 'Do you understand that it is illegal for a witch to reside in or enter Agriterra, and that any suspicion of a witch's presence requires an immediate report to the TADOW Authority?'

'Yes.'

'Would you care to put forward a response to the complaint?'

'I was young,' Tomi said. 'Idealistic. I was in a bad space 10 years ago, as you may have seen from my records. A few months before, I'd been demoted from attending officer to general officer.'

'Yes, I see you graduated with top marks from the academy. What was the reason for the sudden drop in your performance?'

'Personal,' Tomi said. 'But I was performing better again by the time of this... incident.'

Judge Stock rifled through her stack of parchments until she found what she was looking for. 'Your written response states you witnessed a witch using magic to steal several flatcakes from a stall at the Traders' Market.'

'Yes. I chased the witch down a side street.'

'But you willingly gave up pursuit.'

'Yes.'

'Why is that?'

'She turned around, and I could see she was close to starvation.'

Commander Parsons spoke up. 'That should have been more of a reason for you to arrest her. Being taken into custody is safer than being out on the streets.'

'TADOW would've deported her,' Tomi said.

'She was living here illegally.'

'I understand that now. I won't make the same mistake again.'

'Yes, well, it would be a shame to punish you for an incident that occurred 10 years ago.'

Tomi straightened, hopeful.

'However.' Commander Parsons leaned forward. Her lips were painted ice-blue, contrasting with her cropped, wispy red hair. 'The case you're currently investigating has a victim who's a witch, and I hear there's probable cause to suspect the killer is a witch too.'

Her words rang in the room. Iloura whipped to face Tomi, her eyes wide.

It took Tomi a few attempts to speak. 'How did you know?'

'Early findings from Particulars. I'm afraid we cannot allow an officer with witch sympathies to investigate–'

'I have no witch sympathies,' Tomi said hastily. 'It was a matter of compassion. I saw a hungry young woman steal a couple of flatcakes, and I let her go without thinking of the repercussions. It was a decade-old lapse in judgement. I understand now that my job is to uphold the laws of Radaza, not judge them.'

Commander Parsons and Judge Stock exchanged glances. Wendyn Gracer continued to scribble notes.

'I have complete confidence in Officer Cardozo,' Iloura said. 'As you can see from my personal testimony, I trust no one on my team more than her. She's spent the last 10 years building an outstanding career while sustaining a blotless record. Don't take away Radaza's best JO because of a cookie error.'

'I admit, I'm in agreement with you,' Judge Stock said. 'But there's no way she can continue investigating the Jupel murder.'

'You would miss a precious opportunity to allow her to show the court – and the public – that she's on the right side of Radaza law.' Iloura stood and approached the table. 'I accept personal responsibility for the outcome of this case. I know for a fact that Tomi Cardozo will do everything in her power to track down the killer, whether they're witch or human.'

The entire back of Tomi's thigh was freezing from the wet patch. Prickleflesh needled down her leg.

Wendyn Gracer cleared his throat. 'I don't know if we can risk her failure. It would look very bad for the Justice Department.'

'It would look worse to take her off the case,' Iloura said. 'People will start asking why she's allowed to remain in her job at all if you don't trust her to investigate witches.'

'I concur.' Commander Parsons pursed her ice-blue lips into an almost-smile. 'Let's give her a chance to redeem herself. Catch us that witch, Officer Cardozo.'

'On the condition of probation,' Judge Stock said. 'We will reconsider your position and check the progress of the case in four days.'

'Four days isn't enough,' Iloura said immediately. 'Especially if the frost settles in that time.'

'The frost shouldn't stop a JO from doing their job.' Commander Parsons met Tomi's gaze, challenging her to argue. Tomi wanted to – the frost could cause a huge upheaval during a case. But she kept her mouth shut. Commander Parsons seemed to be looking for weaknesses.

'Well then,' Judge Stock said after a silence. 'Are we all in accord?'

Wendyn Gracer and Commander Parsons lifted their hands in agreement.

'I suppose,' Iloura said, glancing questioningly at Tomi.

Tomi nodded.

'Very well,' Judge Stock said. 'We'll reconvene on the fifth day of Harrow. Our office will send you the schedule for the follow-up hearing. Thank you for attending; you're now dismissed.'

Eight

DAMIAN WAS SITTING ON THE FOUNTAIN WALL WHEN TOMI ARRIVED at the station. He stood as she climbed off Finley. There was a gingerness to his movements, and his face was lined with exhaustion. He examined her, expectant, hopeful.

'I'm on probation,' she said. 'But I can still work the Jupel case.'

He let out a slow exhalation, looking as if he'd been released from a life debt. 'Of course you can. They'd be addled not to let you.'

'Are you well?'

'Running like a river.'

'You sure? You seem...'

Iloura rode up on her grousdu before Tomi could figure out how to finish her sentence. 'You can go straight in, officers. I arranged to have Tailor Happershift brought in for 10 bells – she should be waiting for you in the interview room.' She dismounted. 'I'll speak to the staff. If anyone gives you trouble, report them to me immediately.'

Tomi doubted the taunts and pranks would stop now the hearing was over. Her reputation was damaged, perhaps beyond repair.

But she'd collected herself on the journey back from the Supreme

Court. She'd survived darker pits than this. The committee had given her a second chance, and she would use the opportunity to prove herself loyal to Radaza.

'All right,' she said to Damian. 'Let's find out why this Weaver was tussling with our victim.'

She led him into the station. Tailor Happershift wouldn't be a witch, considering she followed the Way of the Weavers. But she'd failed to mention her fight with Jupel during yesterday's interview. Was she ashamed? Or did she have something to hide?

The interview room was on the ground floor, down a corridor away from the general officers. A GO stood outside the room. He handed Tomi a folder with the parchments she needed and remained stationed outside the open door.

Tomi walked in, Damian on her heels. The woman waiting for them was in the light-blue cloth of the Weavers, a white sash draped over her shoulders. She sat primly, hands in lap. Her hair gleamed yellow in the light of two oil lanterns hanging from the walls.

Tomi took her time flipping through the parchments in the folder. She'd found what she was looking for, but was in no hurry to speak. Instead, she read through the notes a second time.

Out of the corner of her eye, she saw the tailor squirm.

'Tailor Harley Happershift,' Tomi said. She pulled out the incident report from the South River Archives and slid it across the table. 'Would you care to tell me about this?'

Happershift glanced at it without picking it up.

Tomi gestured to Damian, who was scribing in the corner. 'We have a statement from you yesterday saying you had had little to do with Professor Ivan Jupel. Yet this incident report, signed by Chancellor Gloudling, says you were in a fight with him last season.'

'I hardly see what that has to do with anything,' Happershift said.

'Where were you on the twenty-seventh night of Harvest?'

'What, you think *I* murdered him?'

Tomi took a seat across from the tailor. 'You had a problem with Jupel, and now he's dead.'

A snort escaped Happershift. 'Is that all you have to go on?'

'It's a start. Now answer the question. Where were you on the twenty-seventh night of Harvest?'

There was a pause. Happershift looked at Damian, still scribbling notes, before speaking. 'I was working at the University until the first bell after midnight, then I headed home.'

'Did anyone see you during this time?'

'Some other tailors in my department. We're in the process of writing a discourse on the cleansing of threads before they're rewoven. And,' she added, 'in case you're about to caw on about religious unity and conspiring, Beacon Guillip was there too.'

'Thank you. We'll follow up on that.'

Leaders from the two main religions scraped against each other over certain discrepancies between their creeds, but they agreed on plenty of other matters. It wasn't improbable that tailors from the Weavers and beacons from the Followers of Light collaborated on essays.

'As for the fight with Ivan,' Happershift said, 'I'm afraid that's a personal matter.'

'Did it have to do with him being a witch?'

'Don't be ridiculous. If I'd had any idea he was an abomination, I would've reported him to the authorities.'

Damian cleared his throat. 'Didn't the Tassela tell you he was a witch?'

There was a note of humour in his voice. Tomi allowed it to pass without comment. Tailors claimed they communicated directly with the Tassela – the five brightest stars in the heavens, who were said to weave life onto the Great Loom. It was, apparently, a tailor's job to pass holy messages onto the public. All tailors agreed that witches were once humans who had attacked the Tassela Clemency and stolen her magic, leaving her with wounds that made her shine red in the night sky. Everything else about Creation and the world, however, was debated fiercely among them. From the sounds of it, they didn't communicate directly with anything, including each other.

'The Tassela let us work through these mundane problems on our own,' Tailor Happershift declared grandly in answer to Damian.

'All right,' Tomi said, as Damian scoffed behind her, 'if you didn't know Professor Jupel was a witch, what else could you be fighting about?'

Silence.

Tomi tapped the incident report. 'Tailor Happershift, this argument was so heated it came to blows. You had an official report written up about it. If you think I'm going to let this drop without learning more, you're wrong. I'm investigating Professor Jupel's murder. I'm not going away.'

'Don't be ridiculous. You have my alibi!'

'That doesn't mean you didn't send someone else to kill him.'

'How dare you? I would never!'

'Then tell me what the fight was about.'

Happershift picked up the ends of her white sash and began tracing the embroidered patterns with her fingers. Her expression was mild, but Tomi could practically see the gearwheels ticking in the older woman's mind. She was calculating whether it was worth living with the lingering presence of the Justice Department to keep whatever secret she was carrying.

'Fine,' she said at last. 'I'll tell you, under the proviso that the Church will not be held responsible for anything I mention here.'

'I can't promise that.'

'This isn't about the murder. This is about... sanctuary.'

Curious. What sort of sanctuary was the Way of the Weavers providing?

Tomi sat back in her chair and waited for Happershift to continue. She couldn't make any assurances to protect the Church, especially if it was involved in something explicitly illegal.

'Do you want to find your killer or not?' Happershift said.

A vision of Commander Parsons' ice-blue smile flashed through Tomi's mind. Four days to go.

'Is your church breaking any laws of Radaza?' she said.

Happershift shook her head.

Tomi figured that was concession enough and nodded at Damian to stop taking notes. She gestured at Happershift to continue.

'People under the thrall of ices come to us for help. We assist them with recovery and rehabilitation. We have places outside the city to house them until they're ready to return home.'

Happershift was right – there were no laws prohibiting the refuge of addicts. But users, distributors and makers were all hunted by the Illicit Substance Elimination Force. If someone was under the influence, they were immediately imprisoned, and the penalties were severe.

'What kind of ices do these people use?' Tomi said. 'Dorvmin, plink–'

'There's no discrimination. We take everyone.' It was a noble sentiment, and Happershift declared it with pride. Tomi would've been more impressed if she wasn't acutely aware of the more hateful aspirations of the Weavers.

'What does this have to do with Professor Jupel?'

'I noticed he was exhibiting the same kinds of symptoms as one under the thrall of cutlass.'

Tomi stiffened.

Happershift smiled smugly. 'Ah. You didn't know ghost was back on the streets. Yes, Officer Cardozo, it's returned with a vengeance. And Jupel was showing all the signs. Incapable of concentrating, dilated pupils, loss of memory, mild drooling. And, without fail, around the end of every month he'd start to get withdrawal symptoms. About six months ago, I caught him behind the church, trying to scratch holes into his arms. When I offered to assist him, he called me an ignorant old croach and attacked me.'

'You didn't mention any of this in the incident report.'

'Of course not. We tailors shouldn't be linked to ices in any manner, in order to protect our charges.'

Tomi glanced back at Damian. Happershift's description of Jupel's behaviour matched what Professor Quaide had said. Was it possible Ivan Jupel was an addict? If so, was his death connected to illicit substances?

And how did witches fit into all this?

Damian spoke up. 'The night of his death, Professor Jupel was complaining about not being able to trust one of his colleagues. Do you think he was talking about you?'

'I doubt it,' Happershift said, lifting an eyebrow. 'Jupel and I hadn't spoken since the incident.'

Well. Tomi had never expected interviewing Happershift would lead to the killer, but it certainly was illuminating.

Nine

DAMIAN STRUGGLED TO HOLD HIMSELF UPRIGHT AS TOMI KNOCKED on the next apartment door. They'd been questioning residents of Jupel's atrium all afternoon, trying to catch the people who hadn't been in yesterday. So far no one had had anything useful to tell them, and all Damian wanted to do was lie down. His ribs ached from last night's beating. Blossoms of purple, black and yellow stretched across his chest. It hurt to move, especially considering he was trying to hide it.

Tomi called through the door. 'Justice officials here. We have a few questions.'

He couldn't tell how she was feeling, but she didn't seem as happy as he would have expected after the results of the hearing. Maybe there was more pressure with the probation than he knew.

He didn't know how he would've lived with himself if she'd lost her job. Giving Vittam vital information on her – and knowing he'd have to do it again – made him feel like milkmoths were eating at his life threads. His very essence was riddled with dirty holes. He would've handed in his resignation this morning if he thought it would help. But Vittam would come for him and maybe punish Pa further if Damian gave up his position.

While what Vittam had done to Pa wasn't legal, the indenture was.

Damian was lawfully contracted to the King of the Streets, and courts often overlooked injuries and abuse done by those who were owed coin. The higher the debt, the more creditors got away with.

And when it came to Vittam, the law practically twisted itself in knots to clear him.

Pa was back at home now, being tended by *Bamki* Rivers. They'd spent all night at the hospital. The medica mavens had done what they could, but the nerves were damaged and he would probably never regain full movement in his hand.

He would lose his job as a grousdu minder. When he'd lost his job at the docks, crippled by a falling crate, he'd turned to gambling to try solving their financial strife. It had almost ruined them. What would he do this time?

The apartment door finally opened, revealing a woman in her early twenties. She wore a sheer red nightgown and had a sleepy zimarool draped like a shawl around her neck. The zimarool lifted its head to sniff hopefully in their direction. Sensing nothing to eat, it yawned, stretched its legs and feathery wings, then fell back to sleep.

Tomi introduced herself and Damian. The woman stepped aside to let them in.

'You'll have to excuse the mess,' she said in a breathy voice. 'It's coming to that difficult time.'

Damian did a quick scan of the room. He couldn't see a single thing out of place, unless it was the newscloth draped on one of the lounge cushions.

'We understand,' Tomi said without irony.

The woman closed the door, revealing a rack along the wall holding various coats. Damian discretely nudged Tomi when he spotted armiene suede in the collection. She nodded in acknowledgement. He took out his parchment book as the woman began to speak.

'You're here about Ivan, I suppose. Such an awful thing to happen. And this is supposed to be a safe district.' She picked up the newscloth to tuck it under the low lounge table. Damian glimpsed a portrait sketch of the professor on the front. 'I don't feel safe anymore. You're trying to catch who did this, aren't you?'

'Yes, that's our job,' Tomi said. 'It's *Leya* Linn, correct? The records say the Linns are in this apartment.'

'That's correct. Veraminta Linn. I would offer you a drink and smallfruits, but...'

'We're working,' Tomi confirmed. To Veraminta's credit, it was the first offer of smallfruits they'd received. 'I don't suppose you happened to hear or see anything the evening Professor Jupel died?'

'No, I was out at the Central Lights Rave all night.' Veraminta sank onto a couch as if she were exhausted. The zimarool climbed off her shoulders and snuggled onto her lap where she could stroke its russet fur. 'I didn't come back until the afternoon – Evelynn Portio invited me to her place in the Black Ivory District for breakfast, which turned to lunch. You know how it is. Have you met Evelynn Portio?'

'I can't say that I have.'

Veraminta gestured a slender arm towards the newscloth. 'She's always in the social pages. Such a dearling. We're the closest of friends.'

'I see. Is *Seno* Linn here?'

'I'm afraid not. There's no such thing as a rest day this close to the frost. He owns a mill, and they're working overtime as people begin to stock up. He leaves at some dreadful hour in the morning.' She let her head flop back dramatically.

Damian watched the diaphanous curtains billow in the sea breeze as Tomi said, 'Does that mean he was the first to leave the atrium yesterday morning?'

'Yes, he would've been.'

'Did he happen to say whether the frost doors were locked?'

'Yes, actually.' Veraminta lifted her head again. 'He mentioned it after I got all worked up over that appalling murder. As if it would make me feel better. If someone can break in even when the frost doors are locked, then we could be slaughtered in our beds!' After an exaggerated huff, she added, 'I had to take myself to the steam spas to calm my nerves, even though I was only there the day before.'

Damian coughed as he scribed her comment. Let the record show that Veraminta Linn was *so* distressed that she had to sit in fragranced baths for two days in a row while lesser people pampered her.

There wasn't a hint of judgement in Tomi's voice as she said, 'It appears the suspect didn't break in. They were invited inside the atrium by Professor Jupel. Then they let themselves out after the crime and must've locked the door behind them, if what your spouse says is correct.'

'My brother,' Veraminta said.

'Pardon?'

'*Seno* Linn is my brother. Oh, and here's my darling niece.' She rolled her eyes as a frizzy-haired girl came out of one of the bedrooms.

'You're the soffs?' the teenager said. 'Because I totally know what happened to Jupel.'

Veraminta groaned. 'Don't start, Kaya.'

'He got killed because he was dealing in ices.'

Damian looked up from his notes to meet Tomi's gaze.

'He was not,' Veraminta said.

'Was too. I've been saying it for ages. I called Father as soon as I heard the professor had been done in. He wanted me to go straight to the mill just in case. *He* believed me.'

Tomi jumped in before Veraminta could respond. 'What makes you think the professor was dealing in illicit substances?'

'He always meets that shipping bloke, Herliz, in the communal parlour next to the oven fire.'

'They have a pot of tea and a smoke,' Veraminta snapped. 'There's nothing wrong with that.'

Kaya gave her the superior look only a teenager could pull off. 'On the second-last day of every month, Herliz gave Jupel a pouch.'

'We spoke to *Seno* Herliz,' Tomi said. 'He said it was a supply of triller herb.'

'There!' Veraminta said triumphantly. 'You see? All your plots and conspiracies. You'll wind up in the Southeast District, my girl, with talk like that.'

Damian lived in the Southeast District, but at least none of his neighbours had been gutted in their own apartment.

The zimarool, who had been forgotten in the argument, yipped for more pats. Veraminta lovingly obliged.

'It's not a conspiracy,' Kaya said. 'Do people check their triller herb like this?' She mimed hefting a pouch in her hand.

Veraminta burst into laughter. '*That's* what you're basing your entire argument on?'

'You've seen people get triller herb,' Kaya said to Tomi. 'They go like...' She pretended to open a pouch and dig through the contents with her finger.

'She's got a weird sort of point,' Damian said.

Tomi's features sparked. She'd put something together – something that made her very happy.

'Thank you for your time,' she said, then grabbed Damian's arm and practically dragged him from the apartment. Hot pain shot up his ribs from the jarring move.

'You're welcome!' Veraminta sang after them as Tomi shut the door.

Damian dropped the wince before Tomi noticed. 'What is it?'

'Herliz gave Jupel his monthly supply of triller the night of the murder, right? Enough to fill that lovely ornamental box, were his words.'

'Right...'

'So why was the box half-empty when we got there? I knew something didn't make sense in the initial inventory. No one could smoke that much in a few hours. Maybe the pouches don't have *just* triller in them.' Tomi mimicked Kaya hefting an invisible pouch. 'They might have something else. Something heavier.'

'An IS?' Damian said.

'Maybe. Let's go to Eversea Shipping and find out.'

Ten

IT HADN'T ESCAPED TOMI'S NOTICE THAT SOMETHING WAS WRONG with Damian. He had only worsened since this morning, and she couldn't decide whether he came from an abusive home or whether he'd gotten himself into some strife last night. It wasn't uncommon for cookies to get ahead of themselves, their new badge feeling like armour as they ventured out into the city after hours. If Damian had picked a fight with someone he shouldn't have, that was his own fault. But if something else had happened...

Tomi wasn't sure whether to ask. It was none of her business. Then again, maybe things would've been different if her own mentor had stepped in to help when she was falling apart as his AO.

She and Damian left their grousdu in a public enclosure filled with other saddled birds and headed towards the bustling docks. While they walked, she chewed on the idea of simply prodding. A casual question, perhaps about what he'd got up to last night? No one slept easy after seeing their first corpse on the job, even if they jested about it during the day.

Damian didn't seem to notice her attention. His gaze was on the scene before them. Heartbeasts hauled cargo up ramps to a grand sailing ship. Burly men and women worked around native Agriterran plants, which sat waiting in soil-filled crates. A system of pulleys lifted plump raizelets onto the deck. The creatures squealed and snorted as they were winched up.

'Bit different to when I worked at the docks,' Damian said.

Unlike the rest of Radaza's merchant docks, which were built along the Madeira, Eversea Shipping's warehouses and piers were built to the north, on the white sands of the Parif River. The company's precinct backed onto the Shores District, the sparkling azure of the river contrasting against the cream buildings capped with red clay roofs. The company must've been raking in the coin, considering the area was like its own tiny village. There was even a three-storey tower with a timekeeper on the top.

Tomi stepped around a steaming pile of heartbeast dung. 'It seems people are willing to pay plenty of jingle for a couple of curios.'

'That looks like the main building,' Damian said, pointing to the tower. He strode ahead purposefully.

Tomi hesitated before following. It was probably best to wait a few days. If Damian's exhaustion and injuries continued, then she'd talk to him.

'Officer Cardozo.'

Georgio Herliz hurried up to them before they reached the main office doors. He wore an embroidered waistcoat, his dark hair slick and moustache pristine. Sweat dripped down his face, but Tomi doubted it had anything to do with manual labour.

He looked from Tomi to Damian, his complexion paler than when they'd interviewed him. 'How can I help?'

'We've come to ask about your smuggled goods,' Tomi said.

Herliz laughed nervously as he pulled out his well-worn handkerchief. 'What do you mean?'

'The smuggled goods,' Tomi said. 'That's why your business is here, rather than on the main docks. You don't want to be paying import tax for expensive items, and you certainly don't want Border Control finding anything illegal in your shipments. Right?'

'I – I have no idea what you're talking about.'

'I think you do,' Tomi said. 'You've been bringing illicit substances into the country, hidden in pouches of triller herb.'

Herliz dabbed at his face with his handkerchief. 'That's an outrageous statement!'

'How outrageous will it sound when we have Particulars test the triller herb in Ivan Jupel's "lovely ornamental box"? What will we find traces of in there?'

'Nothing, because there's nothing to find.'

'No?' Tomi surveyed the area. 'How about I call Border Control down here now? I'll encourage them to have a nice, long look through your goods.'

'You can't do that. We're due to sail at twilight.'

'This ship won't be going anywhere if Border Control have a reason to keep it docked.'

'But the frost–'

'Will be the least of your worries if you don't cooperate.'

Herliz hesitated.

'You found the body,' Tomi said. 'You saw what was done to the professor. If you're part of this smuggling business, how do you know the killer won't come after you next? And if you were *behind* the killing, I promise you, I'll get the evidence I need to ensure you're prosecuted to the full extent of the law.'

'What? No! I didn't kill Ivan. He was a friend.'

Tomi moved closer, lowering her voice beneath the chaos of the docks. 'Was he? Or was he nothing more than a link in your smuggling chain? What happened, Herliz? Did Professor Jupel change his mind? Did he decide he no longer wanted to be part of this? Did he threaten to go to your grandfather and tell him what you'd been up to? I doubt Park Herliz would let anyone get away with using his company to import ices, even if it were his grandson. Is that why you decided to murder Ivan Jupel? To save your job?'

'No!' Herliz's sweaty face flushed red. 'I don't know why you're accusing me. I told you Ivan had a visitor that night.'

'You could've been lying.'

'I wasn't. I'll prove it. My grandfather knew about the pouches, and it had nothing to do with ices.' He stuffed his handkerchief into his breast pocket. 'Come with me.'

Damian shot Tomi an impressed smile as Herliz led them towards the tower. Tomi didn't smile back. The knot in her chest had loosened but only slightly. Convincing someone to talk was usually only half the battle. Unless Herliz had names, there was still a lot of work to do.

And the first day of her probation was almost over.

It was much cooler inside. A cleaner mopped the tiled floor, but the fragrance of the cleaning products was citrus rather than bitter pinjora. Tomi was able to keep her tremors to a minimum as they followed Herliz up a winding eggstone staircase.

'At the beginning of the monsoon season, my grandfather approached me for a favour,' Herliz said. 'He had a pouch of triller herb; said it was a special order for a man in my building. I hadn't spoken much to Ivan before then, but these special orders came in once a month, and we found a bond in our love of collectable items.'

Damian started to slow. Tomi glanced over her shoulder and saw that he was leaning forward, as if trying not to double over.

'My instructions were clear,' Herliz continued, unaware. 'I was to give the pouches to Jupel as soon as he returned home. I was never to open them.'

'And you didn't?' Tomi said.

'I was curious, I admit. But my grandfather made it clear that the less I knew, the better.'

'What ship did the pouch arrive on?'

'Whichever was returning from Elumina at the right time. We have several loads sailing back and forth through the monsoon and wild seasons. The pouches didn't seem to be linked to one specific vessel or one specific captain.'

'So it was arranged by someone in authority at the other port,' Tomi said, silently cursing. Agriterra's Justice Department had no jurisdiction in Elumina.

'My grandfather's partner works at our other port. I imagine she was the one arranging it.' Herliz stopped at the top of the stairs and turned to face Tomi. 'I'm only telling you all this because it's not as bad as you think.'

'How can you say that? A man was murdered.'

'I doubt very much Ivan's death had anything to do with what was in the pouches.' Herliz furrowed his perspiring brow. 'Where's your AO?'

Tomi turned. Damian was no longer behind her.

'I'm here.' His voice echoed from further down the winding passage. 'I'm just horrifically unfit.' He tried to sound cheerful, but she heard the pain laced in his voice.

She sighed. If these injuries were going to affect his job, she would need to talk to him after all.

'Keep going,' she said to Herliz. She followed him along a hall to an office at the end with *Park Herliz, Owner* inscribed on the door plaque.

'The pouches contained a stone,' Herliz said. 'I could feel it inside. It was yea big.' He stretched his thumb and index finger as wide as they could go.

'A stone?'

'Just one stone, yes. That's all. Nothing to do with illicit substances.'

Kaya had seen Jupel hefting the pouch. That would make more sense if he were feeling for something heavy like a stone rather than a packet of ices.

But Tomi hadn't seen a stone that size in the inventory list. Had Jupel already passed it along?

'Did Jupel leave his apartment after you gave him the pouch?'

'No.' Herliz stopped outside the office door and rapped gently. 'Grandfather?'

So either the stone was still hidden in the apartment or the killer had taken it. Tomi was pondering the chances of them missing a second secret hiding place when Damian caught up.

'Jupel owned a lot of precious stones,' he said, breathless from catching up.

Herliz's voice must've echoed down the hallway.

'Yes,' Herliz said. 'Take the parillion gemstone on his thumb ring. It would've been worth a small fortune. But that one was acquired legally.'

Damian got out his parchment book and started writing. His hands shook.

'All Jupel's rings were missing,' Tomi said.

'It was mentioned in his insurance list,' Damian said, scribbling it down. 'But there weren't any descriptions. What does a parillion gemstone look like?'

'Red, with gold flecks.' Herliz knocked on the door again. 'Very rare. Haven't seen another one in Radaza.'

Damian glanced up. 'I have.'

'Where?' Tomi said.

His brow furrowed. 'I can't remember. But I've definitely seen one recently.'

Tomi turned to Herliz. 'What kind of precious stone is as big as the one in the pouch?'

'I'm not sure. You should know, though, it had a horrific odour. Grandfather!' Herliz knocked, this time louder. 'What's he doing in there?' After pressing his ear against the wood, he said, 'Grandfather, I'm coming in.' He opened the door.

Tomi knew what had happened the moment she heard the ragged, terrified breath drag itself into Herliz's lungs. What she hadn't suspected was the how.

The body of Park Herliz, co-owner of Eversea Shipping, sat slumped in a chair, illuminated by the orange glow of the setting sun. The entirety of his skin bubbled with red sores. Blood dripped from his mouth, staining his waistcoat. His eyeballs had been removed, and, as Tomi peered closer, she realised that so had his tongue.

There was no doubt about this one. Park Herliz had been killed by a witch.

Eleven

TOMI DESPERATELY NEEDED A BATH. A LONG, HOT SOAK ALWAYS did wonders for her spinning mind. It allowed her to settle her thoughts and fit gearwheels together. When the frost came and baths were restricted, she found she took longer to close cases.

She'd spent the evening questioning dock workers and employees at Eversea. The cleaner should've been the most help, considering he'd been mopping right beneath Park Herliz's office. But no one had seen or heard a thing: not a scream, not a footstep.

Supposedly impossible, but TADOW always warned that nothing was impossible when it came to witches.

Border Control had swarmed the place, confiscating all kinds of goods. It seemed, despite what Georgio Herliz had believed, his grandfather had been in the business of smuggling. It was impossible for previous raids to have missed this, which meant someone in Border Control had been in Park Herliz's pocket.

No longer, though. Herliz Senior was dead, which meant his bribery or blackmail or whatever he'd been doing was over. In the soil of the native Agriterran plants, Border Control had found what Tomi suspected was the payment for Jupel's stone: dozens and dozens of bones and teeth. More specifically, ossicles and molars. Tomi didn't know what purpose the three types of ear bones and chompers served, but, as she'd learnt from Jupel's secret stash, witches required all kinds of ingredients for potions.

Her next question was, who was supplying them?

She wanted to stew on it in a bath, lounged and warm and steamy. There was so much to contemplate, so many threads to untangle. Unfortunately, there wasn't enough time before her midnight meeting.

The Clinker District bells were chiming 11 as she dismounted Finley. Unlike at Jupel's atrium, the frost doors of hers were never locked. Sometimes homeless people wandered into the communal area seeking warmth and scraps, but they'd never caused a problem.

The oldies were still up; Tomi could hear them singing by the fire ovens. She led Finley towards the entrance. There would be barely any time to change before she had to leave again.

'Tomi.' A familiar man stepped into the light of the entrance.

Tomi's fists instinctively tightened around Finley's reins. She stopped, unable to keep the snarl from her voice. 'What are you doing here?'

Grundy Shard was in a midnight-blue jacket and trousers. His shirt was tight, the neckline dipping in a low valley to reveal tufts of dark chest hair. It was the perfect encapsulation of Grundy – a combination of professionalism and narcissistic theatre. He rubbed his fingers along stubble that had never made an appearance while they were dating.

'I heard about the results of your hearing,' he said. 'I'm so glad you were acquitted.'

He had this way of batting his thick eyelashes that made him seem innocent, but also as if his brains were concrete.

How had Tomi ever been in love with him?

No, that wasn't fair. She'd been in love with someone she *thought* was him. The appearance he'd put on for the rest of the world – an ambitious, interesting, vibrant individual – was nothing more than the sprayed-on sheen of a butterlin shell being sold as a duskpearl. There was a laziness, a stagnancy, in his personality. He always played the same sort of parts with the same sort of lines and was too afraid of failure to attempt auditioning for a larger role. Her infatuation with him had clouded her ability to see the shortcomings.

'I wasn't acquitted,' she said, leading Finley through the frost doors. 'I'm on probation. And I don't have time for this.'

Finley rasped. Tomi half hoped he was cranky enough to peck Grundy right in that pretty face.

But Finley remained disappointingly well-behaved, and Grundy scurried after them. 'I wanted to say I'm sorry. I didn't expect this to get out of hand.'

'*Really?*'

'Yes, really. I made a mistake. I was angry and whispered a few things into your colleagues' ears–'

'You were angry I broke up with you? What did you expect after what you did?'

The oldies stopped singing. They'd spotted Grundy. Lyrica, who'd been conducting the drunken recital with *Leya* Marsh's paintbrush, whipped around so that her golden skirts shimmered in the glow of the fires and oil lanterns. She stumbled in her heels but covered it grandly.

'Tom-eee,' she trilled. 'Lovely for you to join us.' She brandished the paintbrush like a sword towards Grundy. 'Shall we eject this man violently from the premises?'

'That won't be necessary, thank you, Lyrica. He's just leaving.'

'No, I'm *not* just leaving,' Grundy said.

'Stab him,' *Leya* Marsh said, leaning keenly across the table. She didn't notice her elbows were in the remnants of her supper.

Grundy huffed. 'I'm trying to apologise, may the Tassela damn you!'

Tomi ushered Finley into the central enclosure with the other grousdu. 'Your apology is heard and not accepted.'

Grundy had the nerve to look offended.

'Did you think your words wouldn't be taken serious by the Justice Department?' Tomi said. 'Of course the other JOs had to report it. Of course my boss had to write an official complaint.'

'I had no idea–'

'Go home, Grundy.'

She didn't want to do this now. Well, she didn't want to do this ever, but especially not now. She had to get to the southern shores by midnight.

She started up the winding balcony. Grundy, infuriatingly, followed her.

'Do you know how long I've been waiting for you? Hours, Tomi. And you won't even give me the time to say sorry. You see, this was the problem. Your work was your life.'

'Push him over the railing!' Lyrica called from below.

'If that was your problem, you should've talked to me instead of bedding the Honeybun Girl,' Tomi said.

Umbrine had chatted with them on multiple occasions when Tomi had visited Grundy on his work breaks. She'd sold them sweet rolls and treated Tomi like a friend. It was possible she was a selfish, manipulative woman. It was also possible Grundy had spun his lies and tricked her into thinking he was in a miserable relationship. Tomi didn't blame Umbrine if that were the case. From the exterior, Grundy Sharp was something to behold. An insurance assessor by day, a minor theatre actor by night. Who wouldn't be interested in that?

'I might've talked to you, if you ever stopped moving long enough to let me speak,' Grundy said. 'You never paid me any attention. Even when we were together, your mind was always on the case you were working. In the whole year we were together, you barely came to any of my shows.'

'You're a terrible actor, anyway.'

Behind her, Grundy sucked in a breath. 'That's fine,' he said. 'I understand you're upset–'

'Grundy.' Tomi spun around. Below, Lyrica was conducting a new song about witches who'd once ravaged the land, castrating all men as they went. 'I get it. You're feeling guilty. But this case is extremely important–'

'Yes, yes, they always are, aren't they?' Grundy said with a dismissive wave.

'Yes,' Tomi said slowly and clearly so that he understood. 'I investigate *mur-ders*. I stand for people whose threads have been ripped apart before their time. I take killers off the streets. My work will always be important.'

The top of Grundy's lip twitched in the hint of a sneer. 'If that's so, then you'll never find a partner.'

'Maybe,' Tomi said, and she meant it.

The thought of never binding wasn't as alarming as it used to be. Lyrica had never bound, and she was perfectly happy. At least this way Tomi could focus.

Grundy seemed to think he'd won the argument. 'Well then,' he said, stepping backwards. 'I suppose the only thing to do now is wish you the best.'

He paused, as if expecting a reciprocation.

Tomi turned on her heel and continued stalking up the balcony without saying anything. The gearwheels were ticking, and she had somewhere to be.

While she was changing, she heard the jeers on the ground floor that must've been the oldies booing Grundy out of the atrium. She smiled as she rebraided her long hair.

She had sidestepped a pothole when it came to Grundy. Despite thinking herself desperately in love, certain hers and Grundy's life threads were forever entangled, some part of her had been cautious enough to keep her other secret.

Her *real* secret.

Grundy – and almost the entire world – still had no idea who she really was.

Twelve

It was closer to midnight than Tomi would've liked. The bridge was almost empty, so she could race Finley across it at top speed. Her belly was full from a hasty meal of leftovers, courtesy of Lyrica. Tomi often forgot to eat during cases.

She leaned forward, relishing the feel of the rushing wind, the sight of the cobblestones blurring beneath them. Here was the second-best place to think, after a bathtub.

There were so many variables now, so many officials involved. As well as Border Control, the TADOW Authority had part-jurisdiction over the case and would be questioning Park Herliz's family. Plus, she'd had to inform ISEF about the possibility of cutlass being back on the streets.

Witches, ices and smuggling. Professor Ivan Jupel's death was the equivalent of harpooning a norhl for meat and finding its gizzards filled with flesh-eating mogworms.

Damian had been no help. She'd had to send him home after he started slurring his words from exhaustion. Georgio Herliz had to have soporifia elixir to calm his hysterics and couldn't answer any questions. No one knew why Park Herliz had been tortured. Tomi's only clue was the missing stone.

A letter had been sent to Park's partner in Elumina. They were worried she'd be next, but the letter would take half a month to arrive.

Tomi pushed Finley harder, arriving at the southern shores slightly later than the midnight bells. After she'd tied Finley to a tethering post, she headed down to the beach.

'You're late,' the skipper said.

Moonlit waves rolled across the sand. Dune bushes shivered in the wind.

'Got a case,' Tomi said, tossing him a pouch of coin. 'I've put extra in there for your troubles.'

He grinned, his teeth yellow within his beard. 'Appreciated.'

She followed him to the jetty. Neither spoke as he prepped the idling steam engine of his small fishing boat. They'd done this too often to feel obliged to make small talk. Bleak Isle – unfortunately named, thanks to its first owner, *Seno* Bleak – sat further out to sea, visible in the glow of its lighthouse. Tomi watched it draw nearer as the steamboat fought the choppy waves. Twenty-three years she'd been doing this, and still her heart sprinted on the journey out.

It took less than an hour to reach the island. The skipper tied the boat to the jetty and sank into the seat nearest the engine for warmth. He lit a pipe and waved goodbye as Tomi started the trek up the path towards Bleakhouse. Some of the windows were open. A wail drifted out, clear across the night. It startled a haunting owl, which took flight from a twisted salt tree. Tomi put her head down and kept climbing the slope.

Beacon Joan opened the door. She gave a reverent bow as she stepped aside to let Tomi in. They treated her like royalty here. An annual donation of 50 gold coins had brought her respect nothing else would.

She signed the ledger then followed Beacon Joan up the winding balcony. The lanterns were turned down, so the place glowed softly. There was no grousdu or minnisk enclosure in Bleakhouse's centre. What would be the point? Instead it was a communal garden with flourishing plants, hedges and blossom trees, among which residents could sit, eat, socialise or play games. There was even a small pool near the oven fires for exercise.

No residents were out at the moment, although a few holy leaders patrolled the balcony. The wailer had fallen silent.

Beacon Joan unlocked the room at the end of the balcony and Tomi stepped inside.

Harpsigold sat on a chair by the window, wrapped in a fluffy blanket, looking out at the city. Her grey-streaked curls hung freely, long but limp. She was 38, but she looked more like she was in her fifties.

'You have a visitor,' Beacon Joan said.

Harpsigold didn't turn around. Beacon Joan gave Tomi a kind smile. 'May the Tassela watch over you,' she said before walking from the room.

Tomi pulled up a second chair to sit by the window too. 'How are you, Happy Harps?'

Harpsigold didn't react. She watched the moon, the lights from Radaza reflected in her eyes.

Tomi reached out to take her hands. They were warm against Tomi's cold skin.

'It's the first night of Harrow,' Tomi said. 'The frost is coming soon.'

This elicited a shiver from Harpsigold. At least she was listening.

'Don't be afraid. I'll come back after the thaw. I always do.' Tomi squeezed Harpsigold's fingers. 'How was your day?'

Sometimes, Harpsigold was lucid enough to say a few words. They even played cards or clatterboards once in a while. Tomi always let her win, grateful there was enough sense in Harpsigold to understand and follow basic game rules. Tonight didn't seem to be one of those times.

When the silence stretched on, Tomi said, 'All right. I'll tell you about my day instead. The case I'm working on involves – wait for it – *witches*.'

It was only because she was watching Harpsigold carefully that she noticed the slightest intake of breath.

'Harps?'

Harpsigold blinked rapidly. She was trying to convey something.

'What's wrong?' Tomi said

'B-Bad.'

'It's all right. I'll be careful.'

'*Bad.*'

Tomi reached out to stroke Harpsigold's hair. It was unusual to see her worked up about a case.

Harpsigold's breathing turned to sharp gasps. 'Bad!'

'Hey,' Tomi said soothingly. 'It's fine. We won't talk about that.'

She got up and took Harpsigold's doll from the white-clothed nightstand. Harpsigold practically snatched it from Tomi's hands. She rocked in her chair as she stroked the frayed knitting, humming to herself.

When she had calmed, the doll sitting in her lap, her eyes turned cityward once more, Tomi changed the conversation to Grundy. She was pleased to hear annoyed grunts as she described his visit. Harpsigold had never met Grundy – Grundy hadn't even discovered she existed – but she knew enough about him to know what a creeg he was.

Tomi was careful not to mention the hearing. She hadn't said anything to Harpsigold about her legal troubles in case it upset her. Instead, she explained about her new AO.

'He's got a keen eye,' she said. 'A willingness to learn. And he's sort of funny.' She stood and flopped on the bed. 'His academic record was fine, you know, the usual. Nothing different from the applications I'd gotten in the past. I'm never impressed by fancy bloodlines. The only reason I accepted him was because his training officer said...' She trailed off. 'Huh.'

Her mind had snagged again, not on the training officer's statement but her previous sentence. She sat up. It occurred to her why Damian's comment about going to a local parish had caught her attention yesterday. Parishes were more common south of the river, but in his personal details, his address was listed in the Shores. How could someone who lived so close to the Church District have never seen the inside of a proper church?

And, more importantly, did the discrepancy have anything to do with his injuries and exhaustion today?

Harpsigold had turned her face slightly, an indication that she was waiting for more.

'It's fine,' Tomi said. 'I think he might not be telling me everything.' She walked back to Harpsigold and ruffled her hair. 'But his secrets are nothing compared to ours, hey sis?'

Thirteen

Tomi was late. Damian lingered outside the morgue. The clouds were so thick, it barely felt like morning. Puddles gleamed beneath the streetlamps and water dripped from the eaves. From an undercover stall, a teenage boy sold newscloths to well-dressed people riding grousdu or minnisks to work.

Above, a flock of crooners flew northeast. Their bodies streamed like reeds in a grey river, an omen of the impending frost. How much would the settling affect Damian and Tomi's ability to close their case? Everything would be more difficult, that was certain.

And things were difficult enough. Pa slept fitfully, disturbed by pain. The numbing elixir only helped so much; Damian could do nothing as he listened to Pa whimpering through the thin wall between the bedroom and the lounge. His exhaustion had cost him – Tomi had sent him home early yesterday during the interviews at Eversea. It couldn't have made for a good impression.

All the while, the threat of Bunter Vittam loomed like the chayuli, the shadowy monsters in old Khvu stories. The difference was, the chayuli were a myth told to frighten unruly peasants into obedience. Bunter Vittam was very real and very capable of violence.

Damian needed this case closed. He wanted time to think, to figure out how to handle this. He couldn't – wouldn't – be used as a spy against Tomi or the Justice Department. He had to find another arrangement with Vittam.

Tomi arrived with the first drops of the next downpour. She and Damian hurried into the morgue as the clouds burst.

'Nice timing,' Damian said, hoping his breathlessness came across as a result of the short run and not from the pain in his ribs.

'Sorry I'm late.' She gave no further explanation, but she looked more tired than normal.

Guilt prickled at his threads. She would've gotten more sleep if he'd been at the crime scene to help with interviews. 'How did it go last night?'

'What? Oh. Fine. The usual.'

Damian didn't know what 'the usual' meant, but Tomi seemed distracted, so he didn't push it. She'd catch him up later.

They headed downstairs. Damian shivered in the chill of the tunnels that led to the autopsy rooms deep under Lilac Bay. The compacted rock was unnaturally smooth and polished. The medica maven, Payana, was waiting with Jupel's corpse on the dais.

'You didn't come to dinner the other night,' she said as soon as they walked in.

Tomi sighed. 'I told you, I'm working.'

'That's no excuse. Mia's going to burst if she doesn't tell you the news soon.'

'I didn't get fired, by the way,' Tomi said.

'Yes, yes, I heard. Come to dinner tonight instead.'

'I can't–'

'Did I mention how Mia's going to burst? Besides, I got you a present from Evidence.' Payana dangled the small key Tomi had found in Jupel's apartment. A tag had been attached through the loophole with the case number on it. 'Thought it might be useful if you come across whatever it opens.'

Tomi reached out, but Payana yanked it away. 'Uh uh. You have to promise to come to dinner first.'

'May the Tassela damn you to the Umbra, cratter.'

Damian would've gotten a whack from *Bamki* Rivers for using language like that. Payana just smiled prettily. 'Dinner. Tonight. Promise.'

'*Fine.* Can I have the key, please?'

'Catch.'

Payana tossed it over Jupel's corpse. Tomi snatched it from the air and pocketed it in one smooth movement.

'It looks like the dead are in good hands,' Damian said.

'Welcome to the morgue, cookie.' Payana passed a few rolls of parchment over the body to Tomi.

Tomi unrolled them. 'Have you seen Park Herliz's body?'

'Yes.' Payana frowned slightly. 'He looks like he was tortured. Do you know what the killer wanted?'

'Not yet.' Tomi shifted so Damian could read the reports too. 'Jupel's cause of death is the torso wound, as expected. No organs missing. No marks to suggest a struggle, no skin under his fingernails–'

'What about these?' Damian said, pointing to the scratches down the corpse's arms.

'They were made earlier, days before his death,' Payana said. 'There are scars like that all over his body.'

That matched what Tailor Happershift had said about Jupel suffering withdrawal symptoms.

'You've put the time of death around midnight,' Tomi said. 'That's later than Herliz saw the stranger leave.'

'Maybe he got the hour wrong,' Damian said.

'Maybe.' Tomi glanced at Payana. 'Ices in the system?'

'Nothing that showed up in the tests.'

'Cutlass doesn't show up in tests.'

Payana swung her stunned gaze between Tomi and Damian. 'He was on cutlass?'

'Apparently,' Tomi said. 'It'll be hard to confirm, though.'

The two of them seemed grim.

'It can't be worse than plink,' Damian said. One of the residents in his atrium had been addicted to plink. He'd watched as the woman had become so withered and wasted, her grousdu refused to go anywhere near her. She'd ended up suffocating in her own vomit in the ablution block.

'Don't they talk about cutlass in the academy anymore?' Tomi said.

'They touched on it, but it's been gone from the streets for years. The worst wave of it was before I was born.'

'It still ripples through on occasion,' Payana said. 'The problem is defining it. They don't nickname it "ghost" for nothing. Users have clear cravings and withdrawal symptoms, but we can't find anything in their system to confirm its existence.'

'Which means ISEF can't charge them for illicit substance use,' Tomi said. 'And the Justice Department has never confiscated an official sample for testing. They claim that they have, but...' She shook her head. 'The results vary. Experts can't agree on what it consists of. Whoever makes this stuff, their knowledge is way beyond our medica mavens.'

'Is it just me, or does that sound like witches?' Damian said.

Payana gestured to Jupel. 'If it's true he was using, this would be the first time we've ever had a clear link between witches and cutlass. But yes, we suspect it's a potion rather than an IS.'

'You think Jupel was brewing it?'

'Unlikely,' Tomi said. 'People who manufacture cutlass are rarely addicts themselves.'

'From the little research we have, users seem to die within a few years of their first taste,' Payana added. 'I say "seem to" because there's no discernible cause of death. They just keel over one day. And it's so addictive, sometimes they die from the withdrawal symptoms alone. Scratch themselves to death. I suppose that would explain the scars.' Payana nodded to the report. 'I did find something of interest in his stomach contents. I can't tell exactly what it is, but it matched the substance found in one of the goblets.'

'You can't tell what it is?' Tomi said.

'It's a combination of organic materials. Nothing toxic, as far as I'm aware. It looks like soporifia elixir but more potent.'

'A witch's sleeping potion?' Damian said.

Tomi frowned. 'I understand sedating Jupel for a robbery, but changing tactics and murdering him violently while he was unconscious? That's where they've lost me.'

'They could've done it the other way around – killed him then taken his things,' Damian said.

'There are no traces of blood, or that red dust, near any of the empty spaces in the bookshelves, which means the theft happened first. And I don't get why the killer didn't just poison him from the outset if they were going to slip something in his drink anyway.' She pointed at the parchment from Particulars. 'Look at this. The red dust was found on the blade of the kitchen carving knife.'

'The makeup of the dust appears to be nutrients, salts, proteins,' Payana said. 'If I didn't know any better, I'd assume it was blood without the water.'

'Blood powder,' Tomi said. 'Just like I suspected. We're definitely looking at a killer witch, and the carving knife was the murder weapon.'

Payana moved about the room, tidying the equipment. There was a sink that had water running straight from the bay – she filled up a bottle to mix it with cleaning fluid and began spraying surfaces. Damian could've sworn he felt Tomi flinch beside him, but when he glanced at her, she looked fine.

'Did you see there was salitenine grease on the handle of the knife?' Payana said. 'If we're looking at a chemical that stops a build-up of salt, it means your killer worked with machinery on or near the sea – like a barge train, ferry, or shipyard – the day or so before the murder.'

Damian glanced at Tomi. 'Someone from Eversea Shipping?'

'Maybe.'

'Here,' Damian said, touching the bottom of the report. 'Traces of animal dung were found on the snow bear rug.'

'Herbivore dung,' Payana said. 'So not grousdu or minnisk. It looks to belong to one of the greater beasts of the Elumina Prairies. It's fresh, maybe a few days old. If I were to guess, I'd say either the killer or the victim took a trip to the menagerie recently.'

'It wasn't Jupel,' Tomi said. 'At least according to his travel log.'

'There are ways of getting around without having things recorded in your travel log,' Damian said. Being Vittam's runner had taught him how to move through Radaza without leaving a trail.

Payana glanced over her shoulder as she wiped down benches. 'Are any of the people you've questioned so far actually involved with the menagerie?'

'Not that we know of,' Tomi said. 'Why?'

'When's the last time either of you went to Whimsy Holm?'

'Never,' Damian said.

'Not since I was a kid,' Tomi said.

'Then maybe you've forgotten, but the greater prairie beasts can only be viewed from a platform a safe distance away. There shouldn't be that kind of dung on the bottom of any shoes unless they've had access to the enclosure.'

'Like a special visitor?' Damian said.

'Or an employee.' Tomi rerolled the parchments. 'Looks like we're taking a trip to the menagerie.'

'Medica Thraseep?' Payana's attending medica walked in with another report. 'Initial examination of Park Herliz.'

Payana checked the report. It seemed to take her a long time to read.

It was only after she'd been staring at the page for some time that Damian realised her eyes weren't moving.

'Payana?' Tomi said.

Payana's gaze snapped up to her. She looked haunted.

'What's wrong?' Tomi said.

'I have to talk to you.' Payana glanced at Damian, grimaced, and added, 'Alone.'

Fourteen

What were they hiding?

The question plucked at Damian's threads as he and Tomi made their way to the Ariela Park Ferry Terminal. Payana had found something in Park Herliz's autopsy report. What was it, and why hadn't she let him hear?

And why did Tomi, after talking in private to Payana, look like she'd come across a chayuli?

Dark clouds rolled across the sky, dumping showers with increasing regularity. Damian tried not to obsess, but he couldn't stop.

This could be about Bunter Vittam. There was no question Vittam was involved in the shadowy side of Radaza, and there was a distinct possibility that he was behind both Jupel and Herliz's murders. Damian wouldn't be surprised to learn Vittam had witches on his team.

But what if there had been evidence left behind that suggested Damian was involved too? What if, somehow, Payana had spotted proof that Damian was indentured to the King of the Streets? What if that's why Tomi was so quiet – because she was thinking of what to do with him?

Damian had tried not to ask, considering his role as an AO was strictly to watch and take notes, but by the time they reached Ariela Park, he couldn't take it anymore.

'What did Payana find in the report?'

His question seemed to drag Tomi out of her thoughts. 'Nothing,' she said after a moment. 'She noticed a similarity in a case from the late '60s, but that doesn't mean it's connected to the Herliz murder.'

Damian let her words settle around him like a blanket. It had nothing to do with Bunter Vittam. Or him.

Of course it didn't. She would've arrested him immediately or at least asked him about it. His guilty conscience was starting to leak paranoia.

But then–

'She just happened to know a specific detail from a case twenty-something years ago?'

'It was a major case.'

'She looked shocked.'

'Sure.' Tomi gave a casual shrug. 'If she's right, it'd be huge. No one's ever been able to prove witches were involved in the Glisk murders–'

'The Glisk murders?' Damian's interest flared like a freshly lit wick. 'She thinks our case is connected to the biggest case in Radaza?'

'I wouldn't say it's the biggest–'

'Every cadet in the academy had a theory on how it happened. My neighbour said people were using Glisk cleaning products as far as the Epoya region.' Damian pushed down his curls, laughing in disbelief. 'Imagine if we caught the people who murdered the Glisks.'

'Slow your threads. Payana only spotted one minor parallel to the Herliz murder. That doesn't mean we're dealing with the same killer.'

'What's the parallel?'

They steered their grousdu down the slope towards the terminal building on the riverfront. Its walls were made of coruscat glass – dark and reflecting on the external side but transparent from the inside.

Tomi dismounted. 'The preliminary examination found indents on Herliz's wrists, suggesting he was tied to the chair, but there's no pattern in the skin to indicate a rope or a cord and no leftover fibres. It's the same as what happened to Sharlie Glisk. That's it. That's all Payana was going on.'

'It's strange though, right? Why would the killer take the bindings in the first place?' Damian gingerly climbed off Brix. His ribs were even more tender than yesterday. It was difficult to move without flinching.

'It would've been a waste of time,' Tomi agreed. 'Unless it somehow points to their identity.'

'The Justice Department never thought the Glisks had been killed by witches?'

'There were investigations into it, but nothing about the murders suggested magical involvement.'

'Except this weird binding thing.'

'The JOs decided the fibres had been dislodged during the investigation,' Tomi said. 'An error on the medica mavens' part.'

Damian scoffed. 'I guess they were wrong. Because it's pretty obvious Park Herliz was killed by a witch.'

This was huge. No wonder Payana had looked so astonished. If the Glisks had been killed by witches, then it opened up a whole realm of new possibilities.

The murders had been brutal. Anatole and Sharlie Glisk were Black Ivory residents, two of the richest people in Radaza. *Bamki* Rivers had asserted that no other household cleaning products worked as well as Glisk's Rise and Shine.

On the night of 1069's frost settling, Anatole Glisk had been force-fed his own bleach, while Sharlie Glisk had been bound to a chair and shot in the head. Tomi was right – there was nothing specifically linking the event to witches.

Except with this new evidence, maybe there was.

Tomi was quiet as they walked their grousdu towards a public enclosure. Damian couldn't believe she wasn't more excited.

'If you were on the case back then, you would've solved it,' he said.

A soft snort escaped her. 'We've all tried to solve it, Damian. That evidence nook is the most visited one in the archive. But no one's gotten any further than the original investigation. The JOs were thorough. They had to be on a case that big.'

'They didn't know they were looking for magic.'

'No. I suppose they didn't.'

They reached the enclosure and paid the grousdu minder. Finley scratched his sharp claws in the dirt before stalking into the flock. Brix fluffed her feathers and plonked herself down right in front of the entrance.

'Ah, trat's droppings,' Tomi said abruptly. 'I forgot to feed Fin his worm paste and gizzard stones.'

Damian had a flash: Pa dropping the gizzard stones, easing his wooden leg to pick them up, the blade going into his hand.

Pa's screams.

'I usually do it on the first of every month.' Tomi's voice sounded far away. 'But it's hard to concentrate when you're on a case. That's something you'll soon learn. Sometimes I even forget to eat.'

Pa wouldn't be sorting pouches of gizzard stones anymore. His damaged hand was beyond repair. Would he turn to gambling again? Or would he fall to the bottle? Ever since the accident at the docks, Pa had suffered bouts of darkness, unable to cook, unable to speak, unable to get out of bed some mornings. During the first days, at just 13, Damian had had to find food and clean and pay the residency bills with their scraped-together savings.

'Damian?'

Thank the Tassela for *Bamki* Rivers. She'd been their saviour back then and was still looking after Pa now. But would she be enough this time? It was all crumbling, perhaps to the point of collapse. One leg gone, one hand useless, a debt that would take generations to repay, a monster who kept knocking on their door in the middle of the night...

'Damian!' Tomi waved a hand in front of his face, breaking him from the growing panic. 'Are you well?'

He summoned a bright smile as thunder rumbled across the sky. 'Running like a river.'

'It can be tough, jumping into this job headfirst. If you ever want to talk–'

'It's raining again. Let's get inside before we drown.'

Tomi's brow was furrowed, but she dropped the subject. They headed through the arched entryway in silence. People squelched past, hair soaked, umbrellas dripping. The tiles were slick and slippery. Every now and then, lightning flashed through the gloom.

This was the largest ferry port in the city. Boats came and went from the menagerie, the University, Deep Water Bay, the traders' markets south of the river and the Overland Terminal. Damian knew the place well. When he hadn't been sneaking ferry rides, he'd been using it as Vittam's drop point. It was almost strange being here during the day, on an official trip. It had been refurbished since his last visit – new floors, new lockers, new ablution blocks. The place practically sparkled.

They joined the short queue for the boats. Through the coruscat glass, they could see the river churning. Disembarking passengers looked alarmingly unwell.

Ravern Furling was on duty at the first turnstile. Despite everything, Damian was grateful to see her.

'Damian Kamara, as my threads are woven,' she said. 'Look at you! Is that a JO tailcoat I see?' She was only half his height, but her booming voice more than made up for it.

'Better believe your eyes.' He spun around so she could get the full picture. 'I'm officially an AO now.'

'*Very* nice. Oi, Katty, check this out! It's Damian Kamara!'

Katterina Piers glanced over from the customer assistance desk. She nodded once to Damian before returning her attention to the woman she was speaking to.

'She's thrilled to see you,' Ravern assured Damian.

He doubted it. Messengers had complicated relationships with employees of ferry terminals. Slipping on and off boats without getting a travel log stamped, using lockers without identification, passing coins under the table – it was a delicate business. More importantly, it mattered who the messenger represented. Official messengers for the postal service, government departments and private companies didn't know about these underhanded techniques. But messengers representing someone like Bunter Vittam weren't allowed to mention their employer. So even though ferry workers didn't know which messengers were which, if they sent away the wrong person too many times, they could end up floating facedown in the river.

Ravern didn't have any of those problems. She let everyone jump the turnstile, as long as the boss wasn't looking.

'And how are you, Officer Cardozo?' she said as Tomi handed over her travel log.

'Can't complain,' Tomi said.

'Where are you heading?'

Tomi spoke louder as Ravern leaned her good ear towards them. 'Whimsy Holm.'

'Ha!' Another flash of lightning illuminated the place. 'Quite the day for it.'

'It's for business,' Damian said.

'Oh ho, would you listen to that? Business indeed. You're showing off now, *Officer* Kamara.'

'Have you ever met a professor by the name of Ivan Jupel?' Tomi said.

'Yes, I know the professor. Or... I knew him. Saw his face on the front cloth, poor blassard. They won't leave his memory in peace now they know he's a witch.'

Good old Ravern. She could talk anyone into a coma, but at least she paid attention to who she was speaking to.

'Did you see him heading to the menagerie around four days ago?' Tomi said.

'Not the menagerie, no. He came from the University fairly regularly to walk around Ariela Park.'

So Quaide was right – this was where Jupel was disappearing to at lunch times.

'What about anyone else visiting Whimsy Holm?' Damian said. 'Someone you've seen the professor with?'

Ravern tipped her dark blue ferry cap to one side and said cheekily, 'I'm afraid that'll cost you.'

Bolocha. She was veering into dangerous territory. If Tomi picked up on the fact he'd been an unofficial messenger, she might start asking questions he couldn't afford to answer.

'Ravern Furling.' A tall, slender man with a striped suit moved towards them. He had a greying moustache that joined smoothly to wide sideburns. While his pace was slow, his hands clasped casually behind his back, there was something slightly threatening in his approach. 'You're holding up the line.'

'Sorry, *Seno* Notch.' Ravern quickly signed and stamped Damian's travel log.

If it felt strange being here during the day, it was nothing compared to standing in plain sight of Talcott Notch. Notch owned all the main ferry stations and was known to assist the soffs in fugitive and criminal pursuits across Madeira River. Unofficial messengers steered well clear of him.

'My apologies,' Tomi said. Her tone was friendly and light. As a JO, she would've had a very difference experience dealing with Notch. 'We were just asking Ravern some questions for an investigation.'

She and Damian stepped out of the way so the final few people who were braving a ferry trip in the storm could have their travel logs stamped.

Notch's severe expression relaxed when he recognised her. 'Officer Cardozo. Lovely to see you. What can I do for you today?'

'Can you ask your employees to make a list of anyone they remember going to the menagerie about four days ago?'

Notch tapped his hand to his heart. 'I'll see to it at once.'

'Thank you.'

'It's a pleasure to help the Justice Department, Officer Cardozo.' Notch barely gave Damian a glance before walking away.

Damian caught himself feeling grateful for being overlooked. That wasn't good. JOs weren't supposed to be wary of people like Talcott Notch. How long would it take to trim the habits of his old life?

More importantly, how long would it take to trim the *people* of his old life?

They headed down the rain-splattered glass corridor to the ferry. Their travel logs were checked again at a second turnstile before they got onto the ferry. Steam poured from the funnel – it was almost time to depart.

'I hope you have a strong stomach,' Tomi said as the ferry lifted and dipped with the swell, 'because this trip isn't going to be pleasant.'

Fifteen

IT DOESN'T HAVE TO MEAN ANYTHING.

Tomi clung to the thought, because if she didn't, she was going to end up in Bleakhouse with her sister. So what if there was a link between the murders of the Glisks and Park Herliz? It was a small commonality, a tiny matching fragment in a world's worth of death.

Payana had struggled to tell her. Both knew what this could turn into.

It had been a long time since Tomi had let herself think about the Glisk case. She felt like a recovering addict who'd just been presented with a vial of plink. Her hands shook as she gripped the ferry railing; the craving to fall back into that pit was almost too much to bear.

She'd managed to distract Damian for now, but it wouldn't last. She hadn't expected such enthusiasm from him – the murders had happened before he was born. And the fact that fresh cadets were still theorising... When would this case ever leave the public's attention?

It was important to concentrate on the case at hand. Turning her whole attention to work was one of her strategies to manage the addiction.

Whimsy Holm appeared through the mist and she prepared herself for what was to come. The island was in the middle of the Madeira River, its entire space taken up by the menagerie. There was a faint, musty smell of animal as they stepped onto the jetty. It was a relief to be off the ferry. While the rain had eased to a drizzle during the trip, the river had been almost as rough as the sea last night on her way to Bleakhouse.

The breeze was salty. The Madeira River was technically a tidal estuary, where water from the ocean mixed with fresh water flowing out to sea. Salitenine grease was used along the docks and terminals of this river – and at the menagerie.

Damian had managed the journey well enough, but the four other passengers swayed sickly as the group set off up the slope to the entrance. An employee stood under a tall archway, which had *Welcome to Whimsy Holm* inscribed into the iron.

'Tickets here,' he said pleasantly.

Tomi unclipped her badge from her belt and held it up for him. He found a manager, who took them past the bird exhibit into an expansive, empty employee lounge. The place reeked of coin. Oil lanterns illuminated leather couches, gold-framed portraits and various species of plants. Tall, white candles dripped wax down candelabras. The manager told them to wait while he fetched the menagerie's owner.

The lounge had a wall of coruscat glass that offered a view of the grassy plain that lay down the slope. An iron fence ran around the perimeter of the prairie.

'Look,' Damian said, standing beside her. 'I think that's a halicort.'

He pointed to a horned creature with a leathery hide grazing beneath the overcast sky. Beyond, a herd of audfoot were drinking at an inlet. A lone bird circled above them.

Tomi had a brief memory of dragging her father from enclosure to enclosure, exclaiming in awe at the wild and wondrous creatures.

'Sorry to keep you waiting.' They turned as a lithe woman in her late seventies swept into the room. Several young minnisks tumbled about her turquoise heels. Her dress, draping and supple, was the same colour as her shoes, and a sheer shawl was slung around her shoulders.

'My,' she said, examining Damian, 'they start them young these days, don't they?' Her accent was high society, and she moved like one of the queens of Perlia. She touched a hand to her heart in greeting. 'Shiver Whimsy, at your service.'

Tomi had a gut-lurching realisation that she'd met Shiver Whimsy before. It was always a risk when she took on cases in the glimmer districts. Her only armour was the impossibility of her existence and the multiple folds of time.

'Whimsy?' Damian said, tearing his attention away from the kits, who were playing and rolling around on the rug. 'The island's named after you?'

Shiver Whimsy's laugh was a practised, tinkly bell. 'Not me, exactly. The island was gifted to my family during the Resurgence. It's been our honour to care for it since.'

She smiled at Tomi. There was no sign of recognition. It would've been unlikely, considering they'd met when Tomi was six or seven, but there was always that one sliver of chance. Tomi's brown, freckled face hadn't changed as much as she'd needed.

'*Leya* Whimsy, I'm Officer Cardozo and this is my AO, Damian Kamara. We've come to ask about Ivan Jupel.'

'That poor professor?'

'Yes. We have reason to believe the menagerie is linked to his death.'

'The menagerie?'

'Traces of fresh animal dung were found at the crime scene. It looks to be from one of your greater prairie beasts. I'm going to have to question everyone in the menagerie who has access to the enclosure.'

Whimsy's smile vanished. She pressed a hand to her cheek. 'Yes, of course. Whatever you need. By the Tassela, how dreadful. If you wait here, I'll have my manager send employees up.'

Tomi thanked her, and then the woman was gone, sweeping from the room as regally as she'd arrived. The kits scampered after her. All that remained was a hint of pearlblossom perfume and tufts of baby minnisk fur.

Tomi allowed herself a breath of relief. A potential disaster averted.

Feeling more relaxed, she wandered to the portraits. There was Shiver, much younger, holding a baby minnisk in her lap. To the left were three more portraits – two women and a man. Tomi could pick their generations from the fashion. To Shiver's right was a family portrait with a youngish man, woman and rosy-cheeked baby.

Tomi and Damian made themselves comfortable on the leather lounges facing the windows. It wasn't a terrible place to have interviews. Rain gusted across the island all day as they questioned employees. There were moments when sunlight streamed through the clouds onto the prairie, and rainbows lit the sky.

No one claimed to have heard of Professor Jupel. Animal carers had little to do with the intellectuals, as one of the dung muckers wryly commented. There was a hopeful moment when Tomi learnt that contractors would often go to Elumina to collect more specimens, but one hadn't been to Radaza since at least Harvest's half moon. It wasn't recent enough to have left fresh dung from the plains in Jupel's apartment.

When the last of the employees had been questioned, Tomi stood, disappointed.

'One of them could be lying,' Damian said, pulling on his tailcoat. 'The killer could've been sitting right across from us, and we had no idea.'

'Frustrating, isn't it?'

Damian exhaled and turned to look out the window. The clouds had disappeared at last, the afternoon soggy but bright.

'Let's take a walk, clear our heads,' Tomi said. 'I'd like to see the volfe enclosure before we go.'

It was the strongest memory she had of Whimsy Holm: the hushed voices, the gasps, the shift of black monsters in the forest.

She and Damian took the long way around, past the breakfast pavilion and through the mountain region so they could watch the raizelet cubs playing. The cubs were spotted, with little spikes on their backs that looked like razors. At this age, the spikes were spongy rather than sharp, and the cubs were cute rather than ferocious. Tomi's father used to call her his little raizelet. She wondered whether she had grown up ferocious enough.

They headed towards a glass dome that took up the western quarter of the island. While the other animals had special underground caverns for the frost, the volfe enclosure was kept steam-warmed, mimicking their tropical habitat. The cost of heating must've been exorbitant.

'I've never seen a volfe before,' Damian said.

Tomi pushed open the frost doors and let him go first. They were immediately hit by heavy humidity. Tomi's boots clacked on the damp wooden planks that made up the visitor bridge. The dome was dug deep, so the bridge hung high above the forest floor. Lush tropical trees and bright flowers filled the space. Colourful machaflies fluttered by.

'Where are they?' Damian whispered.

'They're hiding,' Tomi whispered back.

The bridge split into several directions, but Tomi and Damian stayed together. They were the only visitors in the enclosure. Every now and then they found an information plaque hammered into the railing, talking about the eight volfe living in the enclosure, their breeding habits, diet and size. According to one plaque, a mature volfe was three times the height of a human, its wingspan just as long. Despite their enormity, the plaque added, they were shy creatures that were selective about who they trusted.

'So,' Tomi said, keeping her voice down, 'tell me what you've learnt about this case so far.'

Damian collected his thoughts, then said, 'A person in an armiene coat visited Professor Ivan Jupel late on the twenty-seventh night of Harvest. That same night, Jupel was sedated and stabbed, and several of his possessions were stolen. Powder that has the same composition as blood was found on the floor and the professor's carving knife. The knife had salitenine grease on its handle, suggesting whoever used it had been working with sea-based machinery. Animal dung found in the apartment points to a person who had access to the menagerie's prairie enclosure. Then Park Herliz was tortured and killed in his own office, with no one hearing anything or seeing anyone go in. From the boils on his skin and the removal of his eyes and tongue, it appears he was killed by a witch. How am I doing so far?'

'You forgot the smuggling. And the ices.'

'I'm getting to that. Witness accounts suggest Professor Jupel may have been addicted to an illicit substance and may have been smuggling precious stones into the country through Eversea Shipping, which were probably exchanged for bones and teeth found in the soil of plants to be shipped to Elumina.'

'So far we have no proof that Jupel was actually using illicit substances,' Tomi pointed out. 'We're just assuming it's cutlass based on what Tailor Happershift told us.'

Something rustled in the bushes. Tomi and Damian stayed very still, waiting. It was difficult to see through the thick vegetation. If a volfe was directly below, there was no real way to tell. After long enough had passed with no other movement, they continued, slightly disappointed.

'Who are our suspects?' Tomi said.

'Georgio Herliz is the key link between his grandfather and Professor Jupel. And he works at the docks – he could've come into contact with salitenine grease. If I hadn't seen his distress after finding Park's body, I would've assumed he was the killer.'

'It could've been an act, so yes, that's possible.'

'Then you have Professor Quaide, who told us himself that his grandmother was a witch. We don't know for sure he didn't inherit her magic. And did you notice how closely he watched Jupel's assistant–'

'Nomik Noritof.'

'Right. When Nomik was going through Jupel's things, Quaide seemed worried.'

'I did notice that, yes.'

'So maybe he's got something to hide,' Damian said.

'Maybe,' Tomi agreed. 'However, here's where we run into a problem.'

'Who's connected to both Jupel and Herliz, and has access to Whimsy Holm's prairie?'

'Exactly.'

They stopped at the next information plaque.

Volfe are often hunted by witches, who use parts of the animal in their potions. While the Volfe Protection Act has been established in Elumina in collaboration with Whimsy Holm, animals are still found dead in the wild, slaughtered by poachers.

'Witches sure know how to make it gruesome,' Damian said.

Tomi touched the plaque. She thought of the indents on Park Herliz's wrists. No patterns, no fibres.

Just like Sharlie Glisk.

'Do you think Professor Jupel killed animals like that?' Damian said.

Tomi dragged her focus back to him. 'Not necessarily.'

'There were animal parts in his secret stash.'

'Humans kill animals for their meat and skin and fur. It's possible witches are getting their hands on the offal and bones from those same animals.'

'Or they're sending poachers to murder animals like the volfe.'

'I doubt most witches do that.' Tomi lifted an eyebrow. 'What's the matter? Have you suddenly decided you're anti-witch?'

'It's not that. I mean, my grandparents were from Elumina. They lived and worked with witches without a problem. But then you hear stories about what witches have done in Radaza, and seeing what happened to Park Herliz...' He trailed off. 'Even our victim was involved in shady business. Smuggling, ices, bones and teeth–'

'Do you still believe that Jupel deserves justice?' Tomi said.

'I believe we need to get his killer off the streets.'

'That's not good enough. Not for me.' Tomi leaned on the railing, breathing in the heady scent of tropical blossoms. 'We stand for the victims because they can no longer stand for themselves. These people – witches or human – had lives and communities and hobbies and passions. They experienced horror and joy, faith and doubt. Most of them woke up on the last morning of their life with no idea someone was going to rip their threads apart. They might be addicts, Damian. They might be smugglers. They might have done terrible things in their past. But no one deserves to have their life taken by another's hand.'

'Have you killed anyone in the line of duty?'

Tomi faltered. She hadn't expected that question. But she should've – it buzzed in the mind of every graduating cadet.

'No,' she said. 'Though it's always possible. When going after killers or infiltrating gangs, sometimes you shoot or you hit or you push to survive, and it doesn't always end the way it's supposed to.'

'Have you ever been tempted to kill someone you've been chasing? Working in Unseemly Crimes, you must've come across murderers who've done some truly terrible things.'

'There's no need to sully my threads any more than they already are,' Tomi said, turning away from the view and propping her elbows on the railing. 'If I've done my job right, there'll be enough evidence to cage them for the rest of their lives.'

There was an exception, of course – she didn't have any idea how she'd react if she found the Glisks' murderer.

Even as she was thinking it, Damian said, 'Your threads aren't sullied.'

She laughed, as scornful as she was amused. 'What makes you say that? There's still a lot you don't know about me.'

'Please. I've met people with filthy threads, and I promise, you're not one of them.'

It was a sweet comment. She liked how much he believed in her.

As for the people he'd met with filthy threads, did they have anything to do with his current injuries? Just how much trouble was he in?

He leaned on the railing, mimicking her posture from earlier to scan the forest below. She turned to look too.

'You're right,' he said after a silence. 'I've done some bad things in my life, and I wouldn't want that to stand in the way of a fair investigation if I were killed. Jupel still deserves justice.'

'Yes, he does. Be the sort of officer you'd want on your own case, Damian Kamara.'

He shot her a teasing grin. 'I will, Tomi Cardozo.'

And then, as if reacting to some unknown signal, all eight volfe lifted from the forest below and soared towards the glass roof. The creatures, covered in downy black fur, wheeled and dipped and looped across the dome. While their heads were large and ungainly, the volfes' long, sharp beaks snapped skilfully at machaflies and moon pixies.

One volfe circled so low, the tip of its membranous wing brushed against the top of Tomi's head. A bright yellow eye looked right at her before it joined its flock.

Forget church. *This* was reverence. Watching these giant, magnificent creatures was the closest to seeing the true form of the Tassela as they were ever going to get.

Tomi's heart soared. She was light and carefree, filled with wonder...

And faith.

It ignited like an inferno, filling her with an urge she couldn't ignore. She wanted, suddenly, to bring Damian into the hidden parts of her life.

'Come to dinner tonight,' she said.

Damian glanced at her in surprise. 'What?'

'A friend is going to tell me something important. I want you to be there too.'

'Are you sure?'

'Yes.' She took her gaze from the volfe to look at him. 'If we're going to work together, and if this case is heading where I suspect it is, you should be there. I trust you, Damian.'

Something akin to pain crossed his face, but it was gone in a flash. She dismissed it and returned her attention to the volfe.

She couldn't help it. They were, in a word, enchanting.

Sixteen

She'd invited Damian to dinner. Not just any dinner. *Tonight's* dinner.

What had she been thinking? Payana was going to kill her. The Trio had always been cautious about keeping her secret, but Payana was especially uptight about it.

Part of Tomi knew it wasn't a sensible idea to have Damian there. The other part, the one that had made the decision, didn't care. He was going to be useful. He was clever and loyal and perceptive. She needed someone like him on her side.

At least she wouldn't have to deal with Payana just yet. She had to make a stop before heading to the northern suburbs. She sent Damian to the station to check if any new information had come in, then headed to the University to meet Professor Quaide in the gardens as dusk gathered on the horizon.

'How goes the case?' he asked as they strolled the puddle-filled path, weaving between bushes and plants. He might have been asking about an essay she was writing rather than her investigation into the murder of his colleague. But there was an eccentricity to him that made his lack of grief unsurprising.

'Complex,' she admitted. 'It's difficult to put the pieces together.'

She had brought Finley along for the outing. He wandered behind her at his own pace, having been given a loose rein. Occasionally, he snapped at a moon pixie or scratched in the dirt for worms.

'That's why I've come to you,' Tomi continued. 'I wanted to ask what you knew about witches. Their lifestyles, their habits, their idiosyncrasies–'

'TADOW questioned me relentlessly about those things,' Quaide said. 'They used the information I gave them to flush out a whole treasury of witches hiding in Radaza.'

'They were living here illegally.'

Quaide stopped to examine the bright, blue petals of a jessandra bloom. The scars on his face shone in the fading light. Finley cocked his head. Tomi had a bad feeling he was eying Quaide's flat cap. Ahead, a groundskeeper was climbing a ladder to ignite a hanging lantern, which dripped from the day's rain.

'Jupel's killer was also a witch,' Tomi said.

Quaide glanced at her, his fluffy eyebrows lifted.

'I want to get inside their mind,' Tomi said. 'Figure out what they wanted, why they did certain things and not others.'

'Your answers won't come from magic,' Quaide said. 'Those things – logic and anger and passion – are human. Witches are technically humans too, you know. Despite what TADOW says–whoa!'

As Tomi had foreseen, Finley darted forward and pulled Quaide's cap from his head. He shook it several times before throwing it into the bushes.

'Fin,' Tomi scolded, fetching the cap. 'Sorry, Professor.'

Quaide chuckled as he dusted it off. 'Your grousdu's a bit like the one I had growing up. My grandmother used to use his tail feathers in a duster to ward off unwanted guests. Worked a charm.' He set his cap back on and steered clear of Finley. 'Wish it had worked on TADOW.'

They continued in the direction of the groundskeeper. 'Why would a witch kill another witch?' Tomi said.

'Why would a human kill another human?'

'But the killer left proof behind that they used magic. Jupel was given a sleeping potion. And the killer turned his blood to dust, which was just as messy as bloodstains anyway. They've caught TADOW's attention unnecessarily.'

Quaide considered her. 'Why does any killer make mistakes?'

'Because they were unprepared. Or because they didn't plan to kill in the first place.'

Quaide spread his hands as if to say, *there you go.*

Finley fluffed his feathers as if he were about to plonk himself down in the middle of the path. Tomi tugged his rein sharply to keep him moving. Once he was down, it was tricky to convince him to stand up again.

'Professor Quaide,' she said, 'any JO is unequipped to hunt killer witches because we know so little about them. Our only option is to turn to TADOW, and honestly, I'd prefer to explore other options first. So I'm asking you now: what can you tell me about witches? What do you remember about your childhood?'

Quaide tugged on the brim of his cap. 'Mostly, my childhood wasn't much different from anyone else's: school, frost festivals, holidays to Deep Water Bay, dinners in the atrium. Being without the magic thread, I wasn't involved in rituals or blessings. It was only small things I noticed. My grandmother grew her own herbs and blooms. We observed special days to mark the seasonal changes. The apartments were cleansed during the first rains of the monsoon.'

'Plenty of people do those things.'

'Witches act more like us than you realise, Officer Cardozo.'

'Fine. What specific magical things do you remember?'

They stopped before reaching the groundskeeper, who seemed to be having some trouble lighting the lantern.

'I remember an altar,' Quaide said, gazing at the darkening sky. 'There were different things on it for different seasons. I remember what it was like in the frost especially. It was covered in a cloth of silver and light blue, and dusted with spices. Cinnamon. Nutmeg. Clove. Orange.' He sucked in a breath, as if smelling it now.

They were common scents during the frost. Tomi remembered them vaguely from the children's home, and the Trio often decorated for the season, but her strongest memories were embedded much earlier in life. Clove-pierced oranges and cider spiced with cinnamon, and aromatic wreaths of gold and brown. They touched upon happier times.

'There were crystals,' Quaide continued. 'The bare branches of moulash trees. A small cauldron. An offering of bread. A goblet of spiced wine. A silver chalice.'

'What about spells?' Tomi said. 'How would a witch make a sleeping potion, for example? Or turn blood to dust?'

Quaide tore himself from his reverie to squint at her. 'I suppose it depends on what type of magic the witch practises.'

'Type of magic?'

'Sure. You've got your moon worshippers, your fire mages, your animal magic, poppet craft. Then there are the witches who worship only the Tassela, and those who invoke nature deities. I couldn't give you an entire list, they vary so much.' He shrugged. 'As far as I'm aware, Radazan witches are pretty heavily into seasonal magic, what with the frost being such a large part of our life and all.'

Tomi massaged her temples. This was already getting complicated. Finley, bored of standing in one place, started investigating the nearest hedge for bugs.

'Oh, and then you've got your specialist witches,' Quaide said. He seemed to be enjoying Tomi's mounting confusion. 'Individuals sometimes have extra abilities. My grandmother was a brewer. That meant she could sense the potency and potential of plants just by feeling their energy. She could make a potion out of just about anything.'

'So the killer is a brewer.'

'You mean because they brewed a sleeping potion? No. All witches can brew potions. It's like how all humans can cook. A brewer, however, would be the equivalent of a human walking into a kitchen with only an egg, a spoonful of salt and a jug of water and still being able to create a feast. Besides brewers, there are dreamwalkers, star readers, qora readers–'

'Wait,' Tomi said, tugging at Finley, who had started ripping at the hedge. 'What was that last one?'

'Qora readers?'

'Right. What are those?' Even as the words left her mouth, Tomi's mind snagged. She'd heard that phrase before. She'd seen it, written down.

Where?

Professor Jupel's scrawled notes from his satchel.

Difficulty comm. with new stlmnts – qora readers, watch for prblms during talks –

'Professor Jupel was considering using a qora reader for communicating with Elumenese settlements,' she said.

'That'd be right,' Quaide said, grinning. 'Qora readers are witches who can see our threads.'

'Our threads?'

She'd always thought the thread thing was a metaphor, something the churches used as a way to explain how Tassela weaved life into the world.

'According to my grandmother, they're not so much threads as streams of energy,' Quaide said. 'A qora reader can see them and tell what we're thinking, tell what we're feeling – they can even see whether we're witch or human depending on whether we have the magic thread. But they're rare, apparently. I don't know how Ivan–'

Finley screeched. He darted forward before Tomi could stop him, leaping at the groundskeeper's ladder as if defending himself against a predator.

The groundskeeper cried out and toppled off, landing hard on the path.

'Fin!' Tomi yanked Finley back and rushed to the groundskeeper. 'I'm so sorry. It's getting dark, and I guess the shadow confused him.'

'You ought to keep blinders on him,' said the groundskeeper with a groan.

Tomi recognised that clipped, Perlian accent. 'Nomik?'

'What are you doing here, boy?' Quaide demanded.

Jupel's young AP climbed painfully to his feet. 'My part for the University, if you don't mind.' He rubbed his backside and gave Finley a sour look. 'I'd better check to make sure I haven't broken anything. Good day, Professor Quaide. Officer Cardozo.'

Tomi watched as Nomik limped off, a little more hurried than necessary.

'His part for the University my foot,' Quaide said gruffly.

'You think he was trying to eavesdrop on us?'

'I don't know, but I wouldn't put it past him.' Quaide patted Finley's neck. 'Jupel and I suspected he's been stealing. Things have gone missing in the office since Nomik joined our faculty.'

'Isn't he rich?'

'Well, that's the thing, isn't it? He comes from an elite family with enough coin to fill a treasury. So what's he stealing from *us* for?'

That was an excellent question.

Tomi watched as Nomik disappeared into the shadows. Twilight had fallen. Afflaris was out, shining brightly to lead the way for the other stars.

'I have to go,' Tomi said. 'Thank you for your help.'

'I helped you because you're trying to find Ivan's killer,' Quaide said, all cheerfulness gone. 'But that's no excuse to start hunting down witches.'

'That's TADOW's job. My concern is justice for Ivan Jupel.'

Quaide nodded. 'When you find his killer, give them a kick from me. They've taken a good man from this world.'

Tomi thanked him one last time and headed for the exit. Night had fallen, which meant it was time to put work aside.

Instead, she would have to deal with her friends. And on occasions like these, they were just as hard to handle as catching killers.

Seventeen

'ARE YOU, AND I SAY THIS BECAUSE I CARE, OUT OF YOUR TASSELA-blessed mind?'

While Tomi had been prepared for the pushback from Payana, she hadn't counted on being famished. She'd forgotten to eat today, and her stomach was starting to turn inside out.

She gazed longingly at the communal dining area. Payana lived in one of the wealthier parts of the Northern District, the residents of her atrium made up of mostly Elumenese from the Zim Mah region. That meant the residents ate together each evening, no exceptions, and the central space was filled with large share bowls of curries, fruit dishes, flatbreads and sweet oil cakes. The smell was intoxicating.

Damian was currently swamped by Payana's welcoming cousins, aunts and uncles, all in their traditional *damiseyak* – an outfit of loose trousers and long, hand-woven tunics with fluffy collars. They sat around him on the cushions, feeding him with their fingers, making him try each of the dishes they'd brought to the table.

Tomi wished she were being stuffed with food right now.

'I trust him,' she said. 'Can we please talk about this later?'

'You're not going to tell him anything, are you?'

'I might have to if there really is a link between Park Herliz and the Glisk case.'

The craving came as quick and sharp as the nip of a grousdu. She pictured herself taking the evidence from the archives, reading and rereading the notes, surrounded by the victims' bloodied clothing, allowing the case to be etched into her threads.

She pushed the thought away. It was a precarious drop into that pit. She would only start down the slope if she absolutely had to.

Payana pulled a face. 'Of all the times for you to get an AO. Since when did you decide you wanted to be a mentor anyway?'

'Tomi, darling!' Mia flounced over. Her curls, muddled with vivid reds, oranges, browns and dark shades of yellow, were loose tonight, fire-bright against her brown skin. She gripped Tomi's hand like an excited teenager. 'He's adorable. Where can I get one?'

'Mia,' Tomi said in a low voice. 'Please save me. I'm starving.'

Mia twirled to Payana. 'What have I said about coming between our Tomi and her food? The woman needs to eat, and you know what she's like when she's working a case.'

'We should discuss this,' Payana said. 'At least wait until Zef gets here.'

'Sure, whatever. Just let me *eat*.' Tomi stalked towards the food, her eyes on the bowl of salted meese strips she'd bought for the table.

Unfortunately, having attended these dinners for years now, she was too well known among the residents. People blocked her way to clasp her hand, pull her close and kiss her cheek in their customary greeting. Payana's parents asked about the result of her disciplinary hearing, while the youngest daughter of the family wanted to show off her first tattoo.

Tomi was starting to get lightheaded. Dinner was so close, smelling so good, and she was going to die of starvation right next to it.

'Carve the way. Our guest is going to miss out on the good stuff.'

Warm hands clapped on her shoulders from behind. She caught a hint of carmao incense as she was steered through the crowd towards the food.

'May the Tassela bless you,' she said weakly, sinking to the cushions.

'Let me guess. You haven't eaten all day.' Zef, currently her favourite person in this cruel, cruel world, dropped to the ground beside her.

They knew each other well enough to skip the greetings and the decorum. Tomi dipped her hands briefly in a washing bowl before shovelling food in her mouth.

Zef unwrapped his long scarf. His collared shirt and black trousers were streaked with dirt from work. The only clean part of him was the earring – a tiny silver thurible – hanging from his left earlobe.

'You've had a haircut,' she said, eyeing the sides of his head, which had been sheared so his tight black curls sprang only from the top. His beard had been clipped close to the face too.

She wondered who the girl was this time.

'Your observational skills continue to impress me,' he said.

She narrowed her eyes, and he gave her a quick grin. The conversation paused as she sampled from each dish, trying to fill her cavernous stomach. They shared a bowl of vallia pieces coated in sugarloaf shavings as an after-supper sweet.

'Better?' he said.

'Getting there.'

'Payana told me about the hearing.' He poured her a cup of *irrabin*, a wine distilled from oborios nectar.

'Mm. I have two more days to prove I'm not a witch sympathiser.'

'I'm sorry.'

'Why are *you* sorry?'

'Grundy never seemed right to me. I should've said something.'

With a groan, Tomi threw back her wine in one gulp. 'Grundy,' she muttered, then swiped the back of her hand across her wet lips. 'You know, he came to my atrium last night. He seemed to think an apology would fix everything.'

'Hey, if you want him to disappear, just say the word.'

'Don't be ridiculous. I'd obviously have to help you get rid of the evidence.'

He laughed.

Across the room, music started. People had been feasting and drinking well before Tomi had arrived. The main supper was finished and instruments had come out, encouraging dancers to flood the empty space in front of the grousdu enclosure.

Grundy had danced with Tomi in this very atrium with these very people.

She poured herself another wine.

'You know the worst thing?' she said. 'I was so sure about him. I really believed...' She slung back her drink. 'And to think I hadn't felt that way for anyone since – well, since you.'

Shameful. Her frost fling with Zef had been *nine* years ago. Nine long, lonesome years of courting people who couldn't stir the same feelings Grundy had tricked from her.

'How could my judgement be so terrible?'

'You can't blame yourself.'

'Zef, I catch killers for a living. I must be the worst soff in Radaza for not seeing Grundy for what he was.'

'It's not–Who's that?'

Tomi glanced up to find Damian extracting himself from his dancing partner and heading towards them. She'd forgotten he was there.

'That's my new AO.' She climbed to her feet. 'It looks like you fit right in, cookie.'

Damian grinned. He was flushed, his eyes shiny from either the dancing or the alcohol. 'What can I say? People love me.' His gaze fell questioningly to Zef.

'Zef, Damian,' Tomi said. 'Damian, this is Zeffir Amaida, Payana's brother.'

Damian tapped a hand to his heart in greeting.

Zef didn't return it. He said to Tomi, 'I didn't realise you were inviting someone.'

'I wanted you to meet him.'

Zef turned his attention to her. 'You know what Mia's telling you tonight.'

'Yes.'

'So why did you bring a stranger?'

'He's my apprentice.' There was an annoyed screech from the grousdu enclosure – two of the birds were bickering. 'What is it with you and Payana tonight? Isn't it *my* choice whether he's here or not?'

Zef didn't answer. She wondered whether he was thinking of Grundy. Did he privately agree that her judgement was off?

Payana and Mia were already making their way up the winding balcony to their apartment. This was happening whether Tomi was willing or not, and she should be allowed to bring whoever she wanted to hear this news.

She turned on her heel and stalked after the pair.

'Tomi!' Zef caught up with her at the start of the balcony. 'I'm sorry. I didn't say anything about Grundy and I should've. So this is me telling you now. Don't get the kid involved.'

'This isn't a romantic entanglement.'

'I know, but my objection stands.' He moved closer, lowering his voice beneath the music. 'There's a reason you haven't talked to anyone except us about this. Your whole life is built on secrets to keep you safe. Why do you suddenly trust this guy?'

'Look, it was a whole moment today. We were at the menagerie and the volfe were flying around us–'

'The volfe?'

'Yes, and they were beautiful and amazing, and it was all sort of transcendent–'

'Wait. You made this decision in the presence of the volfe?'

Tomi's argument died on her tongue. Zef's expression was unreadable. 'Yes. Why?'

'Nothing.' He shook his head. 'My people used to believe... No. It doesn't matter.'

Tomi didn't know what to say. Zef never talked about where he'd come from. The only thing she'd learnt, when hearing Payana's parents had adopted him at 16, was that he was a refugee from Elumina.

'All right,' he said, sounding reluctant. 'If you want him there, I suppose none of us can stop you.' His gaze flicked to Damian, who was following them. 'But promise me you'll be careful.'

'I will,' Tomi said.

She was still planning to tell Damian the truth.

Just not the *whole* truth.

Eighteen

ZEFFIR AMAIDA CLEARLY DIDN'T TRUST HIM. WHETHER IT WAS because Zeffir was suspicious of all strangers, or whether it was some possessive thing over Tomi, Damian didn't know. But he sensed the way Zeffir watched him as the group shared a platter of smallfruits and sweet wine in the quiet apartment.

Colourful rugs covered the stone tiles, and the archway between the spacious rooms was decorated with black and white zigzags. Candles sat on every surface, their flames flickering in the draft of an open window.

Damian watched Payana open another bottle. He'd rarely seen a person from the Zim Mah region without family tattoos. Swirls and patterns adorned her siblings' necks, and her cousins had interlocking blossoms inked onto their arms. Even the teenagers had a symbol or two. Payana was untouched, and while he might've assumed it was due to an allergy or health reason, she also didn't wear the *damiseyak*, either. Even dressed casually, she remained in current Radaza fashion.

It had been hard to gauge Payana's personality while they were at work. She had had little patience and acted frosty, but he imagined working in a morgue required some emotional disconnect.

But tonight, he saw that she separated herself from family, too. It was as if she were determined to be an outsider.

And yet she'd swapped wine cups with Mia during the first meal. That meant they were partners, maybe even bound. He caught the small touches and shared looks between the two.

Mia's wildfire hair and brown skin marked her as from the Epoya region. Wealthy, from the looks of her clothes, and bursting with delight about every aspect of life. She'd *hugged* Damian upon introductions. He'd heard people from the Epoya region were physical with their affections, but that had been unexpected.

So how did someone like Payana end up with the endlessly sunny Mia?

And how did Zeffir fit into this? He was supposed to be Payana's brother, but he had a different blood name, and his skin was as black as silkslate.

How did these three fit together?

Damian shouldn't be thinking about this. He shouldn't be taking in anything from Tomi's personal life. Everything could be used against her – Bunter Vittam would see to that. Zeffir was right to be wary.

The noble thing for Damian to do was walk away. He didn't know what Mia's announcement was, but from the reactions of the others over his presence tonight, he felt it was important and private. It might hurt Tomi if Vittam found out.

But Damian didn't want to walk away. He wanted Tomi to trust him. He wanted to be a professional partner she could count on. She looked so relaxed tonight, her hair loosely tied back and tumbling down to her waist, her clothes loose and soft, her feet bare, the guarded expression melting away with each cup of wine. She smiled a lot with her friends. It was so different from her demeanour at work, where her colleagues were her rivals and she could never turn her back.

Damian wished he could relax too, but Zeffir sat opposite him on the wide circle of cushions, his careful gaze never wavering.

Mia chatted about her boss – from the sounds of it, she worked at a law firm. Apart from Tomi, she was the only one who seemed unaffected by Damian's presence.

Zeffir poured Damian another cup of wine. Damian wondered whether Zeffir was trying to make him drunk enough to pass out. Considering Damian had learnt to hold his drink in Vittam's gambling dens, it would never happen.

'Where do you live, Kamara?' Zeffir said as the conversation lulled.

Tomi glanced at Damian over the rim of her cup. He remembered only at the last moment that he'd put his mother's address in his employee information.

'Nowhere as nice as this,' he said.

Mia beamed, her light-brown cheeks flushed from the heat of the exposed chimney.

The place really was beautiful. There was something comfortable and welcoming about it. Damian sipped his wine as smoke furled from a stick of bygrass incense by the window. 'How do you all know each other?'

'Family friends,' Zeffir said shortly. 'Why did you choose Tomi as your mentor?'

The question was pistol-quick; Damian wondered whether he was about to receive an onslaught of them.

'Who wouldn't?' he said, but before Zeffir could ask another, he added, 'And what do you do?'

'Aha!' Mia lifted her cup in delight. 'You're the budding detective. You tell us.'

Damian took in Zeffir's posture, his hairstyle, his calloused hands. Zeffir had changed into a casual cottonelle outfit with a high collar and white seams, but his clothes upon entering the atrium had been caked with dirt.

'You're a labourer,' Damian said. 'Not from the docks – I worked there before joining the academy, and we never got that filthy. Unless you're inland, with the snarfles? But no, you don't smell like them.'

Tomi grinned as she sipped her wine. Damian was keen to keep impressing her.

'You could be a miner or a farmer – you look strong, and your hands are rough from holding tools.'

Zeffir swirled his wine in his cup, never taking his gaze from Damian.

'But did I get a whiff of carmao incense from you earlier? And the thurible trinket in your ear – that suggests you perform religious rites. Religion, carmao, digging up dirt... I'm going to go with *saccuveirro*.'

Mia trilled her tongue in victory. 'Exceptional work, young apprentice. Yes, Zef is a glorified grave digger.'

Zeffir seemed neither impressed nor disappointed at Damian's deduction.

'So, medica maven working at the morgue,' Damian said, gesturing at Payana with his cup, 'guardian of the dead' to Zeffir, 'and... lawyer?' he asked Mia. 'That's quite the combination.'

'Zef wasn't always a *saccuveirro*,' Tomi said. 'When I met him, he was a family liaison in the children's court. Suits, salary, success was our Zeffir.'

'That's a peculiar career change,' Damian said.

'Go on,' Tomi said. 'Ask him why he did it.'

Despite feeling like he was being led into a trap, Damian asked the question.

Zeffir refilled Tomi's cup. 'I prefer the peace and quiet of the cemetery.'

Damian glanced questioningly at Tomi, who shrugged. 'That's the same answer I always get. If you ever find out the truth, let me know.'

'Enough chatting,' Mia said. 'Now we've done the small talk, it's time for my big announcement.'

'Wait,' Zef said. 'Tomi, are you sure–'

'*Yes*, Zef.' Tomi turned to Mia, sounding strangely resigned as she added, 'Go on.'

'Tomi Cardozo. After 10 years of waiting, Brackenlong Manor will finally be yours!'

There was a silence. No one except Mia looked excited.

'Brackenlong Manor?' Damian said.

'A residence in the Black Ivory District,' Tomi murmured. 'Where the Glisk family used to live.'

'I – What? *How?*'

'I decided to fight for ownership,' Tomi said. 'I'm one of the legatees of the Glisk estate. My mother was the *ama sector* of the household, and the Glisks were very appreciative. They wanted to leave something to show their gratitude. Because the entire extended family and all business partners in their company disappeared, I'm the only one left to receive the inheritance.'

Words choked in Damian's throat. There were too many questions – too much to say and think and ask.

If Tomi's mother was the *ama sector*, she would've been in charge of everything to do with the Glisk children, which meant she probably lived on the premises.

Which meant Tomi had spent her childhood in the Black Ivory District.

'You grew up in the Glisk household?' he said at last.

'Until I was eight, yes,' Tomi said. 'When the Glisks were killed, my mother disappeared with everyone else, and I ended up in a children's home.'

'Where did they go?'

'I have no idea. We assume they were scared away by what had been done to the Glisks, thinking they'd be next.'

This couldn't be common knowledge. Whenever anyone spoke of Tomi

Cardozo, they mentioned her case closure rates, her unbeatable records and her high-profile cases. Damian had never heard stories of where she'd come from before entering the academy. He couldn't imagine the kind of coin she must've been surrounded by as a kid. And now–

'Now you *own* Brackenlong Manor?'

'Not officially,' Mia said. 'She still has to inspect the property before signing the contract. But yes, more or less, the manor is hers.'

The manor. Where Sharlie and Anatole Glisk were brutally murdered. Damian and Tomi would have access to the location of the biggest crime scene in Radaza.

'I know what you're thinking,' Tomi said. 'But I don't want to go there yet. We have an open case to work on, and I only have two more days before I have to show the court my progress.'

'We have progress. Good progress.'

'It's only good progress if the name leads to something useful.'

Talcott Notch had sent bundles of lists to the station that evening. True to his word, the portmaster had got all his employees to write down everyone they remembered visiting the menagerie four days ago. One name had stuck out. *N. Whimsy* – a relative of Shiver Whimsy, surely, and someone who may have had access to the greater beasts enclosure. Tomi would call the menagerie in the morning to confirm.

'You should inspect the manor before the frost hits,' Mia said.

'The cases could be connected,' Damian added.

'There's only a slim chance of that.' Tomi picked up an oborios fruit and dug her thumbnail into the skin. She looked strangely uptight. And unhappy. Who would be unhappy after inheriting a residence in the richest district in Radaza?

'I thought you wanted this,' Mia said.

'I'm sorry, Mia. I know I'm acting ungrateful. It's just harder than I thought it was going to be.'

Payana squeezed Tomi's shoulder. 'We'll come with you to inspect the property if you like.'

Tomi didn't answer. It occurred to Damian that her reluctance could've been more than sadness.

'Tomi,' he said slowly, 'were you in the house when the murders took place?'

She nodded, swiping a stray strand of hair from her face with the back of her wrist.

'Tomi, don't–' Zeffir started, but Tomi spoke over him.

'I was the one who found the bodies.'

'You *what?*'

'Kamara,' Zeffir said before Tomi could answer. 'I couldn't help but notice you're injured.'

Payana and Mia turned to Damian.

'What does that have to do with anything?' he said.

He'd been trying to hide the tenderness of his ribs, even during the dancing. He was sure he'd done a good job of it.

Obviously not.

Tomi ripped the oborios into its two segments. 'Do you mind, Zef? I'm explaining to Damian what happened to me.'

'Tell us how you got hurt,' Zeffir said to Damian. He sounded almost aggressive. 'Has Tomi already gotten you into a fight?'

'No, of course not.'

'You get robbed on the way home?'

'No.' Damian forced a chuckle. 'It's a funny story, actually. I got drunk the other night and fell off my grousdu–'

'No you didn't.'

'What?' Damian looked to Mia and Payana, hoping for help. From Mia, at least – she had been so welcoming.

But the two stayed silent. Waiting.

And then it hit him.

Zeffir knew.

Somehow, Zeffir was aware that Damian was an informant for Bunter Vittam. Maybe he was part of Vittam's inner circle. Maybe Vittam utilised grave diggers for 'necessary services' like hiding bodies.

Zeffir knew that Tomi had been betrayed. He was going to expose Damian.

'It's late.' Damian got to his feet. His heartstep had accelerated to a sprint. 'I should go.'

'No,' Zeffir said. 'Tomi's told you more than she's told anyone else outside this room. She's put herself in danger by doing so. Do you know what would happen if the Glisk killers found out she's still in the city?'

'I won't–'

'Tell anyone? Are you sure about that?'

'Zef, what are you doing?' Tomi got up too, standing next to Damian. 'Didn't we already talk about this? It's my choice who I tell.'

'Ask him why he's injured, Tomi.'

'What does that have to do with anything?'

'Just ask him.'

Payana and Mia stared at Damian with open mouths. They hadn't questioned Zeffir's hostility. But why would they? They knew Zeffir; they trusted him. Damian was a stranger, and he was every terrible thing Zeffir was about to accuse him of.

He couldn't do it. He couldn't be here when Tomi found out the truth.

'I have to go. Um. Thanks for dinner.' He headed for the door, certain Zeffir was going to physically prevent his escape.

But besides Tomi calling his name, no one tried to stop him.

Nineteen

There had been a break in the case, but Damian hadn't shown up.

Tomi paced the area in front of her newly purchased desk, wondering whether she should do the interview without him. She didn't like the thought of taking a GO in to scribe. General officers were sloppy compared to Damian. He commented on things in his notes – strange pauses, peculiar gestures, interesting points. He underlined what needed to be followed up on and marked places where he suspected an interviewee was lying. It was unprofessional, considering the notes were supposed to be unbiased and used in court. It certainly explained why he'd failed the scribing course in the academy.

But it was useful. Tomi liked seeing the interviews from his perspective, even if it was just a wry comment about the glimmery Veraminta and her trips to the steam spas.

The upstairs floor was quiet. Most JOs were out working – it was always a rush in Harrow to have a case closed before the frost settled. The urgency hadn't stopped someone from scribbling *witch lover* on her murder board, though. It was written next to the sketch of Park Herliz's desecrated body.

Tomi had received transcripts from TADOW, who had questioned

Park's friends and family. If the general officers' notes seemed neglectful, it was nothing compared to the officers at TADOW, who didn't have the same training as everyone else in the Justice Department. Their courses focussed on combat against magic, which meant their basic investigation skills were unrefined. Tomi wished she'd had time to question Park's contacts herself. She would've spotted the nuances TADOW had missed. All they cared about was exposing witches – this stone-smuggling business wasn't their concern unless it turned out to have something to do with magic. So far, they had no way to tell whether the stone was simply a precious gemstone or whether it was a potion ingredient.

When the timekeeper at the top of the station rang the midday bells, Iloura came out of her office. 'Haven't you got a suspect waiting in the interview room?'

'Yes, but–'

'Then go. Interview. Get a confession, a statement, something.' Iloura ushered Tomi towards the staircase. 'I stood up for you in that hearing, and I need you to get results.'

'I will. And thank you again. You didn't have to accept responsibility for this case.'

'I know I didn't. Yet here we care.' Iloura's mouth was a tight line as she studied Tomi. 'Don't let me down, Officer Cardozo.'

That was the last thing Tomi wanted to do. Ever since arriving at the North Central Station, Iloura had taken Tomi into her nest, giving her room to grow and learn. One reason Tomi's case closure record was so high was because she never wanted to disappoint Iloura.

Tomi relented, realising she would have to question her suspect without Damian. But as she headed downstairs, he came trudging up.

'Damian,' she said, relieved. 'Thank the Tassela you're here. I'm sorry about last night. I had no idea Zef would behave so terribly.'

They stopped on the stairwell, she two steps above him.

'Zef was terrible? Huh. I hadn't noticed.' He hesitated. 'Did you talk to him?'

'If by "talk" you mean "yell", yes I did.'

'What did he say?'

'Nothing, as well he should have. Again, I'm really sorry. My friends are very protective of me. They've been keeping that secret about my past for a long time. I promise you, though, they're good people. They're like my family.' She descended to Damian's step. 'I know you're going through a rough time. And I understand that it's personal. You don't have to explain anything to me. Believe it or not, I know what it's like.'

There was a silence, where all they heard was the chatter from the ground floor. Damian shoved his hands in his pockets. 'I think I need to give up my position.'

'What? Don't you dare!'

'It's for the best.'

'No, it's not. Look, do you remember me telling you that I could bust you down to general duties?'

'Yes.'

'And do you also remember that I said I knew that from experience?'

Damian's brow furrowed.

'When I first started my apprenticeship, I had access to the archive,' Tomi said. 'Which meant I had access to the Glisk nook. I started investigating and, Damian, I went down a dark pit. I was obsessed. I lived and breathed that case, but there was nothing new to find. And, with my mind on the Glisks, I couldn't concentrate on my job. My mentor fired me three months after I became his AO. He didn't try to ask what was wrong, and I didn't trust him enough to tell him. I know what you're going through isn't the same, but I'm always here if you need someone to talk to.'

He nodded, still looking like someone had killed his pet poffin. She paused to give him a chance to explain. The silence dragged on.

He started to speak. She straightened hopefully. Then he changed his mind and shut his mouth again.

Disappointing, but not entirely unexpected. She knew he was in trouble. Someone was hurting him, possibly someone close to him. His evasiveness about his home life made her suspect he was being abused by a parent or other family member. It was bringing him down, making him doubt himself. But she'd chosen him for a reason, and she wasn't prepared to lose him over this.

She clasped his shoulder. 'Cheer up. I called the menagerie first thing this morning, and you'll never guess who Shiver Whimsy's grandson is.'

This, at least, sparked some curiosity.

She grinned. 'If you want to find out, you'll have to come with me.'

They headed downstairs to the interview room. Tomi tried not to let hope burble too much as she took the parchments from the GO guarding the room. The evidence connected, but there was still a lot missing.

Damian snorted softly when they stepped inside.

'Nomik Noritof,' Tomi said. 'Or should I say, Nomik Whimsy?' She dropped the parchments onto the desk and sat in the chair opposite Jupel's assistant. 'Why did you lie?'

Nomik flashed her a smile. He seemed completely unruffled, despite the fact she'd headed down to the University with two general officers that morning to haul him into the station.

'It was too funny to pass up,' he said.

Tomi clasped her hands on the table.

'Come on,' Nomik said, laughing. 'Everyone knows who I am. It wasn't meant to be obstructing justice or whatever you're charging me with. A quick check with Professor Quaide or Chancellor Gloudling and you would've found out I was jesting. It was a novelty, meeting people who hadn't heard of me.'

Tomi's only response was a tight smile. Behind her, she could hear Damian scribing diligently.

'And I know for a fact you spoke to Professor Quaide again.' Nomik rubbed his hip. 'How's your cranky grousdu? Did he win that fight against the ladder?'

'You have bigger things to worry about than your fall, *Seno* Nomik. In case you've forgotten, we happen to be investigating the murder of your mentor.'

Nomik's mirth faded. 'Look. What happened to Jupel, it was awful. Truly. But me lying about my name doesn't have anything to do with–'

Tomi unrolled one of the parchments. 'Particulars found traces of fresh halicort dung in Jupel's apartment. This was only possible if one of his recent visitors had access to the greater beasts enclosure at the menagerie.' She opened Nomik's travel log, which had been confiscated upon his arrival. 'You went to the menagerie four days ago.'

'I'm not allowed to see my grandmother?' Nomik said.

'Shiver Whimsy says you haven't visited her for years. She had no idea you were there. The day and time of your so-called visit, she was meeting with contractors at the Overland Terminal.'

'It was bad luck. I wanted to surprise her, but I'd missed her.'

'If I had a team of sweepers check your shoes, would they find halicort dung on the treads?'

Nomik frowned. He was looking less smug than before.

'All right,' Tomi said, dragging over the next roll of parchment. 'How about these notes? They were hidden in a false bottom in Professor Jupel's office drawer. Professor Quaide was more than happy to provide them to us when he found them this morning.'

She turned the paper around for Nomik to read. His expression soured when he saw what it was.

'Your mentor was going to fail you.' Tomi stabbed her finger onto the parchment. 'These notes state that you have no concept of cross-cultural communications and consistently show an inept understanding of basic languages. For an assistant to the professor, that surprised me. So I asked around. It turns out, many professors admitted to letting you pass their courses because of various donations to the University in your name. Even Professor Quaide confessed to it. He had a bit to say about you, as a matter of fact. Apparently, he and Professor Jupel suspected you of stealing trinkets from their office. He's been keeping a close eye on you. It would also explain why Professor Jupel told a friend the day before his death that he couldn't trust one of his colleagues. He knew you were taking advantage of him. But we'll come back to that unfortunate habit of yours in a moment.'

She sat back in her chair, watching Nomik's expression. 'From the looks of these secret notes, Professor Jupel had had enough. Perhaps the Tassela Verity whispered to his conscience. He wasn't going to let you graduate, which meant you wouldn't have been able to join your parents in Elumina to collect more animals for the menagerie. And dear Grandmother Whimsy only wants a competent, experienced person to inherit the menagerie. I know – I spoke to her about it. She wasn't too happy to hear you were about to fail.'

So far, Nomik hadn't said anything. That was fine. Tomi wasn't finished.

'Is it motive for murder?' she said. 'Possibly. The menagerie is worth a harbourful of coin. That, along with the halicort dung at the crime scene, was enough to grant me access to your vault ledger.'

She opened one of the books on the table and turned it for him to see. 'For the heir to a fortune, you sure have a lot of spendings. In fact, your vault is almost cleaned out. I suspected a gambling problem. I called the ferry terminal this morning and had a chat to the employee who remembered seeing you visit the menagerie five days ago. Turns out, she used to work at Whimsy Holm. She claims to have helped you sneak out to a friend's boat on many a night, back when you lived on the island. You'd return before dawn and occasionally give her a pouch full of coin – part of your winnings, I'm sure, and probably good hush jingle. More proof you have issues with gambling.'

She shut the ledger.

'Which leads us to your stealing. Things were taken from Professor Jupel's apartment: trinkets, rings, imported knick knacks. If you owed a gambling den, that would be a good way to repay your debts. But perhaps you kept some things. A crystal that caught your eye. A ceramic animal to gift a partner. Tell me, would the team of sweepers that are currently going through your dormitory find anything matching Professor Jupel's insurance list?'

Nomik's eyes widened.

'They'll certainly be checking your shoes for that halicort dung,' Tomi added. 'And your clothes, including the armiene coat you so helpfully told us you owned, one of which happened to be seen at the professor's atrium the night of the murder.'

'Oh, shit,' Nomik said. 'No – wait.' He held his hand out to Damian as if asking him to stop scribing.

Damian didn't stop.

'All right. Shit.' Nomik threaded his hands through his feather-soft hair. 'I was there, I was at the professor's apartment that night. But I didn't kill him. I didn't know. I thought it was just about coin. I had no idea, and when I heard he was dead I couldn't believe–'

'Take me back,' Tomi said, spinning her finger as if winding a timekeeper.

'I had a drink with him, that's *it*.'

'*Seno* Whimsy, I need you to start from the beginning.'

'Right.' Nomik stared at the table as he rocked back and forth slightly. 'I may have a slight inclination for the rollers, and I may owe a touch of coin.'

'Go on.'

A long, low exhalation passed Nomik's lips. He didn't look up. 'Bunter Vittam came to me a few days ago. He said there was a way for me to wipe my debt clean.'

The scratch stick paused.

Despite trying to keep her face blank, Tomi's mouth tightened involuntarily. She hated any case that involved Bunter Vittam.

'He said I had to fetch a shaving of halicort horn and bring it to him,' Nomik said. 'When I did that, he made me come back the next day, gave me a vial of liquid and told me to visit the professor that night. I was to slip the liquid in his drink and leave the frost doors to the atrium ajar on my way out. He said it was a sleeping elixir, and that his people were going to take what Professor Jupel owed them while he was unconscious. I thought they were just going to rob him – I had no idea they were going to kill him.'

'Did you also rob him, *Seno* Whimsy?'

Nomik hesitated, then shrugged. 'I've been stealing from him since I started as his AP. He's so scatterbrained; I just told him he was forgetting where he put things. And it was an easy class. At least, I thought it was. I didn't realise he'd noticed my lack of academia.' He smiled wryly.

'What about the night of the murder? Did you take anything from the apartment?'

'What you said. His rings and a few knick knacks. Thought Vittam could use some appeasing, considering his reputation for wrath.'

'What time did you leave?'

'Just after 11 bells. The professor was alive when I left, I *swear*.'

Tomi glanced at Damian. With a silent gesture for him to follow her, she left the room.

The GO standing guard stepped away politely.

'He's got to be lying,' Damian said after he'd shut Nomik inside. 'He admitted to being at the crime scene. And pointing the finger at Vittam is an easy out. Suspects must blame Vittam all the time. I mean, they're probably right on most occasions, but not this time. Professor Jupel couldn't possibly have been involved in ices, smuggling *and* gambling. Right?' He spoke fast and breathlessly.

Tomi wasn't surprised at his panic. It was a bit unfair for the cookie to have to face Bunter Vittam on his very first case.

'Jupel's vault ledger certainly didn't indicate anything was out of the ordinary,' she admitted. 'But Nomik said he left at 11, and Herliz said the same thing. That doesn't match the time of death.'

'It's close enough.'

Tomi considered her options. 'It would be useful to find out if Nomik's a witch. If he's not, he can't be our killer.'

'You want to call TADOW?'

No. Tomi definitely didn't want to call TADOW. And it was unlikely, maybe impossible, that someone of purely Perlian descent was a witch.

'I think we should check Nomik's story,' she said.

'You want to bring in Bunter Vittam?'

'He always refuses to come, and I don't have any hard evidence that he was involved in this.'

'Then how will you...?' Damian trailed off. 'You're going into a gambling den?'

'That's how we do our job. We go to places. Talk to people.'

Damian looked ill.

'It's not that bad,' Tomi said. As she spoke, she touched the grip of her holstered pistol and checked her inner pocket for her dagger.

Patting her pocket reminded her of something. She went back into the interview room.

'*Seno* Whimsy,' she said, dropping the key she'd found in Jupel's apartment onto the table. 'Have you seen this before?'

Nomik leaned forward. 'Looks like a locker key.'

'Did Professor Jupel have a locker at the University or somewhere else?'

'I don't know.'

Tomi cursed and put the key away. So much for that.

'Um,' Nomik said slowly, 'am I free to go?'

'You are absolutely *not* free to go.' Tomi called for the GO outside. 'Put him in the cells. We'll be charging him with accessory to murder. And maybe,' she added to Damian, 'after speaking to Bunter Vittam, we might be able to upgrade that to plain old murder.'

Twenty

Bunter Vittam punished soffs who involved him in their investigations. Damian hadn't seen it, but he'd heard about it. Tomi must've known, yet she steered Finley through the streets without fear.

Vittam was protected. People gave him alibis. He had associates in every corner of the government. If he did something to Tomi in one of his gambling dens, no one would step forward as a witness. And all she had to back her up was Damian.

Vittam owned several gambling dens around Radaza. They varied in clientele and glimmer depending on their location. His main office was in the den between the Commerce District and the Shopping District. This den brought in the high rollers as well as the tourists, even though it was down an inconspicuous alley and never part of any official tour.

Tomi and Damian left their grousdu in a public enclosure in the Shopping District where they would be safe from Vittam's people.

'May the Tassela unthread me,' Tomi muttered as they walked away from the enclosure. 'I still haven't bought Fin his gizzard stones and worm paste.'

Damian glanced over his shoulder at her bird. 'He should be all right until the quarter moon.'

'Are you sure?'

'Yes. My father is – was – a grousdu minder.'

'There isn't mention of your father in your employment details,' Tomi said.

Bolocha. It was so difficult to remember that while Tomi was opening up about her past, everything Damian said was under scrutiny.

'My parents aren't bound.'

He didn't dare say anything else, and thankfully, she didn't ask.

Her dark-brown hair shone gold as they passed from shadow to sunlight. There was a closed, careful expression that she seemed to wear like a cloak during working hours. Damian had seen it slip away last night in the presence of friends. He realised he shouldn't have been there. He shouldn't be seeing any part of her beneath that cloak. Not while he was acting as Vittam's eyes.

It was as they turned out of the Shopping District, leaving the main crowd, that Damian felt a distinct prickling sensation on the back of his neck. He checked behind them. A few people dotted the streets, dressed in suits and hurrying to their various businesses. No one paid him any attention.

So why did it feel like he was being watched?

'I suppose you have questions for me, too,' Tomi said, breaking Damian from his thoughts.

Yes. He definitely had questions. He wanted to know everything about her past, her parents, the Glisks. Why did she have the right to claim Brackenlong Manor? And why had it taken so long for the inheritance to pass to her?

Then there was the fact that no one knew about her involvement in the case. Why wasn't she more famous? And why did her mother leave her behind?

Instead of asking any of those things, he said, 'Let's wait to see if it's relevant to the investigation.'

'Yes, of course.'

Hopefully, she would be more wary now Zeffir had spoken up. Why Zeffir hadn't completely ruined him, Damian didn't know. It was possible her friend was hiding his own links to Vittam.

Damian should say something. He should tell Tomi right now about his indenture. That he was a liar, a traitor, no better than a common criminal.

But all it took was imagining her expression when he confessed – disbelief, disappointment, anger – to convince him to keep his mouth shut.

They turned down the alley between a tailor's shop and a two-storey department store. In the wall of the department building was a door that led downstairs into darkness.

Damian hesitated at the entrance. The alley was empty except for a few khars hopping around a garbage can for scraps, and the overpowering stench of piss. One of the khars cawed at them before flapping away.

'Don't worry,' Tomi said. 'I'm with you.'

'How many times have you come up against Bunter Vittam?'

'Plenty. In fact, my mentor took me into a southside den during my second month as an AO.'

'And you were fine?'

'Well, no. I ended up with a dislocated shoulder and my first bullet discharged into a person.'

'Was that supposed to make me feel better?'

'I told you my mentor didn't pay enough attention. You're with me this time.'

That might've made Damian feel safer if he didn't already know how Vittam was going to react to seeing them.

Tomi started down the long, narrow staircase. Damian released a shaking breath before following her. The smells and sounds hit them before they reached the bottom. Triller herb. Chatter. Beer. The clack of dice. Jeers and shouts as punters won small and lost big. Damian swallowed the memory of his messenger days. He'd almost started to believe he was free of this place.

They stalked through the blue smoke, past spinning wheels and card games. Oil lamps glowed dimly, giving the patrons no indication of what time of the day or night it was. Besides a slurred 'Fuck off, soffs' and some spit on Damian's boot, they made it to the back of the establishment without incident.

Yaverly and Winsor stood in front of Bunter Vittam's private office. Damian's hand twitched as he thought of drawing his dagger from his inner pocket and slamming it into Winsor's hand the way he'd done to Pa.

Tomi showed her badge. Yaverly looked from Damian to Tomi and stepped aside obligingly.

A rousing cheer sounded behind them as someone won a game, but the noise vanished as soon as the door was shut. Yaverly accompanied them inside. Tomi ignored him as she stalked through the room, which was almost as vast as the gambling den.

Not much had changed since the last time Damian had been in here. The oil lanterns had translucent, colour-tinged cases that drowned the room in reds, purples and dark blues. A musty smell lingered beneath the stench of animals. Breathing it in made Damian's body tired, as if his muscles were remembering the long days at the docks that were followed by him stumbling in here late at night to take Vittam's messages across the city.

He passed the stuffed snow bear, poised as if to pounce. The enormous tapestries, hanging from the ceiling to create a maze, had been Damian's introduction to the female body. The weavings depicted people in all sorts of erotic positions but were interspaced with images of blood and torture. At 14, Damian had been both aroused and sickened, and it had taken a long discussion with *Bamki* Rivers to understand what Vittam was promoting.

An aviary with many species of small, twittering birds took up most of the space in the middle of the room, and several minnisks slept in a heap in the corner.

And there were coins. Piles, pillars, mountains of coins. They lined the room like golden soldiers. There were more than when Damian had last been here.

They headed around the aviary to the back of the room where Bunter Vittam was waiting at his desk, smiling expectantly.

'It must be my lucky night – my favourite soff's returned.' He stood, tapping a hand to his heart. 'Isn't she a doll, Yaverly? Just look at those freckles. A much sweeter view than those pesky officers who keep raiding my dens.'

'I've come to ask you a few questions.'

'I know you have.' Vittam's gaze slid to Damian. He popped a hartmint leaf in his mouth and said, 'You get yourself a cookie?'

Bile rose in Damian's throat. Vittam was playing ignorant, but there was an aggressiveness to the way he chewed. He was angry they had come, and someone was going to suffer for it.

'I want to talk about Nomik Whimsy,' Tomi said.

'Not yet, not yet.' Vittam wandered around his desk to stand in front of Damian. He was a head shorter but still made Damian feel as small as a child. 'Let me take a look at your fresh meat. What's your name, kid?'

'This is Officer Kamara, and I'm sure you're a busy man, Vittam,' Tomi said. 'Why don't you just answer the questions and we'll be on our way?'

'*Officer Kamara*. It's a lovely texture in the mouth, isn't it?' Vittam gave

Damian a playful nudge in the ribs. Damian flinched, only just catching himself before doubling over. The bruises from Yaverly's punches the other night were still black and tender – even that gentle knock brought the pain screaming back.

Vittam smirked and shoved his hands in his pockets. The keys on his belt jingled. Most of them were big and brass, but there was a small one in the collection. It looked very familiar.

Oh no. Damian knew Vittam well enough to know he wasn't a witch. So why did he have a key like the one they'd found in Jupel's apartment?

'Nomik Whimsy,' Tomi said again.

Vittam returned his attention to her. 'Whimsy? Like the island?'

'His family owns Whimsy Holm, yes. Have you heard of him?'

'Nope.' The answer was short and overly casual. Vittam returned to his chair, which looked more like a throne for one of the queens of Perlia, and kicked his feet up on his desk. 'Anything else I can help you with?'

'Where were you on the twenty-seventh night of Harvest?'

He spread his arms. 'Where I always am. Here. All night, every night. You can ask my man Yaverly. Or any of my regular patrons.'

'Nomik Whimsy *is* one of your regulars. He owes you coin, but said you would wipe his slate clean if he did a few favours for you.'

'Hm, let me guess: someone's trying to blame me for their crimes again.' He took his feet off the desk and sat up straight, pouting. 'I'm a victim, Officer Freckles. People are always trying to make me take the fall.'

'So you didn't ask Nomik Whimsy to fetch you halicort horn shavings, then get him to sedate Professor Ivan Jupel?'

'Professor who?'

'Ivan Jupel. Murdered, the twenty-seventh night of Harvest.'

Vittam clicked his tongue. 'Murder. What has the world come to?'

'Nomik Whimsy says Professor Jupel owed you coin.'

'If he owed me coin, why would I kill him? Dead men don't pay debts, right, cookie?'

Damian's jaw twitched, but he remained silent. There was no point scribing this interview. Someone would take his parchment book on the way out if he did, and he'd prefer to keep his case notes.

'How about Park Herliz?' Tomi said.

'Can't say I've had the pleasure.'

'And you stand by your claim that you've never spoken to Nomik Whimsy?'

'Afraid not.'

'Even though he's one of your "regulars"?'

With a smile, Vittam said, 'I have a lot of regulars. They may know me, but I can't possibly be expected to be acquainted with them all. Anything else?'

Tomi may as well have been trying to bail out the ocean. She was never going to get anything from Vittam.

She must've decided that too, because she said, 'That will be all.'

Vittam stood, tapping his heart again. His rings flashed in the dull lighting. 'My absolute pleasure.'

'Wait,' Tomi said. 'Is that a parillion gemstone?'

Vittam glanced at the ring on his thumb. 'I believe it is.'

Oh *shit*.

That's where Damian had seen the rare stone. And he'd been brainless enough to tell Tomi.

'I happen to have looked up the names of all five legal owners of parillion gemstones in Radaza,' Tomi said. 'You're not on that list. In fact, one of the stones was recently stolen by Nomik, who claimed he gave the ring to you.'

'I don't know what you're talking about,' Vittam said. 'I found this ring in the gutter at the docks. Thought it was pretty, picked it up.' He examined it in the blue light. 'Didn't know it was a parillion. How fortunate for me.' He slipped it off his thumb and gave it to her. 'If it's evidence, please take it. I wouldn't want to stand in the way of justice.'

'I bet you wouldn't.'

Damian held his breath. Was it enough proof to take Vittam into the station? Would Tomi bother attempting it?

And what was Damian supposed to do if she did?

But she simply said, 'Thank you for your time,' and slipped the ring into her inner pocket.

'You're very welcome,' Vittam said. 'Please stop by again. And cookie – see you soon.'

Yaverly led them out of the office then stayed in his position at the door as they headed through the gambling den. This time, none of the punters said a word or even looked their way.

'All things considered, that went rather well,' Tomi said, climbing the steep staircase. 'Funny, though. You mentioned you saw a parillion gemstone. It wasn't Vittam's, was it?'

Damian gritted his teeth against a growing headache. He needed fresh air and a moment to think. Tomi was going to figure him out. She was too good at her job.

They reached the top and stepped into the afternoon sun. Two men lingered in the shadows by the garbage can, triller haze from their pipes clogging the alley. So much for fresh air.

Footsteps stomped on the steps behind them. Tomi and Damian spun around to find two more men had followed them from the den.

'Ah,' Tomi said. 'So this is why no one bothered us on the way out.'

Damian swore under his breath.

The four men withdrew batons. This wasn't some assassination attempt. It was punishment for entering Vittam's territory.

And it was going to hurt.

Twenty-One

ONE OF THE MEN GRABBED TOMI FROM BEHIND, LOCKING HIS BATON against her throat. Another advanced from the front. She kicked out, aiming a sharp heel to his stomach. He reeled back. She gave herself enough wriggle room to lean forward then smash her head backwards into the nose of her captor. He released her with a roar. She ducked an incoming punch and spun low to grab the metal lid of the garbage can. It was the perfect shield – she deflected several powerful blows from the batons of the three men around her.

'Tomi!'

The fourth man had pinned Damian to the wall and was lifting a baton to strike him in the face. Tomi threw the garbage lid like a discus. It hit Damian's attacker and sent him reeling sideways. Damian scrambled away, clutching his ribs. He was in no shape to be fighting.

A baton slammed between her shoulders. Someone kicked her legs out from under her and she landed hard on the ground. Wind rushed from her lungs. There was no time to roll away before one of the attackers pinned her down, his hands around her neck. He smirked, assuming he'd won.

She kicked her legs up over his shoulders, locking his arms straight. Using his weight, she rolled him sideways and landed upright with her knee against his chest. She grabbed his baton from the ground and slammed it into his head.

A second baton swung towards her – she blocked it and thumped the owner's kneecap. He lurched. One hit to the shoulder, another to the neck, another to the back of the head, and he was out.

Two men down.

She grabbed the second baton, one in each hand, turning to face the final two attackers–

To find Damian backed against the wall again. He'd taken down one of the men, but another looked like he'd been in his share of bar fights at the docks. Damian drew his pistol.

'Damian, no!'

He fired, the crack followed swiftly by stone crumbling from the wall of the building opposite. The burly man had anticipated the shot and dodged in time. In the space between breaths, he grabbed the pistol from Damian's hand, knocked Damian on the side of the head with the grip, then aimed the pistol at Tomi.

'One less soff on the streets, eh?' he said.

He pulled the trigger.

Tomi flinched, waiting for the bite of the bullet. But the man had jerked while taking the shot. He'd missed her.

He dropped the pistol, still jerking. A look of horror crossed his face before he started screaming.

Tomi watched in confusion as he fell to the ground and began rolling back and forth.

'I'm on fire! I'm on fire!'

Damian grabbed the pistol. He looked a little dazed but otherwise all right. The man he'd taken down gave a horrified gasp and began screaming too. Both men acted as if their skin were aflame, rolling to put out a fire that didn't exist.

Tomi and Damian stared at each other as realisation dawned on them at the same time.

Witchcraft.

They moved together into the middle of the alley, back to back. Tomi drew her pistol too. She scanned their surroundings, searching for where the magic was coming from. The two men she'd defeated started writhing and shouting.

'I don't see anyone,' Damian said.

Tomi didn't see anyone either. There had been a rumour that Vittam had witches working for him, and she wouldn't have been surprised to find it was true. But why would a witch in Vittam's services be helping *her*?

Footsteps rumbled from the stairs of the gambling den. More knuckles were on their way.

Tomi didn't have backup. Damian was injured. They had no idea how to take down a witch.

'Run,' she said.

They sprinted out of the alley and through the Shopping District. Tomi's back was throbbing from where she'd been hit by the baton. With every step, her anger rose.

Bunter Vittam would get away with attacking them. She already knew he'd claim no knowledge of the assault outside his establishment. He wasn't in charge of Radaza's streets – it was *her* job to find the criminals. That's what he'd tell the court.

She had a link between him and Nomik but couldn't disprove his story of finding the ring in the gutter. Judges had thrown away cases with more evidence than that when it came to Vittam. They were either scared of him or under his rule.

TADOW had investigated him and declared him human, which meant Vittam didn't kill Ivan Jupel, at least not with his own hands. But why would he have Jupel – and Park – killed by a witch in the first place? What was so special about these smuggled stones?

And who had helped them in the alley just now?

She couldn't get answers this way. Bunter Vittam was untouchable until she had other evidence.

It was time to see how the Park Herliz side was coming along. And that, unfortunately, meant dealing with TADOW.

Twenty-Two

Eversea Shipping was no longer the bustling enterprise from two days ago. Gone were the heartbeasts and the dock workers. The pulleys hung stationary, creaking in a salty breeze. Crates had been overturned, the soil from the native plants scattered across the ground and raked through for every last bone and tooth. A few members of Border Control and TADOW still searched for illegal products. TADOW were easy to spot – they had long coats cinched with silver belts. Green epaulettes sat on their shoulders with the insignia of the councillors' tower under the five Tassela stars, roofed by a shield. Their tall boots thunked on the wooden ramp into the ship at the dock. They brought to mind the military more than witch hunters.

One officer stepped in front of Tomi and Damian before they could reach the ship. 'This area's out of bounds.' He had a heavily receding hairline and jowls that would put a warbling parlington to shame.

'We're clearly JOs,' Tomi said, tapping the badge on her belt. While she hadn't had much to do with TADOW, she'd heard enough about them to know not to take any of their shit. 'Tomi Cardozo, lead investigator for the Justice Department on the murder of Ivan Jupel and Park Herliz.'

'Park Herliz is under our jurisdiction. And technically, Ivan Jupel should be, too. He was a plant fucker like the killer.'

'Ivan Jupel has no blood family in Radaza. There's no one related to him for you to persecute.'

The TADOW officer curled his lip. 'The boss said you JOs would be sniffing around, trying to take this case away from us.'

'Assuming Jupel and Herliz were killed by the same person, this is a murder case *and* a witch case. That means we need to cooperate. Where's this boss of yours?'

'Good day, officers.' A second TADOW man approached. He had silver tassels on his epaulettes and a brass pin on his folded coat collar. He was in his mid-forties, his hair grey, one eye not quite matching the movement of the other. 'Superior Officer Woods Chadley, at your service.' He had the same clipped tones as Nomik Whimsy. A man from the Perlian elite, then.

'I'm–'

'Officer Tomi Cardozo, of course. Your reputation precedes you.' His smile was wide but lopsided.

'This is my AO, Damian Kamara.'

Chadley tapped his hand to his heart in greeting. The other TADOW officer scowled.

'We've come to compare notes,' Tomi said. 'How are you faring with the Herliz case?'

'You're lucky you caught me – I only popped in to check on my team. I'm usually at TADOW headquarters.' He tilted his head. 'Didn't you think to look for me there?'

'We were hoping to get a list of Eversea employees.'

'You already interviewed everyone who was here the day of the murder. Weren't you the ones who found the body?'

'Yes. But new evidence has come to light–'

'Oh?'

'We suspect Bunter Vittam is involved.'

Chadley cleared his throat and glanced at the scowling officer. 'Dismissed, Rauclay.'

The officer gave Tomi one last scowl before stalking away.

'Vittam, you say?' Chadley said when Rauclay was out of hearing distance. 'We've done a thorough investigation into him and found no witch activities.'

'We suspect he sent a witch to do his work for him.'

'That's a big claim. Can you back it up?'

'We caught the person responsible for sedating Jupel. He says Vittam coerced him.'

Chadley's eyebrows flew up. 'Is that so?'

'Vittam's not owning up to it, of course, which is why I need more evidence. Is anyone you've interviewed so far connected to him? Indentured, even?'

'We'll look into it,' Chadley said. There was caution in his tone.

'The salitenine grease found on the handle of Jupel's murder weapon suggests someone connected to water. If the cases are linked, it might mean the killer was an employee from Eversea Shipping. I'd like to be involved in follow-up interviews. If we could arrange–'

'I'm afraid that's not possible.'

Tomi paused. 'I'm sorry?'

'We'll continue to share all the reports and documents necessary for the case. That should be ample resources for your parallel investigation.'

It took a moment for Tomi to formulate a diplomatic response. 'Officer Chadley, TADOW doesn't normally deal with unseemly crimes. I understand that and appreciate the efforts your team has put into the case. However, their notes have been a little... unrefined. Now, as someone with experience in murder investigations, I feel that I–'

'Look,' Chadley said, dropping his professional manner. 'I don't think it's a good idea you involve yourself in our investigation. You're currently on probation for letting a witch go, are you not?' He glanced at the docks. 'My officers won't appreciate your presence. They'll suspect you of meddling, perhaps even covering up for witches.'

'The committee cleared me to work on this case,' Tomi said, silently cursing. She should've known that TADOW would have been informed of her hearing.

'That's all very well from a legal standpoint. But I can't stop my officers from being wary of a witch-sympathiser.'

'I'm not–'

'It doesn't matter. The issue is, not everyone in TADOW is going to have confidence in you. We can't solve these murders without mutual trust, which is why I believe it's best you stay out of our crime scene and away from our witnesses. Our partnership will have to continue in a strictly written arrangement.'

'You can't be serious.'

'Oh, I'm very serious. And, I'm loath to say it, but if I catch you interfering with our side of the investigation, I'll have to inform the committee in charge of your hearing that you're obstructing justice.'

'What?'

Chadley tapped his chest to her, then, without giving her any further explanation for his outrageous decision, spun on his heel and marched back to the docks.

'Wow,' Damian said. 'Am I allowed to hate him?'

'To be honest, he's the most reasonable person in TADOW I've come across.'

'That can't be true.'

'The things that are happening to me in the station? The pranks and offensive comments? That's nothing compared to how TADOW officers would've treated me if I worked with them.' Tomi let out a long breath and turned back to the grousdu enclosure. 'I guess there's nothing more we can do here.'

'Then what's our next move? If we can't follow up on Vittam, and we can't investigate Park Herliz, what other angle can we take?'

'I suppose we could go to Tailor Happershift and see if she'll let us into her sanctuary. If, by some miracle of the Tassela, one of her addicts talks to us about their cutlass dealer, we could follow up on that.'

'That sounds like a long shot. Starting with convincing Tailor Happershift to give away the location of her sanctuary.'

'Well...' said Tomi slowly. The notion was there before she could stop it. Seductive. Enticing. It reached for her with its sinister tendrils, as it always had.

This time, she found herself reaching back.

'There's another option,' she said. 'But it might be as much of a long shot, if not more.'

Don't do it, don't do it.

'What are you thinking?' Damian said.

Don't do it, don't do it.

Even as her rational mind pleaded, another part of her thrummed with anticipation. The darker, obsessive part of her. They were being blocked at every turn. But this way – this way was wide open. A fresh perspective on an old case. Was it really so bad, just to try?

'Why don't we take another look at that Glisk case?' she said, keeping her voice light.

Damian's eyes widened in excitement. 'Really?'

'Sure. Now that we have a reason to suspect witches were involved, we might find something the JOs missed before.'

'And maybe there'll be other links to the Jupel case besides the missing bindings.'

'Absolutely.'

Damian rubbed his hands together. 'Should we meet at the archives tomorrow morning?'

'No, no,' Tomi said, maintaining her casual tone. 'We don't have long before the hearing. Let's start now.'

'An all-nighter?' Damian said, glancing at the setting sun. 'Sounds fun. I'm in.'

She smiled.

And her addiction, forced into dormancy for so long, bloomed like an exquisite bruise.

Twenty-Three

TEN YEARS AGO, TOMI HAD BEEN SITTING ALONE IN RADAZA'S FANCIEST tea room, nursing one last cup as she prepared to go home and eat a bullet.

She'd just been demoted from attending officer to general duties and no longer had unrestricted access to the archives. For the three months prior, her entire life had been the Glisk evidence nook. She'd paid no attention to her official cases. Nights were spent parsing parchments, lists and records. Rest days were dedicated to hunting down witnesses, company staff – anyone who could explain to her what had happened the evening the Glisks had died.

No one knew a thing.

She'd thought the investigating JOs must've been useless or uncaring or not dedicated enough. Turned out they had examined every alley and avenue available, along with the officers who had come after them and the officers after that. Having been in the manor at the time of the murder, Tomi had assumed she'd do a better job, but all she'd found were the same dead ends her predecessors had.

She had spent years training. Months reliving the horrific experience over and over in order to find something the JOs had missed. And it had been for nothing.

She had fallen into a pit so deep, she could no longer see the light.

The only way out was to finish it. She had no one to say goodbye to. The beacons at Bleakhouse would care for her sister. Her time was done. Her last breath was near, and it was a relief, really, to know the endless pain would finally be over.

And then a fiery head of hair had swum into her vision. It was attached to a cheerful young woman who'd plonked herself down in the chair opposite and started chatting like they knew each other. Two of the woman's friends came over too. The trio practically talked over each other as they explained who they were, while Tomi stared at them blankly, wondering whether someone had dosed her tea with dorvmin.

One of the friends worked as a medica maven in the morgue. She had recognised Tomi from a past case and suggested asking the boss to assign them as partners when Tomi became a JO. Tomi had agreed because she was too bewildered to refuse.

She'd tried to leave. They wouldn't let her. Instead they took her back to their atrium, where Tomi had her first Zim Mah communal dinner experience. They filled her with wine and good food. They danced and sang old songs for her.

It was like they'd known what she was about to do.

It was like they were saving her life.

Around three bells, drunk in their apartment, she'd broken down and told them her entire story. She'd assumed explaining what had happened that night would be like opening a weeping wound, carving deeper into her pain. Instead, it was more like siphoning poison from her body. The relief had been incomparable. It didn't matter who found out now. She hadn't been planning to see the dawn.

But dawn came, and she was still alive, and they stayed with her. They let her live with them for a time, giving her strategies to cope and taking shifts to get her through the nights. They helped her manage the addiction and find meaning in her life – meaning that had nothing to do with the Glisk murders.

She was no longer alone, and that reminder had never been as stark as right now, with Zef standing at the entrance of the underground archives as she came out.

'What is this?' she asked. 'Are you following me?'

Despite her indignation, she couldn't help feeling like a child who'd been caught stealing cakes from the baking tray. She tightened her grip on the crate of evidence. Behind her, Damian had a second crate filled with the Glisks' bloodied clothing. They still smelled faintly of bitter pinjora, even after all this time.

'Tomi,' Zef said quietly. 'You know where this path leads.'

'There's new evidence–'

'Not enough.'

'It is for me.' Tomi pushed past him, heading for the tethering post. Damian trailed dutifully behind her.

'Please, Tomi,' Zef said.

'I've hit a dead end with my current case. I need to take a different angle.'

'That's an excuse, and you know it.'

Tomi buckled her crate to one side of Finley's saddle, then took Damian's crate to buckle it to the other side. Damian shifted uncomfortably as he waited. He avoided looking at Zef.

It reminded Tomi of the argument she and Zef had had last night, of the terrible way he'd treated Damian. Considering his kindness all those years ago when Tomi had needed help, she'd hoped he would've accepted her troubled apprentice.

'I think we've said all we need to say to each other.' Her tone was cool as she swung herself up on Finley's saddle.

Zef stepped back, probably because he knew how temperamental her grousdu was. She was surprised he was letting her go so easily. She'd been bracing for a fight. Had he really come all this way for a few futile words?

Damian climbed onto Brix. Tomi didn't miss the look Zef gave him. It was as if he were mentally digging Damian's grave.

She'd asked Zef last night why he distrusted Damian – of course she had. She wanted to give Zef the benefit of the doubt. But Zef had just repeated what he'd said before: ask Damian where he got his injuries.

As if Zef would know. As if he had the right to judge. Just because Zef had been taken in by the Thraseep family didn't mean everyone in Radaza was well cared for.

Tomi and Damian set their grousdu at a solid pace, speeding into the night. It was a fair distance to the Black Ivory District, which was north and inland from the Shores.

'I was thinking,' Damian said, breaking the cold silence, 'don't you find it strange that Shiver Whimsy didn't mention her grandson was working for Jupel when we were at Whimsy Holm? He was the clear link between the menagerie and the University.'

'Shiver hadn't seen Nomik for years, remember? She probably didn't know he was Jupel's AP.'

'But she was making donations in Nomik's name – that's why the professors let him pass their courses.'

'It doesn't mean she knew who they were.' Tomi glanced at Damian in the light of a passing streetlamp. 'You think she had something to do with the murder?'

'Maybe. She might've found out Jupel was going to fail Nomik and wanted to protect the family name.'

'By murdering him? That's a big leap.'

'I'm just thinking out loud.'

'I called Shiver before we brought Nomik in. She sounded horrified at what he'd been up to.'

'She could've been lying.'

'Why would she send Nomik into the halicort enclosure if she could just go in herself?'

'I don't know. Frame him for the murder?'

Tomi laughed. 'You just said her motive was to protect him from failing.'

'No, I said her motive was to protect the family name. Maybe she wanted to frame him as punishment.'

'Mm. So why did she get Bunter Vittam involved? Why did she kill Park Herliz? And what did the stone have to do with it?'

'I'm still working on all that.'

'Right.'

Damian fell silent. Tomi had been grateful for the short reprieve, but her thoughts soon returned to the task at hand.

The residents of the Black Ivory District had access to the banks of the Parif River and also heated canals where their minnisks could play and hunt. The roads became silkslate; the atriums turned to single-family mansions with sprawling estate gardens. Thick trees spread their roots in this area, ornate lanterns hanging from their branches to light the streets. Minnisk-drawn carriages rumbled past at reckless speeds, their owners unconcerned for anyone in their path.

Tomi's breaths became shallow the closer they got to Brackenlong Manor. When anxiety squeezed at her chest, she curled her fists around the reins. Now was not the time to crumble.

'Here.'

She tugged Finley to a stop and gazed at the overgrown garden corridor that led to her childhood home. It was haunting in the moonlight. Damian pulled Brix up behind her. He gave a low whistle.

'You grew up in this place?'

She stared at the pale, reefstone walls, the sloping roofs, the oriel windows, the vines creeping up the façade.

'It was another life,' she murmured.

Then she spurred Finley onwards. They slowed only when they reached an empty fountain at the foot of the mossy front steps.

'Should we tether the grousdu here?' Damian said, climbing off Brix.

'No. There's a better place inside.'

They climbed the steps to the large, oakendown entrance doors. Musty-smelling gloom greeted them as they walked inside. It was cold in the foyer. Tomi grabbed a flint stick from Finley's saddle and fumbled about for the portable oil lantern kept in the side table.

Damian gawked as he led Brix in after her. Tomi had visited a few times while investigating the case 10 years ago, but it had been long enough since her last visit that she could look at her childhood home with a fresh perspective. Elaborate tapestries decorated the dark wood panelling, and bronze candle chandeliers looped and twisted like vines along the high ceiling. As her eyes adjusted, she could see the dust and cobwebs and mould through the glimmer. The tapestries had been chewed by milkmoths. A creeg skittered across the floor and disappeared under a cabinet.

It really did feel like another life.

Finley rasped, scratching at the tiled floor.

'This way,' Tomi said. She led them straight ahead, past the wide staircase to a long, glass room completely overgrown with plants.

Once, this place had been Sharlie Glisk's pride and joy. She had spent hours cultivating her indoor blooms. Now it could've been mistaken for the wild forests of Elumina, complete with an algae-covered pond. Insects buzzed beneath the stars that glowed through the glass ceiling.

Tomi unbuckled the crates from Finley's saddle. She had to use her dagger to hack away the vines that had grown beyond the threshold so she could shut the door. 'They should be happy in there for the time being,' she said.

Damian was staring at her.

'What?' she said.

'How were these people so rich?'

She shrugged. 'They ran a successful company. Glisk cleaning supplies were shipped all over the continent.'

'Yes, but this is ridiculous.'

Tomi didn't have an answer for him. She hadn't understood as a child the way the Glisks had dripped with coin, and even now her comprehension of commerce and intercontinental trading was limited. The Glisks were rich. That's all she'd known. If it didn't have to do with the murders, she wasn't interested.

'Let's go to the crime scene,' she said.

She picked up one of the crates, the oil lantern balanced on top. Damian picked up the other crate and they headed down a corridor to the left of the staircase. As they walked, Tomi's mind snagged on memories: of chasing her sister down the halls; of learning foreign languages over supper; of knocking over an ornamental plate from the Realm of the Snow Bear Queen and watching it smash to the ground.

It was so long ago.

And yet...

She felt like she'd taken a hit of plink. Her hands were still shaking, but this time it was the thrill of being back at this juncture, of submerging her mind into the details, of reading, comparing, obsessing. It was a state of being she knew and was comforted by.

And that, perhaps, was the scariest thing of all.

'How did the killers get into the house?' Damian said.

'JOs suspect it was through the tunnels. The doors had just been opened for the settling, and it was clearly their escape – there was a trail of blood that led to the tunnel entrance, but it didn't go further. They probably had a grousdu or minnisk waiting. And a guard was missing. They think he was paid off.'

'Did anyone ever find him?'

'No.'

She stopped outside the study. It was a large room with double doors that could be pulled closed from either side, but they had been open most nights during her childhood and never closed again after the murder. There was a stain on the rug by the door where she had vomited before rushing to Anatole Glisk's side.

She stepped in and set down the crate. Damian placed his beside it. She used her flint stick to light more oil lanterns.

'I can't believe it,' Damian said softly. 'This is it. This is *the* murder scene.' He pulled off his tailcoat and rolled up his shirt sleeves.

Tomi moved to the middle of the room. Her mind was already reciting the contents of the autopsy report. Every word of every piece of parchment in the evidence nook had been branded into her brain. 'Here's where I found Anatole Glisk,' she said. 'An empty container of his company's most potent cleaning fluid was here beside him: bleach, fragranced with bitter pinjora.'

– stomach lining, oesophagus and mouth scalded, as is a portion of the intestines –

'The killers poured it down his throat. His blood and bile spread to here, then stopped in the shape of shoe prints.'

– clumps of hair missing suggest head was wrenched back to force the mouth open –

She pointed to the iron chair on the other side of the desk. 'That's where Sharlie Glisk was sitting, shot in the forehead.'

– bruising on wrists and mouth suggest victim was gagged and bound –

'Was there any red dust left behind, like what we found at Jupel's crime scene?' Damian said.

'No.'

He crouched at the spot where Anatole had fallen. He ran a finger along the reefstone tiles, leaving a trail in the thick dust.

'The investigating JOs suspected the eldest daughter interrupted the killers,' Tomi said. 'She screamed, alerting the household. Maybe that's why they shot Sharlie rather than torture her. They had to get out of here quickly.'

'Why were they torturing them in the first place?'

'I don't know.'

Damian frowned, scanning the room. 'Who else was in the manor?'

'It was the night of the settling, so most of the staff had left, but there was still the cook in the kitchen, a butler somewhere on this level, a maid upstairs, the *ama sector–*'

'Your mother?'

'Right. And two minnisk keepers out at the canal. They all gave their statements and were cleared by the JOs.' Tomi paused. 'But if they were witches...'

'They might have had other means of looking innocent,' Damian said, finishing her thought. 'And where were you?'

'Upstairs in my room, getting ready for the neighbour's party. I ran down when I heard the scream and found their daughter huddled in the corner over there. Her mind had been addled by then. She didn't know who she was, let alone what had happened.'

'What about the other daughter? Where was she?'

Tomi hesitated. 'Upstairs as well.' She moved to an empty stone stand, chest height, in the middle of the room. 'The Glisks had set up a game of clatterstones here. It had been knocked over. The pieces were scattered across the floor.' She walked behind the desk. 'The strange thing was, JOs found most of the pieces all the way back here. 21 out of the 32 were past the chair, even though the board was on the floor by the stand.'

Damian moved to the stone stand and mimed tipping over a board. The two of them looked at the distance between the stand and where Tomi was.

'How is that possible?' Damian said.

Tomi spread her hands. 'No one could figure it out.'

He joined her behind the desk, examining the cobweb-laced ink pot and opening the empty drawers. Tomi wasn't sure who had taken out all the parchments. A lot of work was missing. Even the stationery had been taken. Tomi could remember the piles of notes and scrolls, inked with the Glisk insignia on the top: the head of a raizelet, face forward, fierce and proud, with *Lussisco Harldah Buhkasa* written in an arch above it.

'The family motto,' Anatole Glisk had told her. She'd been sitting on his lap while he worked, her small fingers tracing the lettering. 'Light Flares Eternal.'

Even though she hadn't understood what it meant, she remembered feeling the weight of the words.

Lussisco Harldah Buhkasa.

She watched as Damian's careful gaze combed the area, from the handles of the drawers to the skirting board, to the map of the continent stretched across the back wall. She'd never brought anyone here before. It felt as if she were laying herself bare for him to poke and prod as he pleased. And yet he was oblivious to the intimacy.

'This is incredible,' he said, running his fingers across the thick parchment of the map. 'I've never seen one so detailed.'

He traced the line of mountains separating Agriterra in the south from Perlia in the northwest, then up the stretch of land to the east that covered the Freelands of Elumina. To the very north were the snow deserts. There were no cities up there.

'Strange,' he said, probing at a point in the mountains. 'There's a hole here.'

'The Glisks used to have pins all over the map. I think it was where they sold their product. They were shipping cargo across the continent.'

'But someone took them down?'

Tomi held up her oil lantern so he could examine it better. 'I suppose so.'

Damian felt about for more holes in the parchment. He paused at the centre of Perlia, flicking at a small horizontal cut in the parchment. 'What's this?'

'Probably just got torn when someone was taking the pin out.'

'No.' Damian frowned, peering closer. 'It looks like it's been sliced.' He glanced at Tomi. 'The Glisks' game of clatterstones. Was it the Elumenese version or the Perlian?'

'Perlian. Why?'

'So the pieces were rectangular prisms.' Damian walked back to the stone stand where the game board had been. He looked at the stand, then the map.

'What are you thinking?' Tomi said.

He lifted his hand slowly, moving in the same action as skipping rocks across a pond. 'Someone scattered the pieces like projectiles. The pieces would've flown across the room, which explains why most were behind the desk. And it accounts for that rip in the map – one hit the wall with enough force to tear the parchment.'

'What, they just grabbed handfuls of game pieces and threw them? I don't think so. No one could throw that hard anyway.'

'We're looking at this with the assumption the killers are witches, right? So what if it were magic? They moved the pieces with a spell or something?'

'You think the killers attacked the Glisks with clatterstone game pieces before brutally murdering them?'

'They could've. As a show of force.'

Tomi didn't think it was likely, but she was keen to hear new ideas.

'Or,' Damian said, 'maybe the clatterstone pieces were thrown in *defence*.'

'The killers didn't need to defend themselves. They caught the Glisks completely off guard.'

'I'm not talking about the killers.' Damian's eyes shone in the glow of the oil lanterns. 'What if the Glisks were witches too?'

'That's impossible.'

'Not necessarily. The JOs dismissed the idea of the killers being witches because there was no sign of magic and no motive. But what if the motive was witch related?'

'I'm telling you, the Glisks weren't witches. I lived with them my whole life.'

'You were a child – you wouldn't have known if they were hiding it from you.'

'Trust me, I would've.'

'But this explains why their products were so good. What if there was a potion in the cleaning fluid? Maybe other witches were angry they were flaunting their magic and wanted to stop them.'

'Listen to what I'm saying. The Glisks weren't witches. I knew their daughters, and they didn't have magic.'

'You can't be certain.'

'Yes, I can.'

'Well, even if they didn't, that doesn't mean Anatole and Sharlie weren't witches. Remember what Professor Quaide said? His grandmother was a witch, but he didn't have any magic. It's not always inherited.'

'Damn it, Damian! The Glisks weren't fucking witches!'

Damian closed his mouth. Tomi breathed hard, like she'd run up a flight of stairs. She lowered the oil lantern.

'Sorry,' Damian said after a silence. 'I just thought you wanted fresh eyes on the case.'

Tomi didn't answer.

'This is obviously hard for you,' Damian said. 'Maybe I should go.'

'Yes, maybe you should.'

Damian picked up his tailcoat. He waited one more breath, as if hoping she'd change her mind. When she didn't say anything, he left.

She listened to his footsteps thumping down the hall, to him leading Brix out of the conservatory, to the entrance doors opening and closing again.

When she was certain he was gone, she sank down by the crates to pull out all the parchment work and evidence, spreading it out around her as the laterns burned lower.

It had been a mistake bringing Damian here. He couldn't help if he didn't have the complete story. He didn't understand.

Tomi Cardozo was not a real person.

Her name was Maribelle Glisk, joint heiress to the richest company in Radaza, and at age eight, she had walked in on her parents' bodies, tortured and bloody, with her big sister drooling senselessly in the corner.

Justice, fairness, the law – she could speak of those things all she liked, and in quieter moments, she could believe in them too.

But one day, she would find the people who had killed Sharlie and Anatole Glisk – *her mother and father* – and she would take them down.

Twenty-Four

THE FERRY TERMINAL HAD A STRANGE DISSONANCE LATE AT NIGHT. The oil lanterns burned brightly but only made the shadows thicker. Each footstep and comment seemed muffled, as if the night swallowed most of the sound. This wasn't the time for family outings or romantic trysts. The midnight bells weren't far away, and the frost was near. The few passengers were haggard and alone in their travels: night workers, crooks and messengers. Damian recognised a few unofficial messengers from his runner days. Were any of them working for Vittam now?

It unnerved him to think about. It unnerved him to be away from Pa, too. If Vittam decided to do another late-night visit, Damian wanted to be there.

But Tomi needed help. They had only one full day before her hearing, and the more evidence they collected, the better off she'd be. He didn't know for sure whether Shiver Whimsy had anything to do with Jupel's murder, but it wouldn't hurt to double check. He just hoped Vittam was done with his punishments, now he'd sent the knuckles after them in the alley.

Damian headed to Katterina Piers, who was taking tickets for a ferry going south of the river. She stood out with her purple hair, dyed from the crushed petals of a harris blossom.

'Do you ever leave?' he said.

She flicked him a look of disdain. 'I was wondering the same about you.'

'You'd miss me if I stayed away.'

Her long nails, painted purple like her hair, drummed on the metal turnstile. 'What do you want, Kamara?'

'Why, are you busy?' Damian glanced pointedly around the near-empty terminal.

'I'm calling security.'

'Hey, I'm an officer now. I'm here on business.'

'At midnight?'

'A soff never sleeps. So they say.' He pulled out his parchment book. 'I have a question for you about the twenty-seventh night of Harvest. If you can remember any passengers–'

'I wasn't here that night,' Katterina said. 'I had a quarter-moon holiday. My first day back was yesterday.'

'You took a holiday right before the terminal closes for the frost season?'

Katterina met his gaze with a steady stare. 'Just because the terminal's closed, doesn't mean I stop working.'

'Fair enough,' Damian said, writing it down.

'If you want to know who was travelling that night, ask Ravern. She's been doing double-shifts lately.' Katterina jutted her chin towards the corridor for the ferry to Deep Water Bay. Ravern dozed against the turnstile. She was short enough that she didn't have to bend much to slump over it.

Damian thanked Katterina and headed over. 'Ravern Furling,' he said in a deep, drawling voice, mimicking the last time Talcott Notch had wandered up to them at the terminal.

She lurched off the turnstile with a shout. He laughed as she clutched her chest.

'Damian Kamara,' she shouted, whacking him on the arm. 'You scared the threads outta me! I thought you were the boss.'

'He's not still here, is he?'

'Yes.' She massaged her heart sourly. 'This close to the frost, his office is piled high with scrolls.'

'Why are you working so late?'

'Have to do makeup shifts. My kid's been sick and...' She eyeballed him. 'What are *you* doing here? Haven't seen you here past midnight since your runner days.'

'I want to ask you about the twenty-seventh night of Harvest. Did you see if Shiver Whimsy came through?'

'Sorry, no. I went home early. Like I said, my kid's been sick. But Shiver Whimsy doesn't use the ferry anyway – she's got her own boat.'

Of course she did. Damian refrained from slapping himself on the forehead. She could come and go from the menagerie without anyone knowing. That meant she wouldn't have her travel log stamped, either.

Ravern turned her good ear towards him, keen for gossip. '*Leya* Whimsy got something to do with the case you're on?'

'Maybe,' Damian said tantalisingly. 'Actually, you might be able to help me. When you worked at the menagerie, did she and Nomik get along?'

'Not really. He ran a bit free as a kid – though what can you expect, living on an island full of animals? From what I saw, Shiver didn't approve of the way his parents raised him.'

'They're in Elumina now, right?'

'Dunno. Haven't been involved in the menagerie for years.' She brightened. 'Did you visit the enclosures while you were there yesterday?'

'We may have walked around a bit.'

'Tell me you saw the volfe. Aren't they the most amazing creatures? They were my domain – worked with them for almost 20 years.'

'They took flight while we were in the enclosure,' Damian said. 'It felt... strange.'

'In a good way?'

He nodded, remembering how his loyalty to Tomi felt absolute in that moment. And then she turned around and asked him to dinner.

'Consider yourself lucky,' Ravern said, beaming. 'They say when the volfe fly, you–'

'*Bolocha.*' Damian turned towards the wall to hide his face. 'Why is Bunter Vittam here?'

Ravern frowned.

'What is he doing?' Damian said.

'Heading to *Seno* Notch's office.'

Damian risked a glance back. Vittam had Yaverly and Winsor with him. It was better they were here than at Damian's apartment, but still.

Why?

'What does Vittam want with your boss?'

'Couldn't tell you.'

'Have you ever seen him here before?'

'Nope.'

Damian watched the three men head to an archway. Notch's office was up a slope, on a second storey where he could watch over the terminal from a mezzanine walled with coruscat glass. The portmaster could see out, but no one could see in.

'I'm going to find out what they're saying.'

'Damian, don't!'

He ignored Ravern's panicked whisper and scurried across the terminal to the archway. He was resolved, not just for Tomi but for his own sake. If he could overhear something useful, maybe he could use it against Vittam as leverage. He waited until Vittam and his knuckles had closed the office door before creeping up the ramp and crouching to press his ear against the keyhole.

'–cursed *witches*,' Vittam was saying in his raspy accent. 'I don't know whether this particular one is making a habit of hanging around my den, but one of those cratters covered my men with itching powder this afternoon. Let two JOs get away, and let me tell you, I was not happy.'

Damian held his breath, worried even a soft gasp would give him away. Just who was that witch in the alley this afternoon?

'I'm keen to know what any of this has to do with me.' That was Notch's drawling voice. Damian hadn't done his undertone of disgust justice when he'd mimicked him.

'I'm getting to that,' Vittam said.

'I'm an extremely busy man. If you could "get to it" a little faster – don't crack your knuckles at me, *Seno*. I'm not afraid of you. There will be unpleasant consequences if you lay a finger on me.'

He was probably talking to Yaverly or Winsor. Even the thought of them, so close behind the door, caused a throb of pain in Damian's ribs.

'Park Herliz,' Vittam said. 'Friend of yours, I believe. Died a most terrible death at the hands of a witch. The same witch who killed Ivan Jupel.'

There was a silence. Then Notch said, 'Do you know the identity of this witch? I would like to peel off their skin.'

Damian made a face.

'Get in line,' Vittam said. 'This witch came to me, invisible. Threatened me with all kinds of nasty things. Did some of them to me, too. I'll never walk the same.'

There was the scraping of a chair. Notch standing up?

'Tell me,' Notch said. 'What indication did they give of their identity?'

'Nothing. I can't tell you anything about them. But they had me get that Whimsy kid to fetch halicorn horn shavings and gave me a sleeping potion in return. They wanted in to Jupel's apartment.'

'Why?'

'My people on the inside tell me the witch was after a stone. A stone that *your* pal was smuggling. Want to explain who might've had a problem with that?'

Damian choked. Was the portmaster involved in the smuggling? It made sense. He owned the ferry terminals. He had connections and coin. If anyone was in a solid position to be part of a smuggling trade – of stones, ices, whatever – it was Talcott Notch.

Damian hadn't realised the room had gone silent until the door swung open. Yaverly's stocky hand grabbed Damian's jacket and hauled him to his feet.

'What's he doing here?' Notch said.

'Relax,' Vittam said. 'He's one of mine.'

'He's a JO!' Notch pointed a slender finger at Damian. 'What did you hear? Park Herliz was an old friend, but I had nothing to do with his illegal affairs. And if you try to say otherwise, I will have my lawyers breathing down your neck so fast–'

'Notch, please.' Vittam gave Damian a greasy smile. 'He's not going to say anything.'

Damian couldn't bring himself to answer. Yaverly was still gripping his collar, and Winsor glowered from the corner. Beyond the coruscat glass, the terminal was quiet. Ravern gazed up at them, though he knew she couldn't see him.

All Damian could think about was the blade sliding into Pa's hand. Callous, almost casual, like a slap on the back. How easily would that blade slide into Damian's gut? Or Pa's? Or *Bamki* Rivers'?

Notch's face was growing red with fury around his long silver sideburns. 'I have friends in high places. The highest. If you dare imply my involvement in this – I had nothing to do with – Vittam came to *me*–'

'Notch,' Vittam snapped. His easy tone was gone. 'Kamara won't be implying anything. He has a father who requires his silence.'

Damian's stomach clenched uncomfortably.

'Then what,' Notch said through his teeth, 'is he doing here?'

'Good question.' Vittam turned to Damian. 'You spying on me?'

'I–' Damian started.

'Because if you're spying on me, I'm afraid we're going to have to do another home visit. I'm already very irritated at your intrusion into my den this afternoon. Another betrayal could mean I lose my temper for real.'

Vittam wandered to Damian. The keys on his belt glittered in the light of the oil lanterns, including the one identical to the key they'd found in Jupel's apartment. It was so close Damian could almost touch it.

'I have news,' Damian said, his heart sprinting. 'About Tomi Cardozo.'

Vittam waved at Yaverly to release his grip on Damian's collar. Damian shook his shoulders free.

He shouldn't do this.

But how else would he get out unscathed? How would Pa stay safe, now Damian had been caught spying on Bunter Vittam?

It wasn't that big a deal, was it? Tomi was being overly cautious. She didn't really have anything to do with the Glisks' murders. The information would be interesting to Vittam, but there was nothing he could actually do with it.

Right?

Damian glanced at Talcott Notch. Telling Vittam was one thing, but the portmaster shouldn't be here.

Notch arched his thin eyebrows. 'You must think me a fool if you expect me to leave.'

'Don't worry,' Vittam said. 'I have ways of making him squawk.'

'You don't have to.' Damian drew a steadying breath, then said, 'Tomi Cardozo is the daughter of the *ama sector* for the Glisks. She was in the house during the murders.'

After a stunned silence, Notch stroked his chin with long fingers. 'Intriguing.'

'Very much so,' Vittam said, his lips curling upwards.

Damian threw himself at Vittam, gripping his jacket lapels. 'Please! Please don't hurt Pa. That has to be enough information–'

Yaverly wrenched Damian away. Damian saw a fist before black pain strobed in his vision. He slammed to the floor.

'Get him out of here,' Vittam said, sounding disgusted. 'He's lucky he brought me something of use, or I might've had him taken to the docks.'

Someone – probably Yaverly – hauled Damian up and threw him out of the room. Damian rolled partway down the ramp before coming to a stop. For a long time, he lay on the cold stone, gasping as he waited for the pain to subside.

It had been a risk. And he had paid for it.

He smiled, opening his fist to reveal Vittam's key.

Totally worth it.

Twenty-Five

MAMA!

Tomi's memories bled into her dreams. She called for her mother as she ran through the manor. She was breathless from laughing. Her favourite minnisk had just learnt another trick. A somersault? An obstacle course? It had been something exciting.

The monsoon season had finished at last, giving way to the wild season. The first sunshine was always the sweetest. It made her feel as happy as a poffin on a cushion.

She burst into the conservatory.

Harpsigold spun around with a gasp. 'Maribelle!'

Her sister was at a table adorned with blossoms and a pink and green cloth, helping Papa plant a sapling in a small pot. Mama was lighting colourful candles with a flint stick.

'That's all right,' Papa said, beaming at Tomi. 'Hello, my little raizelet. You were supposed to be looking after the minnisks.' His fingers were deep in the soil.

'There you are.' Lameia, the *ama sector*, scooped Tomi up from behind. 'Come on, my naughty girl. It's time to eat pippycakes and drink too much sweetmilk.'

Tomi shrieked with laughter as Lameia spun her away from the room. Everything twirled, around and around, in pinks and greens and browns. Altars and cloth and blossoms and candles and altars and altars and altars—

'Tomi.'

A warm hand brushed her cheek. She stirred. 'Papa.'

'Tomi, wake up.'

She opened her eyes to find daylight fighting its way through the grimy windows. Zef was crouched beside her, holding a canteen. He brushed down the sleeve of her ruffled blouse as she sat up. Mia and Payana stood over them with small cooking pots and finger towels. There was a roll of parchment under Mia's arm.

Tomi's nose was blocked, her vision blurry. She'd fallen asleep in the dust, surrounded by reports and evidence. Zef handed her the canteen, and she gulped the water greedily. The colours of the dream were already fading.

'When's the last time you ate?' Payana said.

Tomi didn't answer, simply because she couldn't remember. Breakfast yesterday... but had she lunched? She couldn't recall stopping for food between interrogating Nomik Whimsy and going after Vittam. And she hadn't been able to think of anything other than the case once she'd stepped foot into Brackenlong Manor.

Payana and Mia set the pots on the floor. They took off the lids to reveal curried sausages, fruit and a hard-boiled egg. Tomi fell into it, too ravenous to care whether they watched her or judged.

There were much bigger things to be ashamed of. She had jumped back into the pit, headfirst this time. She wished she felt sorry, but she didn't. She couldn't.

Mia walked to the study desk and unrolled the parchment. 'This is the contract for the manor. Sign on the bottom, and it's yours.'

Tomi still wasn't sure she wanted it. Then again, she couldn't imagine giving the manor to someone else. They'd renovate it, destroying her past and any evidence that might still be lurking in the shadows.

And there were still new things to be found. Damian had proved that last night.

'Damian has a theory,' she said. 'He thinks my parents were witches. I dismissed it at first, but now I'm wondering. If their killers were witches, maybe it's not totally impossible. It would explain why my whole family fled. They were afraid of being exposed.'

Payana and Mia exchanged glances.

'And I remember something,' Tomi said, grasping for the dream. 'One of Jupel's colleagues told me about altars, and I think... I think I interrupted my parents and my sister dressing an altar when I was very young.' She lifted her gaze to her friends. 'Being back in this house, with a new perspective... it feels different this time. Like I've finally reached the right path.'

The Trio's silence was a weight on Tomi's chest. She felt raw and tender, like an exposed wound. It wasn't just the fresh theory; it was the room itself. Now she wasn't absorbed in reading reports and searching for clues, she felt the complicated pressure of being here. It hurt, but there was a perverse pleasure to it, too. That blooming bruise of addiction.

She couldn't concentrate, couldn't figure out what her friends were thinking. They were probably angry. They'd spent so long trying to pull her from the shadows, and here she was, running back. She couldn't handle their disapproval right now. Her emotions wavered on a precipice, and she didn't know what would happen when she fell.

Mia said, 'Tomi–'

'No,' Payana snapped.

'We can't let her go on like this.'

'We all need to agree, and I don't.'

'This isn't fair. We have to tell her.'

Tomi looked to Zef as Mia and Payana fought. It sounded like they were arguing over whether to reveal something about her parents. But that couldn't be. They hadn't even known about the Glisks before they'd met her in that tea room.

Zef looked tired, as if he'd heard this fight a hundred times before.

Tomi climbed to her feet. 'Do you know something about the case?'

The bickering stopped abruptly. Mia and Payana looked away from each other, from Tomi.

'How?' Tomi said. 'How could you know something about the case?'

Zef looked to Payana. He sounded apologetic when he said, 'I think we have to.'

'No!'

'We can't leave her wallowing in this mess,' Mia said.

'It's better than the alternative.' Payana's words were vicious. Tomi barely recognised her beneath all that rage.

'In case you've forgotten, Tomi is our friend,' Mia said.

Payana's fingers curled into fists, almost hidden beneath the cuffs of her coat. 'She's not one of us.'

That hurt.

Tomi had always felt that she was a bit of an outsider. How could she not? The Trio lived together. They had inside jokes and a shared past. They were family.

But they always welcomed Tomi warmly when she was there. They never acted like she was an appendix to the group: Payana worked with her, Zef had shared a bed with her, and Mia had spent 10 years helping her win back the manor. Tomi was entangled in their tapestry.

Except, maybe not.

'If you know something about the case, you have to tell me,' she said. 'I can't believe you wouldn't. I can't believe you watched me flounder all these years. You let me drown.'

'We *didn't* let you drown,' Zef said. 'That was the whole point. We kept it from you because we didn't think it would make a difference to the case.'

'It's only going to hurt you,' Mia added.

'I found my parents brutally murdered in my own home. What could you possibly think is worse?'

'The Glisks were witches,' Mia said.

Payana let out a strangled cry.

'You were right,' Mia told Tomi, ignoring Payana. 'They were practising witches. In fact, they were the most famous – or rather, infamous – witches in Radaza.'

'How…' Tomi said. 'How could you know that?'

'Mia, don't.' Payana stepped in front of Mia, as if that would stop her from speaking. She wasn't just angry – she was panicking. Tomi couldn't remember ever seeing Payana so emotional before.

There was only one explanation for all this. One thing that made sense.

'Oh no,' Tomi whispered.

Payana whirled to face her, eyes wide.

Tomi stepped back. Her foot kicked the empty bottle of bleach that had killed her father, one of the many puzzle pieces she'd taken from the evidence nook. It spun away. 'I can't know this. I can't hear this!'

'It's all right,' Zef said gently.

'What have you done?' Payana said to Mia.

'She's not going to say anything.' Mia sounded confident. Too confident. Oh, sweet, trusting Mia.

Tomi shut her eyes and said, 'I have to report you. It's my duty. It's the *law*.'

'You see?' Payana said. 'I told you we couldn't trust her. When we asked her why she let that witch go, she said she'd never make that mistake again. We knew she wasn't on our side, and you still–'

'The Glisks were murdered by witches,' Zef said.

Tomi's gaze snapped to him. He looked patient. Unconcerned.

'But we didn't know until Payana found the link. The killers must've gone to a lot of trouble to make sure there were no traces of magic left at the scene. But if your parents were killed by witches, that means we can help you.'

'We know things about magic.' Despite everything, Mia still sounded enthusiastic. Perhaps too enthusiastic. As if she were trying very hard to keep Tomi on her side. 'We can figure out what spells they used. And *why* they were after your family.'

The throb behind Tomi's eye had become a full headache. 'You said my parents were infamous.'

'They were selling potions as cleaning products,' Mia said. 'My parents told me all about it. That's why the sprays and rinses worked so well. The Glisks risked exposing themselves every single day. It's possible some witches were angry about that.'

Tomi pinched the bridge of her nose. 'I can't–'

'We know you can't,' Payana snapped. 'That's why we shouldn't have said anything.'

To her credit, Mia didn't flinch under Payana's glare. 'You suspected Tomi would figure us out the moment you saw Ivan's body. She's too good at her job. It would've only been a matter of time.'

'Ivan?' Tomi said, dredging her mind for the name. 'Ivan Jupel?'

She remembered how strangely Payana had acted at the crime scene. Something had felt off; Tomi had even asked if Payana had known him.

'He was part of my parents' coven when he first came to Radaza,' Mia said. 'But five years ago, he got kicked out. They found out he was pushing the government to talk to witch settlements and didn't want anything to do with him.'

'No one wants to be associated with a witch who could be outed,' Payana said.

'Like my parents,' Tomi said. 'Did they have their own coven?'

Payana snorted. 'Unlikely. They were too public.'

Tomi blinked. She couldn't believe it had taken her so long to realise. 'Wait. Does this mean *I'm* a witch?'

'No,' Zef said. 'You didn't inherit the magic thread.'

'How do you know?'

'Because I can see. I have this power. I'm a qora reader.'

Her memory sparked. The University gardens. Professor Quaide explaining about witches who had specialised magic.

Zef tilted his head, examining her. 'You know about qora readers.' He sounded impressed.

Tomi recoiled slightly. 'You can read my mind?'

'I can see your qoras,' Zef corrected. 'Health, intentions, emotions, thoughts – I've learnt to interpret the spark and shift of each stream of energy flowing inside you.'

'Which is how we knew not to trust you,' Payana said. 'Zef can tell you're more dedicated to your job than to us.'

'That's not true!' Even as she said it, Tomi doubted her words. She had promised the court that she would never make that cookie mistake again. A compassionate act wasn't worth a dereliction of duty.

Right?

She groaned. 'But it's illegal for you to be here.'

'Hey, our families have been in Radaza for longer than yours,' Payana said. 'And, in case you've forgotten, if we hadn't been there that day in the tea room, you wouldn't be here.'

Tomi absorbed this. The tea room. The day she'd decided to kill herself. Part of her believed the Tassela had sent the Trio to her that afternoon to stop her. She hadn't considered the fact Zef, Mia and Payana already knew what they were doing. Zef had seen her qoras, and together the three of them had made the purposeful decision to save her life. They had brought her into their home, knowing that one slip meant she'd discover their secret and expose them.

A golden songrush chirrupped outside the window. Tomi stared at her friends in the muted sunlight. 'You risked everything for me.'

'Yes,' Payana said. 'And you can repay us by doing the same.'

'I–' The words stuck in her chest. It went against everything she believed in.

'Tomi.' Zef looked pained. 'Before you make any decisions, you have to hear what I know about Damian.'

'Damian?'

'He's loyal to you; I can see that. And the fact that you chose to trust him while watching the volfe fly suggests your destinies are connected.

Volfe have always been an important part of witchcraft. It's said that they can see qoras too, and assist people in making the right choices. It's hard to explain, but they help you feel what they can see themselves. They believe Damian's good for you.'

'But?' Tomi said when Zef hesitated.

'But his qoras are tangled in lies. Someone's hurting him, and I'm worried they're doing that to get to you.'

Tomi turned towards the window. She concentrated on the glimpses of blue sky rather than the flood of emotions surging through her.

Even as she tried not to think about it, her mind put together the pieces. Vittam had seemed overly interested in Damian. She'd thought it was because he was happy to see a cookie under her watch, a weakness perhaps – the whole reason she'd never taken on an apprentice in the first place.

But Damian had claimed to have remembered seeing a parillion gemstone somewhere, unable to recall the exact location. She thought of the ring she'd confiscated from Vittam, sitting in the inner jacket pocket of her tailcoat.

It couldn't be, could it? Was Damian working for Vittam? Were her instincts really that terrible?

How could she be a JO after this? She was mistaken about everyone. Damian, Zef, Payana, Mia, her parents – even Grundy. She couldn't investigate murders with such terrible intuition.

'If you give up your badge, you won't have the resources you need to solve your parents' murder.'

She turned to Zef. 'You think I can work for the Justice Department now? Not only am I a complete failure at my job, but I'm considering protecting illegal residents.'

'Cheer up,' Mia said. 'You're already protecting one. What's three more?'

'What do you mean?'

'You've still got a family member left in Radaza,' Mia reminded her. 'And you're certainly not going to turn her in, are you?'

'My sister,' Tomi said in sinking horror.

'It's likely Harpsigold is a witch,' Zef said.

Tomi remembered bursting into the conservatory, Harpsigold planting a sapling for the pink and green altar.

'I suspect you're right.'

But she couldn't allow Harpsigold to be exiled. She wouldn't survive without proper care.

'So we're agreed, then,' Mia said brightly. 'Our secret's safe with you.' She didn't wait for an answer. Instead, she rubbed her hands and said, 'Now that's sorted, let's get to work.'

Twenty-Six

'WHAT HAPPENED TO YOU?'

Minwell Warrick stared at Damian's fresh black eye as Damian walked across the second floor of the station.

Damian flashed him a smile. 'Our case took us after Bunter Vittam.'

'Seriously? Cardozo has insides of steel.'

'No kidding.' A scan of the space told Damian that Tomi wasn't in. Her murder board hadn't been updated – it still had *witch lover* scrawled on the side. 'Have you seen her?'

'Not this morning.' Warrick went back to his inventory list, then frowned and looked up again. 'Is she unaccounted for? Because if she went after Vittam–'

'It's all right,' Damian said. 'I think I know where she is.'

He'd seen the look on her face as they spoke in the study of Brackenlong Manor yesterday. She'd lost her temper. While he hadn't known her for long, it didn't seem like her.

He thought about what Nomik and Quaide had said, about how Professor Jupel had *felt* wrong since the last frost. It was the addiction. It had been the same with Pa and the gambling dens. Tomi had admitted the reason she'd lost her own apprenticeship was because of her obsession with the Glisk case. She was completely engulfed again.

Except her follow-up hearing was tomorrow, and she hadn't prepared for it at all.

Damian sat down at her desk and got out a fresh roll of parchment. Having a thorough report written up and ready to present to the court was exactly what she needed. Besides, it would take his mind off the pendulum of emotions that swung between pride and horror when he thought about what he'd done last night.

Warrick got up from his desk and wandered to the window, hands in pockets. It was cold out there today. Not frost-cold, but it was getting closer.

Another cart of supplies had rolled up to load the underground storage of Damian's atrium that morning. The longer the frost held off, the more they could stockpile resources – jars of preserved fruits and vegetables, salted and dried meats, pots of flour and grain.

'Cookie,' Warrick said. Damian glanced up from his work to find Warrick pulling on his tailcoat. 'Walk with me.'

Damian hesitated. He wanted to get this report written for Tomi, and it was going to take a while. But if the Glisk case was as important to her as he suspected, she might be gone all day anyway.

He joined Warrick and together they headed down the staircase, out into the chill of the morning. The grey clouds were too high and thin for rain, but their breaths steamed.

'Isn't this supposed to be one of your rest days?' Damian said. 'You just solved a murder, right?'

'Ah, if I want to break Cardozo's case closure records, I can't go taking long breaks.'

'Why are you nice to her if you're rivals?'

'A friendly rivalry doesn't mean I have to be like some of those blassards in there,' Warrick said, jerking his head towards the second storey. 'I mean, *no one* wants to be like Jerry Lorenze.'

Damian didn't remember who that was, but he was pretty sure he had been involved in sawing off the legs of Tomi's desk.

'Which is why,' Warrick continued, 'I'm talking to you now. I saw a note about cutlass on your murder board.'

'A witness claims Jupel was using it, but we haven't confirmed anything.'

'That's the problem with cutlass. You *can't* confirm it.' Warrick rubbed his stubbly mouth. 'I worked in ISEF before moving to Unseemly Crimes. We had people showing all the signs of being under the influence of an IS or having withdrawal symptoms, but there was no way to prove it.

Considering Radazan law is so strict when it comes to ices, it's the perfect foil.'

They stopped at the fountain. His voice muffled by the gushing of water, Warrick added, 'There was a name that got thrown around a lot back in the day: Oclavida. He was linked to high-level dealers that we suspected were selling cutlass. He may have been the manufacturer. We thought the guy was long gone, but I have friends in ISEF who are currently investigating a case where that name came up again. A man uttered it while in hospital with an illness that looks a lot like cutlass withdrawal. He died yesterday. And he's not the first to have those symptoms in the past year.'

'Then cutlass really is making a comeback,' Damian said.

'It looks like it. But the head of ISEF is refusing to accept it. He's making excuses, giving other reasons for these strange deaths, pretending it's not there.'

'Why?'

Warrick glanced up at the windows of the station's second floor. He turned away so no one inside could see his face. 'Because it's impossible to fight. We suspected from the start that witches are behind it, and that means we're practically powerless to stop the spread. ISEF don't have the resources to handle this wave, so the big boss would prefer to act as if it's not happening.' Warrick gave a wry smile. 'You look stunned, cookie.'

'They're just *pretending* it's not out there?'

'Sure. It happens all over the government, all the time. Including at the very top.'

'You mean the councillors?'

'Absolutely. They want you to think the witch problem isn't so bad. That TADOW have everything under control.'

'They don't?'

'TADOW don't know nearly as much about witches as they think.'

'And you do?'

'I've had my scrapings with them,' Warrick said, shrugging. 'Interestingly, any mention of witches in my reports gets ignored if it's not easy for TADOW to go after them.'

Damian regarded him curiously. 'Why are you telling me this?'

'Because Tomi's not here yet, and I'm heading off soon. She has to present her progress to the court tomorrow, right? I highly recommend she leave any mention of cutlass out of the report. No one's going to look favourably on her chasing ghost when they want her chasing killer witches.'

'We're struggling to piece together Jupel's connection in the first place. He was possibly under the influence of cutlass, but the murder of Park Herliz tells us this was about the stones he was smuggling from Elumina. Only we don't know what type of stones they were or where they were going or anything.'

'Are you sure the stones and cutlass aren't connected? We don't know how the stuff's made or even what's in it. If witches are involved, they could be using the stones as part of the brew.'

Damian was losing feeling in his hands. He hugged them under his arms then winced, having momentarily forgotten the bruises on his ribs.

'You all right, cookie?' Warrick said.

'Running like a river.'

Warrick lifted an eyebrow. 'Be careful out there, especially if Vittam's involved.'

'Does he have something to do with cutlass or Oclavida?' Damian had never heard the name while working for Vittam, but as a messenger he'd been the lowest in the hierarchy. He wouldn't have been anywhere near the ices business. Besides, he hadn't been part of Vittam's inner circle for the past few years.

'I have no idea,' Warrick said. 'Knowing Vittam, it wouldn't surprise me if he didn't have at least one finger in that pie.' He lowered his voice. 'Word is, Ariela Park was a common place for snagging ghost. If you want to follow that lead, it might be a good start.'

Damian glanced at the street, hoping for any sign of Tomi. They had so much to talk about, and time was running out before her second hearing.

And, well, he hoped she was safe. Stealing Vittam's key was a huge step, but he couldn't help thinking of the last thing Vittam had said before throwing him from the room.

He's lucky he brought me something of use.

Why was Tomi's identity useful to Bunter Vittam? What, exactly, had Damian done?

Twenty-Seven

TOMI WATCHED AS ZEF PROBED THE LARGE MAP ON THE STUDY wall, exactly the same way Damian had yesterday.

'The kid is good,' he said, 'noticing the holes here are different to the ones made by pushpins. I think he was onto something.'

She didn't want to hear compliments about Damian right now. Her insides were a mess of angry serpents, squirming and hissing, unable to untangle from each other. She dropped her gaze to the logo of the raizelet on the empty bleach bottle, which she'd picked up off the floor.

Damian was a traitor.

Her best friends were witches.

Her parents' killers were witches.

Her *parents* were witches.

It was all so much. To know her family had been hiding an entire piece of their life from her. Why had they never told her the truth? Even if she hadn't inherited the magic thread, she deserved to know who her family were.

Lussisco Harldah Buhkasa.

Where had she come from, really?

'But the clatterstone pieces weren't moved with a spell,' Zef said, breaking her thoughts. 'There's no spell that I'm aware of to move objects without touching them. It's a specialised power, the way I'm a qora reader.'

'Are you sure? I thought witches could do impossible things.'

'You misjudge our strength. Most Radazan witches don't practise witchcraft much. They may have altars and basic potion ingredients, but they don't know how to use them. It's too dangerous, and few want to risk teaching the next generation. Mia's family have rudimentary knowledge. Payana's family don't practise at all. I only know some spells because I was born in Elumina.'

'Ivan Jupel was hoping to open communication between Radaza and Elumenese settlements using a qora reader,' she said. 'I heard qora readers were rare, but he mentioned one in his notes. Do you think he was talking about you?'

'Maybe. I never met him personally, but Mia's family could've told him about me. I suppose my power's a bit of a novelty to some.'

His bitter tone perked her curiosity. 'You don't like being a qora reader?'

'Let's just say it's hard to find decent people – human or witch – in this world.'

Tomi joined him in front of the map. He didn't look at her, so she studied the settlements, tracing her finger up the mountain range running through the continent. 'Where are you from?'

'Here.' He pointed to a tiny dot signifying a settlement north of the Zim Mah region. 'It doesn't exist anymore.'

'Why not?'

She'd asked him about it before, but he'd always told her he preferred not to talk about it. Now, he said, 'It was a witch colony. Perlians came through the mountains and burnt it to the ground. They're trying to push their territory into Elumina.'

'Couldn't your people protect themselves with magic?'

'Magic can't stop an entire army. We're not invincible.'

'Did everyone from your village come to Radaza, then?'

'No.' Zef stared at the map, though his eyes were unfocused, as if his thoughts were far away. 'I was the only survivor.'

Tomi opened her mouth. Nothing came out.

'Here we go.' Payana came in, carrying a bag. She was flushed from her quick expedition. 'Your neighbours had everything I needed.'

'What were they like?' Tomi said.

'I only met the household staff.' She put on a false Perlian accent. 'Black Ivory residents don't do mundane chores like lend things to their neighbours.'

Mia bounced in with plant clippings from the conservatory. 'I found some good ingredients in there. Your parents had an excellent supply for potions.'

Of course they did. Tomi shut her eyes, wondering how easily the elements of her childhood would unfold to reveal its secrets. Her mother hadn't been a gardener. She'd been a witch tending to her ingredients.

'Mia's a brewer.' Zef's tone was lighter, as if he were brushing away the topic of their previous conversation. Maybe it was all Tomi would ever get of his past. Maybe it was all she deserved.

'That's right,' Mia said. 'Just wait until you see what I can do.'

Payana rummaged through the bag and brought out a chopping board, a small knife, a wooden box filled with common spices, and mortar and pestle. 'Let's look at how your killer turned Jupel's blood into powder.'

There was a lot of mixing and chopping on Mia's part while the rest of them watched.

A thought occurred to Tomi as Mia worked. 'I don't suppose witches can turn invisible, can they?'

'Yes,' Zef said. 'But it requires concentration.'

He reached into the pocket of his waistcoat and pulled out the black feather of a khar. 'It's called a shadow spell.' He folded the feather in his hand and stepped back, melting into a gloomy corner. He had disappeared.

Tomi's muscles twitched, instinctively preparing to drop into a defensive stance. Every part of her reacted the same way as it did to danger.

Zef stepped into the sun again, opening his hand to reveal the crumpled feather.

Tomi forced herself to relax. 'That explains how Park Herliz's killer was able to get into his office without anyone seeing.'

'Probably,' Zef said, dropping the feather to the ground. 'I was using the spell yesterday when I threw itching powder on those men attacking you in the alley.'

'That was *you*? You were following me?'

'I was following Damian. I told you, he's not to be trusted. And,' he added, frowning, 'can I remind you that I saved your life?'

'I – Yes, fine, thank you for that.'

'You're welcome.'

'Done,' Mia said triumphantly. She'd pummelled a few leaves and kitchen spices into a fine powder.

Payana pulled a glass bottle of blood from her bag.

'Where did you get that?' Tomi asked.

'I killed someone's pet poffin.'

When Tomi choked, Zef said, 'She's jesting. There's a butcher at the district border.'

Payana tipped half the bottle of blood on the floor. 'Watch your prejudices, Tomi. Witches don't randomly slaughter living things. It upsets the balance of energies.'

Mia sprinkled some of the potion onto the pool. The liquid evaporated before their eyes, leaving the same red powder Tomi had found on Jupel's floor.

'Huh,' Tomi said.

'More than that,' Payana said, 'I only got ingredients Jupel had in his home.'

Tomi remembered a strange point on the inventory list: *1x potted carris fern, green, several leaves appear recently torn off.*

'So it really is possible that the killer didn't intend to murder Jupel that night.' She massaged her temples as she tried to put the pieces together. Her mind was crammed and confused. 'If they were able to put that potion together with what was in the apartment, does that mean they're a brewer like Mia?'

'That's one theory,' Zef said.

'And the other?'

'They already knew about the potion and were lucky enough to have most of the ingredients at hand.'

Tomi frowned. 'Is it a common spell to know?'

'Maybe if they work with blood. Like a butcher or a medica maven. Otherwise...'

'Otherwise?'

'They might've used it before. To clean up a murder.'

'You think they've done it before?'

'I don't know.'

Tomi scrunched her fists against her forehead. 'I assumed this was about smuggling, but now I can't be sure.'

'From what Payana's told me about Park Herliz's murder, I think that was planned,' Mia said. 'The killer had a potion to boil the skin. That's not easy to make. And witches use eyes and tongues to assist them sometimes.'

'With what?'

'There are spells that allow you to see with someone else's eyes and hear things a tongue has spoken,' Zef said. 'It's usually used after a person's died.'

Mia nodded. 'I hear it helps solve unexplained deaths in Elumina. Would be useful, wouldn't it? I don't know how to do the spell myself, though.'

'Neither do I,' Zef said. 'And I don't know what this killer was looking to hear or see from the second victim's eyes and tongue.'

'Border Control found a bunch of ear bones and teeth to be shipped off illegally,' Tomi said. 'What do you think they're for?'

Payana and Mia looked perplexed, but Zef's body stilled. Tomi didn't need to be a qora reader to know he had something to tell her.

'Zeffir?' she said.

'They're common ingredients in a potion used by refugees – including myself – to assimilate a language as they cross the border. I didn't know how it was made when I came to Radaza. I bought it out of desperation. I only learnt about it later, when some of Mia's parents' coven asked for the bones and teeth of a body I was performing last rites for.'

'Could the bones and teeth be coming from the cemetery, then?' Tomi said. 'That would explain how there were so many of them at Eversea.'

'If they were, it wasn't from my cemetery. I would've noticed if the graves had been tampered with. Witches are resourceful. They have to be, in this city. But magic is about the flow of energy, both good and harmful. Like Payana said, to hurt or kill things changes the balance, which means it changes the effect of a spell. Even harvesting plants needs care and attention.'

'It's true,' Mia said. 'There's an art to it. And we only use animal products where the animal has been killed in a way that releases their qoras gently back to the Great Loom. You humans might sense it vaguely, but we know for sure when an energy isn't right.'

'That's why it's so unusual that your murderer's a witch,' Zef said. 'Either they never learnt their heritage, or something has driven them to it.'

Tomi rubbed her thumb along her lower lip in thought. 'So far, the only thing I understand about this case is someone's shipping bones and teeth to Elumina in exchange for an unknown stone. But the murderer's cut this trade off. They've killed two men in the smuggling chain.'

'You think Park Herliz was tortured to find more people in the chain?' Payana said.

'It's likely. We may end up with another body if I don't catch the killer soon.' Tomi hesitated before she asked the next question. 'What about Herliz's missing bindings? Does that have something to do with witchcraft?'

And, more importantly, was it also how her mother had been tied up?

'It would've been a binding spell,' Zef said. 'Requires a piece of string and a poppet. You can magically tie someone down without touching them.'

'That's why there was no pattern on Herliz or my mother's skin or fibres left behind,' Tomi said.

'You might be looking for a witch who specialises in poppet craft.'

'Do you know anyone like that?'

Zef shook his head. 'I don't know many witches in Radaza. None of us do.'

'I hadn't heard of that binding spell,' Payana admitted. 'Otherwise, I might've noticed when I studied the Glisk case.'

Tomi looked at her. Witches in Radaza were losing their heritage, their magical knowledge, the same way Tomi had lost the stories and secrets of her own family.

They were just gone. Forever.

A sudden urge to explore gripped her. 'I need to take a walk.'

She hadn't paid much attention to the rest of the house since the murders. The conservatory, the kitchen, the drawing room – she hadn't even given much thought to her own bedroom. Yet it was as much a part of her childhood as the crime scene.

'That's fine,' Mia said. 'I'm going to see if I can recreate the same potion but not leave any powder behind. Maybe that's what your parents' killers did and why the JOs weren't able to follow the blood trail further than the tunnels.'

Tomi nodded numbly. She left Zef, Mia and Payana behind and walked through the manor, looking at it anew. This wasn't just the place where the Glisk murders happened. This was her home.

She climbed the staircase. Her uncle had sent her away to her paternal grandparents in the countryside after the murders. Once the frost had moved on, she'd returned to Radaza to find everything gone. The manor was vacant. Her cousins, aunts, uncle and maternal grandparents had left. The family's wealth, company and factory were cleared out. Lameia Cardozo, the *ama sector*, had given Tomi new identity pages that declared

Tomi was her own daughter before taking her to a Followers of Light children's home.

'Why can't I come with you?' Tomi had said as Lameia breathlessly fumbled to do up the buttons of her raincoat.

'You're safest here, under the name Tomi Cardozo. You need to look after Harpsigold. She lives in Bleakhouse now.'

'I want to go home.'

'I know, starshine. But you can't. None of us can. The people who killed your parents made sure of that.' Lameia kissed her forehead. 'Promise me you'll never tell anyone who you really are.'

'Why?'

'Because then they'll think it's over.'

Then they'll think it's over.

The words had haunted Tomi since that day. Who were the people who had murdered her parents, and what had they tried to end? The newscloths had suggested a blood feud, but Tomi had never heard of any problems with another family.

She stopped at the threshold of her parents' bedroom. The room smelled of staleness. Gone were the oils and fragrances of her parents – death resided here now.

A memory tugged at her: her father loosening his cravat so it hung around his neck, her mother unclasping her duskpearl bracelet. They were tired after a long day, but when they saw their youngest daughter at the doorway, they smiled and invited her in. She sat on the bed while they regaled her with tales about adventurers from faraway lands.

'I'm still not certain we can trust you.'

Tomi jumped.

Payana came up behind her. She was alone.

'I'm still not sure why Mia told me,' Tomi said.

'We've been back and forth on it since the day we met you. But I guess today was the breaking point. Part of me knew it was going to happen. Zef and Mia were worried you were going to spiral out of control again. You reopened the case, after all the time and effort we spent helping you step away.'

'I had to. My parents were killed by witches. It's fresh evidence, and I–'

'No.' Payana's expression was tight. 'You don't understand. You don't have any connections to the witch world. You say there's fresh evidence, but your investigation would've been futile without help. Zef saw the obsession grip your qoras last night, and he thought you were going to end up back in that tea room, drinking your last cup.'

'Why are you so mad at me?' Tomi crossed the threshold into the room. 'None of this is my fault, you know.'

'Before, you were my friend. Now you're a threat, not just to me, but to Zef and Mia and my entire family.'

'I'm not going to tell TADOW.'

'Aren't you?

Tomi began checking the drawers. They had been emptied – only bugs and creegs scuttled inside now. 'How can I? It's not just you three; it's Harpsigold as well.'

She didn't know how to feel. Confused? Paranoid? Relieved? Her entire life was a lie.

She opened the chest at the end of the bed. It was empty too. She didn't know exactly what she was looking for, but she needed to find *something*. Signs of her parents' magical heritage. Spells, potions, amulets. A clue as to why they were murdered.

There were only a few things left behind – the bed, an empty earring rack, a portrait of her parents on the wall.

'Who cleaned the house out?' Payana said.

'I don't know.'

In her late teens, Tomi had travelled back to her paternal grandparents in the country to ask what they knew of the family's disappearance, only to find they had vanished too. Her last connection to her parents, and her last thread of hope, had gone. Their farmhouse was abandoned, falling apart from disrepair. No one in the local town knew where they were.

Tomi's blood family had completely disappeared, as if lost to the void of the Umbra.

Payana studied the portrait, drawing Tomi's attention to it. Her parents had been bright eyed and cheeky back when it was painted. Anatole wore a silver suit and fur hat. He held a porcelain mask in front of his eyes. It was gold on one side and blue on the other. He smiled, without any idea what his future held.

No amount of physical torture would compare to knowing that her precious father had suffered so much. There had been no way to protect him. Anatole Glisk, who had knotted her hollyblossom crowns, who had tucked her in at night and promised the dark was nothing to be frightened of, had died in agony. Her innocent, loving father.

Sharlie was in a top hat and a long black dress lined with fringes, the material slit to her thigh and revealing chunky silver heels. She leaned forward on a cane, her hip jutting out suggestively.

Tomi's mother had been less outwardly doting, showing her love by slipping Tomi an extra sweetbun after supper and lavish presents on her return from business trips. She always came home from those trips smelling of harris blossom.

Their faces had faded from Tomi's mind over time, her memory of them becoming a blur of colour and feelings, but seeing their images again – even as their younger selves – was a cold rush to her nerves.

'They look happy,' Payana said. Her voice had thawed slightly.

Tomi closed the chest. 'They were.'

'They're lucky.' Payana tore her gaze from them, wandered to the bed and sat on the dusty blanket. 'It's hard to be happy as a witch in Radaza.'

Tomi sat beside her.

'The panic I feel,' Payana said, 'day in, day out, from the moment I understood what I was... I'm always terrified I'll do something or say something that will expose us.' She shook her head. 'No one should live like that.'

'I know it's not the same thing, but I've had to hide my true self, too. I've been living in fear that the people who killed my parents will come back for me.'

'At least you're not fighting your very nature. I had to learn to walk in this world as less than myself, like I'd tied my hands behind my back and claimed I'd never had arms to begin with. I can feel the wrongness of the energy around me, but I can't do anything about it. Do you know how sharp and raw the energy is inside a morgue? Do you know how difficult it is for me to not sprinkle protective salt or light a stick of bygrass so I can breathe easy again?'

'You can't just do it secretly, when no one's watching?'

'No,' Payana said, and the word was vehement. 'I would never endanger my family like that. All it takes is one slip-up. I'm surrounded by justice officials and sweepers – people who are trained to look closely, especially at anyone who's Elumenese. I've always tried so hard to pretend to belong.' She held out her arms. 'I even refused my family tattoos, and they're not technically connected to witchcraft. I just didn't want to risk it.'

'But you live with Zef and Mia, who practise magic.'

'Yes, well, that was an accident. Mia and I were together for a while before Zef met her and realised she was a witch. By then, it was too late. I couldn't be with anyone else. It turned out to be a blessing, I suppose. I was certain I would end up alone. It's hard to find a partner when you're living a lie.'

'You would never trust someone else enough to tell them the truth?'

'You told Grundy that you let a witch go 10 years ago, and look how that went.'

It was a good point. An excellent point.

'Most witches are outed by ex-partners,' Payana said. 'It's not worth sharing your secret. We don't even know many other witches in Radaza, except for our own family. Or, in Mia's case, her family's coven. It's just safer that way.'

'I'm sorry, Payana. It sounds like a difficult way to live.'

Payana gave Tomi a sideways glance. 'That's why Zef had to break up with you, you know.'

'What do you mean?'

'He's like I used to be, before Mia. He looks for small bursts of comfort, an occasional partner to keep the chill of loneliness at bay. I don't think he meant to court you for so long. But he had to break it off, because it was unfair to both of you. He could never be himself with you, and you would be living a lie.'

It took some time for Tomi to absorb this. She and Zef had slept together one drunken night a few months after her breakdown. They'd ended up spending the entire frost season together, but on the day of the thawing, as it dawned on her how much she wanted their relationship to be more than a fling, he'd told her it was over.

'He saw my qoras,' she said slowly.

'Hm?'

'That blassard.' Tomi kicked at the bed leg. 'He unravelled our courtship the day I realised I was in love with him. It wasn't a coincidence. He saw how I felt and left me heartbroken in the gutter. If it weren't so long ago, I'd kick his hide all the way back to Elumina.'

'I don't think he *wanted* to break up with you, Tomi. But like I said, it's complicated when you're a witch, and a thousand times more complicated for him. Even our kind don't want to bind to someone who can read their every thought and emotion.'

Tomi couldn't help but agree with that. She didn't like the idea that Zef had always known, and would always know, her deepest, darkest thoughts.

'How do you live with him?'

Payana gave a one-shouldered shrug. 'I say what I think. I'm cynical and pessimistic, and I let everyone know it. I don't have anything to hide from him.'

'Tomi!' Mia burst into the room. Now there was another unscrolled parchment. Mia was the same as Payana in terms of not having anything to hide, but her reasoning was the complete opposite – she was bright and happy and loved life recklessly.

She didn't look happy at the moment, though. Her eyes were wide, her chest heaving with gasps.

'I hope you're ready to face Damian,' she said breathlessly. 'Because he's coming up the garden path.'

Twenty-Eight

AFTER BEING KNOCKED UNCONSCIOUS WHEN HE WAS 16, DAMIAN had gone to the Southeast station to ask for help. He was sick of the abuse, the fear, the exhaustion of working all day and running all night. The general officers on duty had told him, without much interest, that if he were under contract, there was nothing in the law that said Vittam couldn't rough him up a little. Pa owed over 700 gold coins – an intergenerational debt. Damian had limped away from the station, broken and powerless.

It was then he'd decided to become a justice official. He would fight for the people being bullied and belittled by moguls like Vittam. He'd solve big cases, earn hefty bonus pouches and hopefully find a way to cage Vittam for good. It didn't matter that indentured people weren't allowed to enter the academy. He was determined enough to beg his mother, the Treasury Minister, for the coin and her good name. She'd done nothing for him his entire life – not even a brass piece to save his 'no-good father' from debt – but she'd obliged him in this.

Up until this point, he believed he'd put her coin to good use.

He rode Brix up the path towards Brackenlong Manor. Tomi waited for him by the empty fountain with Finley saddled and ready to go. Her expression was cool and unreadable. 'What happened to your face?'

'Long story. I have information on the case.' He slowed Brix to a stop and climbed off. 'As well as a gift. Here.'

She took the offered pouch from him. 'What's this?'

'Worm paste and gizzard stones for Finley. I figured you haven't given them to him yet.'

'No, I haven't.' Her frostiness thawed slightly. 'Thank you.'

'You're welcome.' Damian gazed up at the manor. He thought he saw a curtain twitch. 'Find anything new?'

'Maybe. But Damian, in case you haven't seen your reflection recently, you look terrible.'

He grimaced, his cheek throbbing from the punch Yaverly had landed on him last night.

Tomi pocketed the pouch. 'I think it's time you explained what's going on.'

Maybe she would understand. Maybe she would help.

Or maybe, like the GOs when he was 16, she would tell him there was nothing she could do then cage him for treason. He was a spy for Vittam, after all.

He couldn't bear the thought of disappointing her.

'It's my landlord,' he said, hating himself the moment the words were out of his mouth. 'We haven't been able to pay the rent lately, and he likes to send reminders in the form of his fist.'

'That's highly illegal,' Tomi said, looking aghast.

'My local GOs don't seem to think so. According to them, creditors are allowed to rough up anyone owing coin.'

'Not like this.' Tomi reached for his face.

He flinched away.

'Anyway,' he said, 'that's why I'm injured. I didn't want to tell you because it's embarrassing. I don't exactly live like, well, like this.' He gazed up at the manor. It was a little run down, but it still represented more wealth than he could ever imagine.

'I'm sorry,' Tomi said, drawing his attention back. 'I didn't mean to sound suspicious. I knew it was none of my business, but I guess I just–'

'Don't worry about it.' Guilt burned in his throat. He wished his story could've been true. That the scariest thing his family had to worry about was a lousy landlord. That Tomi's apology was justified, and he wasn't the one in the wrong.

May the Tassela damn him to the Umbra.

Finley rasped, shifted his weight on his scaly feet. Tomi stoked his feathers to soothe him. 'Well then. Now we've cleared the air, tell me what information you have.'

It didn't take long to fill her in on what Warrick had said about cutlass, the ominous Oclavida and Ariela Park being a hot spot for dealers. She listened intently, but when he got to the part about not including it in her report for tomorrow, she spoke up.

'I'm not leaving that out. It might be the motive behind Jupel's murder.'

'Especially if the stones he was smuggling connect to cutlass somehow,' Damian said. 'But we need the hearing to go smoothly, don't we? Just add it in once you're acquitted.'

'That's not how I operate.' Tomi climbed onto Finley. 'I think it's worth doing a scout of Ariela Park.'

'Agreed.'

'Meanwhile, I want you to go back to Jupel's atrium.'

Damian paused with one foot in a stirrup. 'What?'

'I've been thinking,' she said, overly casual, 'with Jupel trying to convince Radazan officials to open communication with witch settlements, his coven might've been scared off. Maybe they didn't want anything to do with him in case he was exposed.'

'That's a good point.'

'So if Jupel had no coven and was the loner everyone in his atrium claimed, how did he get his hands on cutlass? People don't just start an IS habit out of nowhere.'

Damian hauled himself up onto Brix. 'Didn't we decide it could've been payment for smuggling the stone?'

'Jupel was a clever man. He would've known how dangerous and addictive cutlass is. Someone coerced him, gave him a taste, introduced him to suppliers.'

'Herliz?'

'Maybe. Or that frost lover he had last year. I want you to find out.'

'Alone?'

'You'll be fine. Herliz will be at home. Eversea has been shut down while TADOW and Border Control investigate.'

Damian made a face. 'Can't we stick together? There are some other things I want to talk to you about.'

He hadn't risked stealing Vittam's key to hide it away. He had to tell Tomi *something*.

'My hearing is tomorrow morning,' Tomi said. 'The more we uncover today, the better my progress report will look. Splitting up is the best option.'

'I guess I can't argue with that.' Damian spurred Brix into a trot back down the garden path. Tomi didn't follow straight away. She looked back at the manor, as if waiting for something.

Damian wondered whether she was considering blowing off the trip to Ariela Park and returning her attention to the Glisk case. Just how obsessed was she, anyway?

And *how* was Vittam going to use her connection to the case against her?

Damian urged Brix faster. He couldn't take back what he'd told Vittam, but he would do everything possible to help solve the Jupel case. He wasn't going to let this hearing be the end of Tomi Cardozo's career.

And whatever Vittam ended up doing to her, Damian would figure out a way to fix it.

The Shores was the next district over so he got to Jupel's atrium in good time. When he knocked on Herliz's door, however, there was no answer.

'You won't find him there.'

He turned to find the frizzy haired teenager, Kaya, in the minnisk enclosure. She had a crate of fish and was tossing one after another into the water for the minnisks to splash after.

'He's organising the funeral,' she said. 'Which is harder than it sounds, since the authorities aren't releasing his grandfather's body for burial yet.'

Damian wandered over to her. 'How do you know that?'

'I listen. And watch.' She waggled the fish in her hands. The minnisks followed it eagerly with their eyes.

Damian got out his parchment book. 'I don't suppose you know anything about Jupel's... acquaintance last frost?'

'You mean his frost lover?' She gave him an arch look. 'I'm 15, not five. And yes, the professor was cosied up with a woman called Serillia.'

'Are they still in contact?'

'No. *Leya* Notch passed last monsoon season, but I don't know how.'

Damian added a question to his notes about Serillia possibly dying from cutlass. He paused as he recognised the bloodname. '*Leya* Notch? Was she related to Talcott Notch? The portmaster?'

'Sure was. She was his step-niece. Aunt Veraminta was practically falling over herself to get in with the family, especially when she found out Talcott

180

Notch had gifted Serillia an apartment in the Black Ivory District. You should've heard the wailing and sobbing when Serillia died. Not because of the death, mind you, but because my vacuous aunt is stuck sponging off us instead of being introduced to a spouse she could sponge off in the Black Ivory District.'

'Life's unfair, isn't it?'

Kaya threw the fish high. 'Tell me about it.'

It sounded like Serillia Notch was Jupel's most likely introduction to cutlass. Damian could see how it had happened. A long frost. The University closed for the season. Nothing to do, nowhere to go. A beautiful woman, keen to share her deadly habit with a lover.

And the portmaster was involved, after all. Serillia was his step-niece – that couldn't be a coincidence.

'Did Talcott Notch and Professor Jupel know each other?'

'That, I don't know.'

Damian wrote down Talcott Notch's name with a question mark, just in case.

And then it hit him.

He pulled out the small brass key he'd stolen from Vittam. A locker key – from the ferry terminal?

When Damian had been a messenger, the keys were big and brass. But Ariela Park's terminal had just been refurbished.

What if Talcott Notch had been more involved with Vittam than he'd said last night? The terminal's lockers were used as drop points. Damian had thought he'd been sneaky in his runner days, slipping things in and out of the terminal, but what if Notch knew what was going on the whole time?

Tomi was already at Ariela Park looking for potential cutlass dealers. All he had to do was meet her there. And figure out a lie big enough to explain how he'd got the key.

Twenty-Nine

'TELL ME WHAT YOU SEE.'

Zef surveyed the group exiting the terminal, fresh from the latest ferry. 'A lot of cold qoras. Everyone's busy, flustered, upset. The coming of the frost has a strange effect on people. There's a nervous but excited energy. And obviously lots of worry: will there be enough food, is my elderly relative going to survive this year, what if it settles before I get this thing or that thing done?'

Tomi watched Zef as he watched the crowd. She had often felt that his gaze was too perceptive, that sometimes, when he looked at her, she felt as if she were exposed.

Turned out, she had been right.

'I thought you didn't read minds,' she said.

'I don't. I interpret their thoughts based on the flow of their qoras.'

'So you could be wrong.'

'I can tell intention. I'd know if someone was walking around here looking to buy or sell cutlass.'

There weren't a lot of people enjoying the park today. The weather was too cold, too much like the frost. It was a reminder that there were things to be done before the settling.

Tomi and Zef were seated on a bench at the bottom of the slope, close to the terminal. They'd done a few laps of the park, all the way up the hill, around the statue of Ariela Madeira, then back again. They'd bought flasks of hot cider from a vendor who'd been stoking a fire to keep his cauldron bubbling and draw people in with the warmth.

Tomi sipped at her drink, the steam heating her icy cheeks. 'What does a person's qoras look like when they're on cutlass?'

'I'm not sure. I didn't even know what it was before Payana explained. But,' he added, 'I have seen some strange qoras over the past few years.'

'Strange how?'

'Like the person's streams of energy are faltering. Imagine the flickering flame of a dying lantern. Or a river drying up.'

'That's not normal?'

'No, never. As you age, your qoras flow slower. If you make harmful choices, your control qora becomes corrupted – some believe it has to be cleansed by the Tassela before it's rewoven on the Great Loom. But qoras degenerating? That's unnatural. I'm worried the qoras of these people aren't returning to the Great Loom at all. That they're just... decomposing.'

'That's terrifying.'

'Yes. And it includes the magic thread.'

The group from the latest ferry had disappeared. The park was practically empty.

'You can tell people are witches because you can see a seventh thread inside them,' Tomi said.

'Yes.'

'And I'm definitely not a witch?'

Zef shifted on the bench to face her. 'Would you like to be?'

'No. I just don't understand how my parents were, but I wasn't. And my sister...'

Zef hadn't met Harpsigold. Tomi had never taken anyone to see her, even the Trio.

'There are stories about why witches have a seventh qora,' Zef said. 'My people used to say that during Creation, the Tassela Clemency plucked 100,000 threads from her own body to weave witches onto her loom instead of humans. She wanted to share her magic, but the other Tassela found out what she was doing and attacked her. She shines red from the blood she sacrificed to grant us power.'

'Only 100,000?'

'The number changes depending on who's telling the story, but the point is, there was only a limited amount of magic threads. When a witch dies, their magic thread returns to the Great Loom for Clemency to weave the next baby in their bloodline. In our stories, witches are only ever woven from her part of the Loom.'

'What if there isn't a magic thread waiting in the Loom when a baby is born from a witch? Is that why I missed out?'

'They're just stories, Tomi.'

She shivered. 'They might be just stories, but it still happened to me. What am I, if my parents were witches but I'm not?'

Zef put an arm around her, and she was instantly engulfed in his heat. She sank against him gratefully. Even clean, the faint scent of carmao incense lingered on his skin.

It was nice to not be fighting. She and Zef didn't disagree about much – the disastrous dinner the other night was the worst their relationship had been through since the awkward post-break-up phase.

'*Lussisco Harldah Buhkasa*,' she murmured.

Did the family motto belong to her, if she weren't a witch?

'It doesn't have to change anything,' Zef said. 'You're still you, no matter where you come from.'

'But why didn't they tell me?'

'They might have wanted you to grow up peacefully. Keep you safe.'

'Safe,' Tomi muttered wryly. She threw back the rest of her cider. It burned on the way down.

Her parents and sister had been making memories without her. She thought of the pink and green altar, of her father smiling as he helped Harpsigold plant the sapling. They had had a whole secret life, one that Tomi was never invited to join.

'It worked,' Zef pointed out.

'I wouldn't call my life safe. My parents' killers are out there. Not to mention people like Vittam, who would very much like to see me dead.' She gasped and sat up, away from Zef's warmth.

'What?' he said.

'I can bring Vittam down.'

'How?'

'With you, marsh-brain! I can ask him questions, and you can tell me whether or not he's lying.'

'I can't do that.'

'Why not? You said you can read intentions.'

'I mean,' Zef said, 'I don't want to reveal myself to someone like Bunter Vittam.'

'Then go invisible.'

'The shadow spell isn't infallible. Imagine what he'd do if he found out I was a qora reader.'

'I wouldn't let him hurt you.'

'I don't mean what he'd do to me. I mean what he'd make me do for him.'

Tomi scoffed. 'He's not a witch.'

'Magic isn't the only way to force people to do things. I've heard enough about Bunter Vittam to understand how he works. Speaking of...'

Tomi glanced up to find Damian riding Brix towards the public grousdu enclosure attached to the terminal. She crinkled her nose. Zef hadn't seen Damian's qoras during the explanation about his landlord, but he still believed Damian was lying. They'd talked about it on the ride to the park. Zef had latched onto Tomi's original theory of Damian working for Bunter Vittam and wouldn't let it go, even when Tomi told him it was highly unlikely. Cadets were checked for any indentures before joining the academy. It would've been a massive oversight if they'd missed that Damian was under contract with Vittam.

'He's figured something out, from the looks of his qoras,' Zef said. 'But he's even guiltier than the last time you spoke to him. I know you want to trust him, and I know that's partly because you made the decision when the volfe were in flight, but keep your guard up. That's all I ask.' He stood. 'I have to go. I have the late shift at the cemetery.'

'Thank you,' Tomi said, standing too. 'I appreciated your company.' She hesitated. 'And thank you for, you know, telling me the truth. You and Mia and Payana. It must've been a huge risk.'

'I remember the last time you went down this path,' Zef said. 'It almost got you killed. We couldn't let that happen again.'

He kissed her cheek and headed up the slope to the grousdu enclosure on the far side of the park. She gazed after him until he was no longer in sight. Then she went in the opposite direction, reaching the terminal's grousdu enclosure as Damian was coming out. His bruised eye looked even worse.

'That was easy,' he said brightly. 'Didn't know how long it would take to find you.'

'What are you doing here?'

'I went to Jupel's atrium like you asked. Herliz wasn't there, but I found out Jupel was seeing a woman called Serillia Notch during last frost.'

'Notch?'

'Apparently, she's Talcott Notch's step-niece. That got me thinking about the key on Jupel's floor.'

Tomi turned to the terminal's entrance. 'You think it might be the key to a locker in here.'

'Doesn't hurt to check. I hear this place is a drop point for all kinds of criminal organisations.'

'How did you hear that?'

Damian faltered for barely a breath before he shrugged and said, 'Word I picked up at the academy.' Then, just as casually, he dug into his pocket. 'By the way, I happened across Vittam last night, and he dropped this from his belt.'

'You what?'

He held up a key that looked very familiar. She gasped and pulled the evidence key from her inner pocket. Side by side, it was clear they were from the same set, but their teeth were different.

Damian smiled. 'I thought so.'

'Where did you see Vittam?' Tomi said.

'He was walking down the street near my atrium. Must've been chasing someone owing him coin.' Before she could ask more, he started for the terminal. 'Come on, let's check it out.'

She followed him through the frost doors. Was that really the only explanation he was going to give?

'How did–'

Damian stopped abruptly. 'Oh no.'

'What?'

'Stay very still. Maybe she won't notice us.'

Tomi followed his line of sight and saw a familiar woman in a fur coat striding out from the corridor to the menagerie ferry. 'Is that Veraminta Linn? What's she doing here?'

'As long as it's not talking to us, I don't care,' Damian said under his breath.

'Oi, Damian! Back again?' Ravern Furling's booming voice echoed around them. She flapped an old rag in greeting.

Veraminta turned and saw where Ravern was waving. Damian groaned as she changed direction towards them.

'Officers,' she said breathily as soon as she was upon them. 'I'm so glad you're here. I've just come from seeing dear Shiver.'

'You're friends with Shiver Whimsy?' Tomi said.

'Of course. We spent the afternoon playing with her lovely baby minnisks.'

Tomi eyed the delicate green dress beneath Veraminta's fur coat.

'Have you caught the killer?' Veraminta said. 'I can't sleep thinking about it.' She glanced at Damian and winced. 'What happened to your face?'

'It's how I was born.'

'We've made good progress on the case,' Tomi said.

'You'll tell me, won't you?' Veraminta said. 'The moment you make an arrest?'

Damian gave her a big smile. 'You'll be the first person we call.'

'Wonderful, thank you. I must be off – it looks like the weather's about to take a turn.' She swept towards the doors without waiting for a reply.

'Do you think she knows what she sounds like?' Damian said.

'Probably not.'

'I almost choked on her perfume.'

'You'll live.'

Damian puffed his cheeks and blew out his breath noisily. 'I still think Shiver Whimsy had something to do with Jupel's murder. Maybe Veraminta's involved as well.'

'There's a fine line between keeping an open mind and being outright paranoid, Damian.'

They headed to the customer service counter. A bronze plaque on the desk told them they were being served by Katterina Piers. She was a tall woman about Tomi's age. Though her eyebrows were brown, her long hair was unnaturally purple.

Tomi identified herself and they put the keys on the counter. 'Do these belong to your lockers?'

'Yes,' said Katterina after a quick examination.

Tomi flashed Damian a grin.

'Can you tell us which ones?'

'One moment.' Katterina brought out a semi-spherical contraption from beneath the counter. It had a keyhole, where she inserted Vittam's key first. With a click, she turned it, causing a card to pop up with a number written on it. 'Sixty-four.' She did the same with the second key. 'Eighty-two.'

She led them to locker 64 first. Tomi opened it, not sure what she was hoping for, certain she would hate whatever it was.

'Empty,' Damian said, sounding as disappointed as she felt.

'Who hired this locker?' Tomi said.

Katterina returned to the counter to check the ledger. 'Nonne Dafouy.'

Tomi clucked her tongue. *Nonne Dafouy* was a common pseudonym for criminals. It was exactly what she would've expected from Vittam.

'What about locker 82?'

Katterina flipped the page. 'Huh,' she said, pointing to a written note. 'It appears no one's hired it, but the locker's unavailable.'

Tomi didn't have a clue what to expect in locker 82. She wasn't even sure whether it belonged to Jupel or his killer.

'Officer Cardozo.' Talcott Notch strolled up to them, the silver stripes in his suit matching his silver hair and sideburns. 'To what do we owe the pleasure today?' His gaze fell on the ledger.

'We're checking evidence,' Tomi said, holding up the key. 'I found this at one of my crime scenes. Do you know who hired locker 82? It says it's unavailable in the ledger.'

'I'm afraid not. I don't have much to do with the day-to-day of customer service.'

Damian spoke up. 'While we have you, do you mind answering a few questions?'

Tomi wasn't entirely surprised that he was having a go at taking the lead – in fact, she'd expected it sooner – but what did catch her attention was the way Notch dragged his gaze to Damian as if it were an effort to look at him. A slight sneer touched the portmaster's lips, but it disappeared in a blink.

'I'm always willing to assist the Justice Department where possible.'

'We wanted to ask you about Serillia Notch,' Damian said, taking out his parchment book.

There was the slightest pause before Notch said, 'What about her?'

'She's a relation of yours?'

'She was my sister's step-daughter.'

'Were you and Serillia close?'

'Not particularly, no.'

Tomi watched the exchange, curious to see how Damian would tackle the big question.

'I hear you gifted her a house in the Black Ivory District,' Damian said.

'I *leased* her an apartment room, as a favour to my sister. But Serillia died a year ago.'

'Were you aware that Serillia was seeing Professor Ivan Jupel?'

There was a pause. Tomi couldn't tell whether Notch was trying to recall the information or whether he was rapidly putting together a story.

'I remember my sister said something about Serillia seeing a scholar,' he said at last. 'I couldn't tell you more than that.'

'Did she mention Serillia was a substance abuser?'

Tomi glanced at Damian. That was a hefty accusation. They didn't yet know for sure Serillia had used cutlass.

'I'm sorry?' Notch said.

'It's likely Serillia was addicted to an illicit substance.'

'What illicit substance? When? Who told you this?'

'Are you confirming this to be the case?'

'I'm confirming nothing.' Notch's back and shoulders stiffened. 'There were no traces of ices found in her system after her death, and she was never charged with possession. I don't know where you're getting your information, but it's wrong, and I'll thank you for not sullying my family's name with such accusations.' He rounded on Tomi. 'I recommend you keep your attending officer reined in. It seems he'd rather jump to ridiculous conclusions than do proper investigative work.'

'Asking questions *is* investigative work,' Tomi said. 'Just because no ices were found in her system doesn't mean she never used them. How did she die?'

'It was a tragic health condition. And if you're as determined as your inept apprentice to offend me, I'll ask you to leave this terminal at once.'

Tomi held up the evidence key again. 'We're checking your lockers.'

'With my permission, which I'm legally allowed to retract at any time. You're on private property. If you want access to my terminals from here on, you'll have to apply for the required permits.'

'You're not going to let us open the locker?' Damian said in disbelief.

Notch turned a frosty stare to him. 'I think I've seen enough of your face to last me a lifetime.'

By the Tassela, Notch really had it out for Damian.

Tomi touched Damian's arm. 'Come on.'

'But–'

'Damian. Let's go.'

It took a few breaths for him to come to his senses and follow Tomi out of the terminal.

'We were so close to finding out what was in that locker,' he said, stamping his feet in the cold. 'I shouldn't have questioned Notch until we'd opened it.'

'Never mind. We'll request the access permit.'

'But your hearing's tomorrow.'

'It'll get through before then, if Iloura manages to push the right people.'

They hadn't yet reached the grousdu enclosure when a messenger girl ran up with a sealed letter. 'You Officer Cardozo?'

'Thank you,' Tomi said, taking the letter.

She pulled off the wax seal as the girl rushed away. As she read, her stomach dropped.

'What is it?' Damian said.

She folded the letter and tucked it into the inner pocket of her tailcoat. 'I'll meet you back at the station.'

'Why? What's wrong?'

'Nothing yet. Go. See if you can ask Iloura to put together an access request before the end of the day.'

It was only after Damian had taken Brix and ridden away that Tomi headed down to the riverfront path.

Bunter Vittam was waiting for her.

Thirty

IT WAS GETTING COLDER. SOME PEOPLE WERE WEARING THEIR frost coats. Tomi shoved her hands in her tailcoat pockets and ducked her head against a sharp wind coming off the river. It wasn't a far walk from the terminal to the gazebo. She didn't like to imagine how Bunter Vittam had known where she was.

The gazebo was expansive, with white posts decorated in coloured ribbons. People hired it out for birthdays, cultural festivals, even wakes.

Today, it was empty except for Vittam. He stood at the edge, gazing out across the choppy water. His two knuckles loitered beneath a tree close by.

'Make it quick,' Tomi said as soon as she was close enough. 'I'm working.'

'Everyone's always so busy these days. Why don't you stop and enjoy the crisp air?'

'Unless you have information on Ivan Jupel or Park Herliz, you're wasting my time.'

'Tut tut. Is that the way for a soff to speak to a civilian? I thought we were friends.'

The scent of hartmint drifted from him. His blue suit sparkled with silver stripes, bringing out the green in his eyes.

'You haven't found your killer, then?' he said when she refused to rise to his bait. 'Shame. You'd better hurry up – I'm wagering on you.'

She resisted the urge to kick his legs out from under him. 'Why did you call me here, Vittam?'

'I just wanted to tell you I did some research. And I noticed, buried deep in parchment work, that you're in charge of a rather large vault in the treasury.'

Tomi narrowed her eyes. How did he find that out?

'After a few enquiries,' he continued, 'I discovered that you make a sizeable donation to Bleakhouse every year. What an honourable cause. I commend you for caring for those poor, unfortunate people.'

The temperature in the gazebo plummeted. Tomi sucked in a ragged, razor-sharp breath.

Not Harpsigold.

She'd take any punishment, but her sister had already suffered so much.

Vittam flashed his gold teeth in a smile. 'It takes a lot to upkeep that old atrium in the middle of the sea. Sucks coin like a whirlpool. Why, it would practically fall apart without funding from kind people like yourself. And then where would the residents go?'

Tomi found her voice. 'What do you want?'

'To make sure your hearing tomorrow goes smoothly. Like I said, I'm wagering on you.'

'I don't–'

'You need to remove cutlass from your report. If you want to keep investigating this murder – if you want to keep your *job* – ices can't get a mention. Understood?'

'How do you know cutlass is involved?'

'Who said anything about cutlass being involved? I'm simply advising you that your suspicions won't be received well in the courtroom. And if they throw you off the case, well, no one useful will be left to solve this murder.'

'I–'

'And when you do solve the murder, let me know. I'd like to speak to this killer witch on my own, thank you.'

'I'm not doing you any favours, Vittam,' Tomi snapped.

'I'm hurt. By the way, perhaps you should know that I've spoken to a few other donors of Bleakhouse. Turns out they're considering withdrawing their annual funding. Unfortunate, isn't it? If the asylum doesn't get their coin, those residents will be out in the cold.'

Tomi stepped forward. She was taller than him in her heeled boots. 'Are you threatening me?'

'Of course not. I'm just letting you know that if you don't get me my witch, some Bleakhouse patrons may find their vaults a little too empty to spend on donations.'

'You son of a–'

'Uh uh. We're in a public place. Are you sure you want to make a scene?'

Tomi glanced around at the few people still in the park. No one was paying particularly close attention, but they would if Tomi punched Bunter Vittam in the face.

She forced her tense muscles to relax.

'That's better.' Vittam traced a thoughtful finger across his mouth. 'And on the topic of friendly advice, I suggest you keep Talcott Notch out of your report too.'

'Are you telling me he's involved in the murder?'

'I'm telling you he's *not* involved. And he has friends in high places. The highest, in fact. Putting him in will guarantee your removal from the department.' He squinted up at the grey sky. 'It's getting chilly out, isn't it? Might be time for us to seek shelter.' He winked. 'Good luck tomorrow, Officer Freckles.'

Then he sauntered out of the gazebo as if he threatened justice officials on a regular basis.

Which he probably did.

But how? How had Bunter Vittam gotten such private information about her? There was no possible way he could've known she had access to the Glisk vault, unless–

Damian.

The growing rage was more than enough to keep the cold at bay.

Just after she tells Damian about her connection to the Glisk case, Vittam finds her hidden vault? That was no coincidence.

Zef had been right. So had her original instincts when she'd pondered over Damian's comment about the parillion gemstone. She'd tried so hard to believe in him, to believe she'd made the right choice for an apprentice.

But Damian was a traitor. He'd lied to her. There was no abusive landlord. And he'd told Vittam her biggest secret, putting Harpsigold in danger.

He was going to pay.

She stalked towards the grousdu enclosure, her entire body shaking. She was so angry, it took her a while to take notice of the distant clanging echoing across the park. The bell was joined by more, until all the bells from the Church District were ringing.

The hair stood up on her arms. The few people around her lifted their gazes to the grey sky and gasped or groaned in disappointment. The time had come.

The frost was here.

Thirty-One

THE FROST ARRIVED LIKE DROPS OF WINE ON A TABLECLOTH. SILVER-blue ice crystallised on the coldest, wettest places of the city first. Then it spread outwards in every direction until, within a few short hours, the entire city was stained.

When Damian was young, maybe five or six, he had gone outside to watch the frost creep across the street. His father had been working at the docks and *Bamki* Rivers had dozed off, drowsy from a head cold. She hadn't even heard the bells ring.

Damian stood on the kerb in wonder. People ran past on their way to warmth and safety. One woman – the plink addict who had later suffocated in her own vomit – had shouted at him to get inside. Otherwise, no one stopped.

Eyes down, doors locked. That was the saying in the Southeast District. No one interfered in anyone else's business because there were too many ways to get into trouble. Pick up the wrong mail, ask the wrong question, stare too long at the wrong person, and you might end up under the river.

So Damian had been able to witness the wonder of the settling up close.

His little red boots froze first. The ice ate its way over the hilkskin until it had anchored him to the ground. He stared in awe at the way flecks formed on his hands. His nose felt deliciously cold, and his breath curled in front of his face like his mouth was a chimney.

It was only when the cold started to hurt that he realised he couldn't move. He pulled and tugged at his boots, but the frost had claimed them.

He'd cried for his father. The tears froze on his cheeks, fresh drops of wine to stain his face. Ice clawed beneath his woollen beanie. He heard the crackle of it in his ears.

By this point there were no people on the street. A single grousdu scampered past, its frosty saddle empty.

Damian's scream was locked in his throat as he stood with his arms outstretched, reaching for help.

Thirty more breaths. That's how long the medica mavens suspected he'd had left, if *Bamki* Rivers hadn't rushed out and wrenched him from the kerb. Thirty more breaths, and he would've become an ice statue, to be picked up and taken to the collection point for his family to identify later.

Bamki Rivers had thawed him by the atrium's fire ovens, which had been working back then. He had spent the rest of the month weak and feverish.

Damian had barely survived experiencing the settling firsthand, and being outside while the bells rang always filled him with dread.

Now was one of those times. He stood outside the station, beside the fountain. His feet shuffled, his hands shook. As long as he kept moving, he should be safe, at least for the next quarter hour. He glanced towards the station's entrance, which had been sealed. All access was at the back now, from the underground tunnels.

The windows were blocked too. While most buildings had reinforced windows to keep out the frost, Warrick had mentioned the old-fashioned shutters for justice stations had been installed during the early years of the Invasion Era and never updated. Officials were forced to make do with lanterns and enclosed candles that had been donated by the public rather than sunlight and a street view.

Not that anyone would be looking out at him now. Most of the officers had gone home by the time he'd returned. Despite the danger and hardships to come, the night of the settling was a celebration. People left work early for drinks, parties and searching for a frost lover.

Damian had assumed Tomi would go straight to her friends' atrium for more curries and dancing. His own night would consist of attempting to sleep while his neighbours brawled and set fire to things for fun. And, of course, caring for Pa.

Instead, he and Tomi were standing outside as the frost stole across the city. It crackled around them, creeping across the buildings and empty streets.

Damian's breath steamed before him. 'We should go inside.'

'Not yet.' Tomi looked strangely unaffected by the cold. Damian couldn't read her expression. What had been in that letter she'd received at the terminal?

'Iloura thinks the access request won't get through before your hearing,' he said. 'The settling has slowed everything down. We should find someone else to open the lock–'

'You're working for Bunter Vittam.'

Damian's mouth fell open.

'You're going to tell me everything, right from the start.'

'I – I'm not–'

'Do you think me a fool?'

Damian shut his eyes, then quickly opened them again as he felt frost forming on his eyelashes. Of course he didn't think her a fool. He had known he was living on borrowed time – she was too clever, too observant.

'Are you indentured?'

One more heartbeat of hesitation, one more moment where Damian could pretend to be the perfect apprentice. Then, at last, he nodded.

The sound of the fountain stopped as the frost claimed the spray in freezing arcs. Ice spread across the pool.

Tomi let out a long, steamy exhalation. 'How much do you owe?'

'I–'

'How much, Damian?'

He cringed at the force behind her words. 'Seven hundred and twenty gold.'

'Bless'd *shit*.'

'My father lost his job. He tried to win some coin at the dens and got addicted. I took on the debt to save him, paid Vittam what I earned from the docks, worked as his runner at night.' Damian's teeth started chattering. Fear rose in him like a storm, his body screaming as it remembered his near-death experience. 'P-please can we go inside?'

'How did you get into the academy?'

'U-using my mother's name. She has nothing to do with us, so there's no connection to Vittam. Tomi, if we can just g-go inside–'

'Why would you be senseless enough to enter the academy knowing Vittam owned you?'

'I was hoping to earn g-good coin and pay him back. I didn't know he'd u-use me against you.'

'You can't have been so naïve.'

Maybe he had. Or maybe he'd been lying to himself.

Clemency help him, he was so cold. He realised belatedly that he'd stopped moving. He tried to shuffle his feet. Even that simple movement was excruciatingly hard.

Tomi seemed unaware of his slowing body. She paced back and forth before the fountain. 'I can't believe I trusted you,' she muttered. 'I can't believe I let you get away with your lies for so long.'

'I h-have information for you, at least,' he said feebly. 'Vittam didn't plan Jupel's murder. A witch told him to do it.'

Tomi gave a derisive snort.

'I know how it sounds, but it's true. I h-heard him talking to Talcott Notch. The witch was invisible – they threatened him. Tomi, please, let's go inside.'

'We're not going anywhere until you tell me everything. So you'd better talk faster.'

Through clattering teeth, Damian summarised what he'd overheard last night about Talcott Notch's connection to Park Herliz and Bunter Vittam being afraid of the witch, and how he'd stolen the key.

As he spoke, he sank to the wall of the fountain. It hurt to breathe.

'M-maybe the locker was a drop point between Vittam and the witch,' he said between laboured gasps. 'So he could hand over the halicort horn shavings, and the witch could give back the sleeping potion. That way, the witch wouldn't have to deal with Vittam directly. They were using him, but they were being smart about it.'

'And why would a witch involve Vittam at all?'

'They n-needed Nomik to leave the frost doors of Jupel's atrium ajar. The best way to get to Nomik was through V-Vittam.'

'So it had to be someone who knew Nomik was indebted to Vittam. That can't be many people.' Tomi was shivering now too. Frost had turned the pins in her hair white.

'Please,' Damian moaned. He was stuck in that moment from his childhood, envisioning his arms outstretched, his scream stuck in his throat. 'I'll d-do whatever it takes to stop him.'

'How can I know that?'

'M-my life will never be safe with him on the streets. Neither will my father's. I need Vittam gone. Caged, or dead. I d-don't care which.'

'Mm.' Tomi flexed her fingers, which had started to fleck with ice. 'Except you told him I was involved in the Glisk case.'

'I d-didn't think it mattered. He can't use it against you.'

'You have no idea.' Tomi's voice was low and lethal. 'He's found my weakness, and he's trying to exploit me.'

The frost crept up Damian's boots, the same way it had all those years ago.

'You're fired, Damian.'

He'd been expecting it, but he was no longer able to react. His eyes drifted closed. The shivering was uncontrollable.

'Not just busted down to general duties. You are completely, utterly fired, never to work in the Justice Department again. I'll be telling Iloura about your indenture to Vittam, and you'll be charged accordingly.'

That's if he survived. He was surely reaching his last breaths.

He started to slump, but she grabbed his collar and yanked him to his feet. There was a ripping sound – his tailcoat had frozen to the fountain wall. She marched him around the side of station. His legs had forgotten how to work; he stumbled, almost collapsing to the ground again.

They went through the frost doors to find the place empty, though there would be someone on duty somewhere. Oil lanterns flickered at their lowest flame. Parchment work had been left strewn across desks from the officers' hasty departure.

He gulped a breath of warm air. It burned his lungs.

Tomi practically threw him onto a visitor bench. His bruises flared in pain; he curled up to make it stop.

'Return your uniform, weapons, cuffs and badge upstairs.'

'V-V-V–' The word wouldn't come out. He kept trying. 'V-V-Vittam will kill me.'

'Dead men don't pay debts, remember?' She swiped ice from her sleeve. 'You sold me out, Damian. I have no use for traitors.'

Then she walked away, leaving him gasping and alone in the station.

Thirty-Two

THE BELLS HAD STOPPED CLANGING. THEY'D FROZEN STIFF, COATED in silver-blue ice like every building, lamppost and stone in the region. The homeless had flocked to the churches while the bells rang; those enormous, greystone structures became refuges during the season rather than places of worship. The arched doors would now be closed and frozen over. Radaza had turned into a glittering, deadly city.

Even after entering the crowded underground tunnels, the chill knifed at Tomi's mouth and throat. Ice dripped from her skin and clothes and sloughed from her hair. She patted Finley's neck. 'We'll be home soon.'

He rasped to convey his disapproval. He hated the tunnels.

Sentinels stood guard at the exits, their features hidden beneath frost coats, hoods, face scarves and massive gloves. The walls were lined with oil lanterns and bronze signs telling people where they were.

Slowly, the rage that had built up since her meeting with Vittam started to wear off. She'd said everything to Damian she'd needed to say.

It didn't make her situation any better, though. Besides Zef, Mia and Payana, she hadn't told anyone she was involved in the Glisk case. Now, after 23 years, she'd broken her silence to the one person she couldn't trust.

Why?

Why had she divulged her most precious secret, especially so soon after what her ex had done? Why had she put so much faith in Damian?

The nearest tunnel in her district opened a few atriums from her own. She had to go inside the first atrium, climb the curving balcony with Finley and walk across four different skybridges, which had opened now the frost was here. The buildings were alive with people and parties.

There were sentinels at either end of each skybridge. People who had no work during the frost took shifts to ensure non-residents coming through didn't linger.

She welcomed the heat seeping into her. During the season, the oven fires were piled with grakka rocks instead of wood, burning hotter and longer and keeping entire buildings warm.

At last, they made it home. Tomi locked Finley inside his enclosure and he plonked himself in the hay.

'Tom-eee!' trilled Lyrica, who was helping with the food at the fire oven. The communal dining area was packed with residents and their families. 'Are you hungry, sweetbun? I made a plate for you.'

She'd put together a supper of roasted game bird, smallfruits pie, seared vegetables and wine-soaked raisins. Sometimes, it was worth putting up with the old woman's midnight operetta. Tomi thanked her gratefully and headed upstairs with the plate.

She closed her door, drowning out the party sounds. In the warmth and safety of her apartment, her body finally started to relax.

She slid the transparent, reinforced covers over her windows. The frost had already started creeping inside. Before eating, she unpinned her hair and ran her fingers through her long, tangled curls. A mild headache pulsed at the back of her eyelids.

Baths were restricted now, but she needed a wash. Desperately. Today had been... long.

The tub had been a luxury, made of cream ivory and gold clawed feet. She'd used her first big bonus to buy it. It was in the corner of her bedroom, hooked to the single tap in her apartment. The pipes curled around the exposed chimney for hot water. Ferns hung from the ceiling and potted plants surrounded it to form a screen.

While she waited for the tub to fill, she ate her supper and took a small bell and three white ministration candles from her nightstand drawer. She dimmed the oil lanterns, then set the candles on the stone floor.

'Anatole Glisk,' she said, lighting the first candle with a flint stick. She rang the bell three times.

'Sharlie Glisk,' she said, repeating the actions.

As she lit the final candle, she said, 'Harpsigold Glisk', but didn't ring the bell. Her sister wasn't dead. She was just... gone. Alone in the frost. And now, because of Tomi, in danger of losing her only sanctuary.

Tomi undressed and slid into the warm water. After soaping herself down and washing her hair, she lay back to soak, watching the steady flames of the candles. She couldn't celebrate the first night of the frost with everyone else. Her parents had been murdered during the settling. This was a time of grieving, of vigil. The Followers of Light believed the Tassela were soothed by the ringing of bells and weaved life at the Great Loom more kindly. Sharlie and Anatole's threads would've been rewoven a long time ago, but the action was a comfort all the same. Tomi chose to mark the anniversary on the night of the frost settling rather than the actual date of Harrow that they'd died. It felt right somehow.

It was different this time, though. Her parents weren't human. Had they been rewoven, or was the Way of the Weavers correct and her parents cast off the Great Loom, sent to the void of the Umbra because they were abominations? Surely not.

She shut her eyes. Maybe her parents hadn't told her the truth because they were disappointed she was human.

But she didn't believe that. Her childhood had been happy and filled with love. Yes, they were busy. Yes, she'd seen more of her *ama sector* than her mother and father. But they always made time for her when they could.

And now she owned Brackenlong Manor. She would have to walk those halls filled with pain and death, the house too empty for a single person. When Mia, Zef and Payana had dragged her out of the pit she'd fallen into, it had seemed like a good idea to get her home back, to have something of her parents, to not let it fall apart. Mia had sent out messages across the country to find the next owner – Tomi's uncle – and waited the required seven years. Then had come the long, legal battle to prove Tomi had a right to the inheritance, which was difficult under her false identity.

And now she didn't want it.

A soft knock at her door interrupted her thoughts. She willed the person to go away. Everyone in the atrium knew not to disturb her on the night of the settling, but sometimes they grew rowdy and restless, and called through the door for her to join the celebrations.

'It's me.'

Tomi's eyes snapped open. She climbed out of the bath and wrapped herself in a towel before answering the door. Zef stood on the other side, bundled in a frost coat.

'Oh, sorry,' he said when he saw her state. 'I finished closing up the cemetery and thought I'd check on you on the way home. But I can leave if–'

'Get in; you know I don't care.' She stepped aside to let him pass.

He studied her, and she realised his scrutiny wasn't surface-level – he was reading her qoras.

'It didn't go well with Damian?' he said tentatively.

She shut the door. 'He told Bunter Vittam I was connected to the Glisk case.'

Zef flinched.

'Yes,' Tomi said. 'You were right. He was indentured.' She headed back to her bedroom and flushed the bath water down a reinforced pipe along the exterior of the building. 'As you can imagine, I fired him.'

'I'm sorry.'

'I'm never taking on an apprentice again.'

She pulled on a milkmoth robe and carried her candles to the window sill. Zef knew about her settling ritual, and she was comfortable enough to have him here.

'I have a few extra ministration candles,' she said. 'If, um, you want to light some too?'

His entire village had been wiped out. Everything he'd known as a child was gone. He had no home to inherit, no sister to care for. She couldn't imagine the pain he carried.

'Keep them,' he said. 'We all have ways to deal with grief, and I don't want to take from yours.'

He would know. Being a *saccurvierro* meant he lived among grief the way a gardener lived among blooms.

His job had changed now. It was unsafe to dig graves – this season required funeral pyres. The scent of woodsmoke would join the carmao incense clinging to his clothes. It was a morbid sentiment, but she loved the way he smelled in the frost.

Tomi set her used dishes from supper on a tray to take down to the communal kitchen later. Unlike Jupel, she had no sink. Her apartment was much smaller than his, but at least her decor was vibrant. Living in the Clinker District had given her access to brightly patterned cushions, tapestries and rugs. Colourful beads hung from stained glass oil lanterns; multitudes of scented candles dripped wax onto her low lounge table; her couches were low and squashy and comfortable. She enfolded herself in a fluffy blanket and sat beside Zef.

'I have a present for you,' he said.

She laughed. 'I'm not a child demanding frost gifts.'

'I know. But I have one for you anyway.'

Before she could answer, there was a *crack*, and red light flared outside.

'Fireflowers,' Tomi murmured. She got up again, the blanket around her shoulders as she moved to the window. A second explosion seared the sky with colour, this time green. It hung there briefly before frosting into flakes and drifting to the ground.

'Tomi,' Zef said.

She turned. He dug into the pocket of his waistcoat and withdrew a pouch. An image flashed in her mind, unbidden, of Damian handing her a pouch too. Just that morning, at Brackenlong Manor. He had brought her gizzard stones and worm paste for Finley.

Zef hesitated. 'What was that?'

'What?'

'Your qoras... Are you well?'

A groan escaped her. 'I don't know whether it's more or less annoying to understand how you know me so well.'

'I can't help it. It's not always a good thing to see what others are thinking.' The deep blue of a fireflower glowed across his face. 'It's why I had to quit my job as a family liaison officer. I saw too many children enduring too many terrible things. The dead don't have qoras. And they certainly don't mind me hanging around.'

Tomi let this sink in. After the explosion of a purple fireflower, she said, 'Are you trying to make me feel *sorry* for you?'

'Mm.' His lips twitched. 'Maybe a little.'

She returned to her spot beside him and snatched the pouch from his hand. 'Well, I'm fine. I was thinking of Damian and accidentally felt bad. Don't worry, I'm over it.' She unknotted the silk rope. 'What a waste. He had so much potential. I only accepted his application because – what's this?'

The pouch contained a chain with a flat, blue pendant. She tipped it into her palm. More booms echoed across the night.

'It's an ettyspar crystal,' Zef said. 'From Elumina. Rare to find and extremely difficult to enchant.'

Tomi moved her hand away instinctively. 'It's enchanted?'

'It's linked to mine.' He pulled out an identical chain and pendant from around his neck. 'Watch.' When he rubbed his thumb across the gemstone, green swam over the blue until it looked like a completely different stone.

In Tomi's palm, her own pendant changed colour.

'It's warm,' she said, surprised.

'Ettyspar crystals are used by travellers to help find each other.' He pressed his gemstone against hers. They returned to their original temperature and colour. 'If you activate one, the other will lead you to it. I thought it might be useful if you needed me.'

She stared down at the crystal. 'Zef, this is so thoughtful...'

'But?'

The yellow flare of a fireflower shone over them.

'But I don't know if I should be carrying around an enchanted object. Especially since my hearing is tomorrow.'

'No one's going to recognise it, and you can hide it beneath your clothes. Tomi,' he said when she still hesitated. 'I know you can look after yourself. But you're dealing with witches now. And when Bunter Vittam starts spreading the word about your connection to the Glisk case–'

'All right, all right,' she said, slipping the chain around her neck. 'I can't argue with that. I have to say, I'm not a fan of dealing with witch killers. I can't keep up with all the things they can do. My head hurts just thinking about it.'

'Maybe your head hurts because it's late, and you've been working non-stop.' Zef squeezed her knee. 'Try to rest. You have to be ready for your hearing tomorrow.'

'I still have to write my report.' Tomi flopped back on the couch, watching the colour show through the window. 'Vittam found out about my donations to Bleakhouse.'

'What?'

'He's going to put Harpsigold on the streets if I include cutlass in my report.'

Zef sat back so their faces were level. Warmth radiated from his body, seeping into her. 'So you're going to leave it out?'

She hesitated. 'I can't let him dictate my actions. If I'm compromised, I may as well leave the Justice Department.'

'What about Harpsigold?'

'I'll figure something out.' Tomi tried to give a reassuring smile, then realised her expressions meant nothing when Zef could read her emotions. She dropped the smile. 'I have to do this. It's the right choice. I'm sure cutlass is involved in this case, so I can't just omit it. And Talcott Notch, the portmaster, is involved too. If Damian was right about Notch being acquainted with Park Herliz *and* Notch's step-niece was involved with Ivan Jupel, that means he's connected to both victims. Who cares about his lawyers and his friends in high places? I'm not going to be frightened off by bullies.'

Zef had a strange look on his face.

'What?' she said, self-conscious under his gaze.

'Nothing.' He tucked one of her drying curls behind her ear. 'I like your passionate speeches.'

She whacked his arm. 'Shut up.'

'No, no, tell me more about how you're going to stand up for what's right and proper–'

'Shut up!'

But she was laughing, and so was he, and he was very close, one of his hands on her hip, the other hot against her neck.

The night suddenly changed. They stilled, his gaze dipping to her mouth.

Her pulse quickened to a sprint. Was this another foray into a frost relationship? It was the night of the settling, after all. That's what people did.

But she wasn't sure she could go there again. Last time, the tryst had turned into something more – at least for her – and Zef had hurt her deeply.

She thought about what Payana had said, about him not wanting to break up with her, and wondered if maybe... maybe...

Then again, he was a *witch*.

His hands lifted from her. She cleared her throat and wriggled back, putting more space between them.

'Uh.' She snatched at drifting thoughts, trying to pick up the threads of their previous conversation. 'Um. Well. Besides.' The hearing. Vittam's threat. 'I have Nomik in custody,' she said, finding her place, 'and all of TADOW's findings from Park Herliz's murder. Hopefully, no matter what they say about cutlass or Talcott Notch, my progress is good enough to merit staying on the case and prove I'm not a witch sympathiser.'

'Except you are.'

She looked at him. Both of them were still breathless, and her body throbbed with a heat she didn't want to think about.

There was a smattering of explosions outside as the fireflower display reached its climax.

Zef was right. She *was* a witch sympathiser.

May the Tassela unthread her.

How was she ever going to reconcile the fact that her duty was to uphold the law, when she was breaking it with every passing moment?

Thirty-Three

COMMANDER PARSONS' LIP PAINT WAS A SHADE OF MAGENTA. TOMI watched, fascinated, as the colour shimmered with each stretch and purse of the commander's lips. Or maybe it was just easier to think about her mouth than what she was saying.

'—spoken with the head of ISEF and he assured me there's been no confirmed cases of cutlass in a number of years. He's concerned your report might raise unnecessary alarm and suggested you investigate different avenues.'

'I have it on good authority that cutlass has made an appearance–' Tomi started.

'Your source is unnamed in your report.'

'They requested not to be identified.'

Wendyn Gracer, the Justice Misconduct Officer, was taking notes again. He scribbled quickly to keep up with the dialogue.

'Without any further proof, we have no reason to believe they were being truthful,' Commander Parsons said.

'How about the fact that we know witches are involved?' Tomi said. 'And cutlass has been linked to witches.'

'*Suspected* of being linked to witches. Again, you have no proof.'

Tomi had known this would happen, but she couldn't comprehend just how quickly the hearing committee dismissed her suspicions. Hadn't she closed the most murder cases in Radaza for any JO ever? Wasn't she upheld as one of the top officers? Hadn't the councillors given her a personal commendation for catching the assassin who had killed one of their own?

'If this is about cutlass, and I catch the witches manufacturing it, doesn't that prove I have no witch sympathies, not to mention getting a deadly IS off the streets?' she said.

'Mm.' Commander Parsons rolled up the parchment Tomi had spent most of the night working on. 'It strikes me as convenient that putting ghost in your report is the perfect excuse for why you haven't made much progress on the case.'

Iloura, who was sitting next to Tomi, spoke up. 'As her superior, I have to say I'm quite satisfied with Officer Cardozo's progress. She has a confession from Nomik Whimsy.'

'Yes,' Commander Parsons said. 'Again, convenient that he would blame Bunter Vittam. Most criminals stammer out that man's name in the hopes it will save themselves.'

'I noticed you've also linked Talcott Notch to this case,' Judge Stock said. She spoke less crisply than the commander; her statement was more curious than anything.

'Yes,' Tomi said. 'As you can see from my report, he was an old acquaintance of the second victim. And his step-niece was involved with the first victim, plus the key we found in Ivan Jupel's apartment opens a locker in the ferry ter–'

'Talcott Notch can't be held accountable if a locker in his terminal is linked to an unseemly crime, the same way the maker of the carving knife can't be held accountable for it being used as the murder weapon,' Commander Parsons said.

'I disagree. Notch owns the property. It's a private business, therefore he has some responsibility for what happens there.'

'I have here your request for an access permit to the terminal. It's been denied.'

Tomi was stunned into silence.

'On what grounds?' Iloura said.

Commander Parsons held out the form for Iloura to take. '*Seno* Notch claims an attack on his character from both the attending and investigating officers.'

'We asked him about the death of his step-niece,' Tomi said. 'That's hardly an attack on his character. Commander, we have to have access to the lockers.'

'It says here Judge Stock approved the request, but the permission was overruled by the council,' Iloura said, returning to the chair beside Tomi.

Tomi leaned over to read for herself.

Friends in high places.

Vittam hadn't been wrong. Talcott Notch had the highest protection in the city.

'Look,' Tomi said, struggling to contain her mounting frustration. 'The salitenine grease found on the murder weapon suggests the killer worked near water. And I've heard Bunter Vittam uses his lockers as drop points.'

'You've *heard*?' Commander Parsons snorted. 'Again, I wouldn't say that's sufficient evidence. And the salitenine grease is circumstantial. In fact, it sounds like you're pointing fingers at anyone and anything to appear as if you've made more progress than you have.'

'Come now.' Iloura sounded as annoyed as Tomi felt. 'I've never worked with a more professional and thorough officer than Tomi Cardozo. She doesn't twist facts for her own gain. If she says she suspects that cutlass is part of this, I'll stand by her. If she wants to investigate Bunter Vittam and Talcott Notch because there's physical evidence and confessions against them, I'll stand by her. If she swears she's not a witch sympathiser, you can be assured, I'll stand by her.'

Iloura's words were a blade through Tomi's gut.

This had all come about because Tomi had let a witch go. Now she was sitting here, trying to defend herself when she was hiding the identities of *four* witches. The enchanted pendant hung like a noose around her throat.

She wasn't an officer of justice. She was a fraud. Iloura was wrong to put faith in her.

Guilt wrenched at her threads.

Her *qoras*.

She knew the witch word for life threads because she was a traitor.

The Tassela damn her. She couldn't do this.

'Commander Parsons, I accept your criticisms,' she said. 'You're right. I haven't made sufficient progress on this case. I've let down the victims and the justice system.'

Zef had said she wouldn't be able to investigate her parents' case without access to the archives. He was wrong – she owned the manor now, and she knew the reports by heart.

But she couldn't represent the Justice Department if she continued protecting her friends. And after her grievous misjudgement of Damian – and Grundy – she knew her intuition couldn't be trusted.

She drew a long, steadying breath.

'I've done wrong by the system,' she said. 'I wish to resign from my position.'

Gracer stopped writing. A blob of ink spilled onto his notes from his hovering quill. Commander Parsons' red eyebrows flew up.

'Don't be ridiculous,' Iloura said. 'You can't resign. You're the best officer this city has.'

'Officer Minwell Warrick can take over the case. He's a competent, hard-working JO who doesn't have any accusations of witch sympathies. It's what's best for the reputation of the department.'

'I agree,' Commander Parsons said.

'Officer Warrick's already on a case,' Iloura said. 'It'll have to go to Officer Lorenze.'

Tomi's chest tightened. She hadn't expected that.

She could've entrusted Jupel's case to Warrick. But Jerry Lorenze was one of the officers who had been taunting her this past month. He wasn't a witch sympathiser – he was a witch hater, and he had no qualms about outwardly flaunting his disdain.

Judge Stock looked momentarily lost for words. She peered at Tomi over her eyeglasses. 'Are you sure you want to resign?'

'No,' Iloura said, laying a hand on Tomi's forearm. 'No, but she'll be suspended until this case has been cleared up. She can turn her badge and weapons in at the station and brief Officer Lorenze on her work so far. Is that acceptable?'

Tomi wanted to argue, but Iloura squeezed her arm to keep her quiet.

Parsons, Stock and Gracer discussed it among themselves and agreed with Iloura. Tomi was officially suspended.

It was only afterwards, as Tomi and Iloura were walking through the grand halls of the Supreme Court, that Iloura muttered, 'I think you're onto something, suspecting cutlass has turned up again. Officer Warrick and I have discussed it. But until we have proof, it's best not to crack the frosted lake.'

'This isn't about cutlass.'

'No,' Iloura said. Her face was tight. 'It's about much more. Don't give up your position, Tomi. I need you on my side.'

How could she deny her superior officer?

Iloura was silent as they rode their grousdu through the tunnels. Tomi used the time to consider everything that had happened in the courtroom. Either the commander had it in for her, or she was somebody's puppet. Was the head of ISEF pressuring her to keep any mention of cutlass quiet? Or was there something more sinister at play? Like, perhaps, Bunter Vittam? He had been resourceful enough to find Tomi's weakness and brazen enough to threaten her with it. Did he have something similar on Commander Parsons?

And how were the five city councillors involved? Tomi had no idea who to turn to if a councillor was dirty. Was that what Iloura had been talking about?

All these musings were overshadowed by the fact that maybe it didn't matter. She was suspended, for who knows how long. Part of her wondered whether she had been a little hasty offering her resignation. The other part couldn't figure out how she could work for the Justice Department while hiding the identities of witches. There didn't seem to be any right answer.

Her thoughts were so tangled, she almost didn't notice the GO waiting for her when they returned to the gloomy, shuttered station. The place was almost empty. The day after the settling was the only one when it didn't matter what time officials dragged themselves in, as long as they made an appearance at some point.

'Got your suspect in the interview room,' the GO said, handing her a scroll.

She looked at him blankly as she hung her frost coat on the rack.

'Her alibi didn't check out,' he said with a grin. 'And I got to talk to Evelynn Portio. This was the best morning of my life.'

It took Tomi a moment longer to comprehend what he was telling her. She'd almost forgotten she'd left instructions for the general officers that morning.

'No,' she said, unravelling the scroll to see for herself. 'No way.'

But it was true. She had a suspect for the Jupel-Herliz murders. A real suspect.

With great difficulty, she rolled up the report again. This wasn't her case anymore.

'Just for your legal information,' said Iloura quietly behind her, 'you're not technically suspended until *after* you go upstairs to hand in your badge.'

Tomi grinned and started for the interview room.

'Aren't you going to wait for Damian?' Iloura said.

Tomi glanced back in surprise. They hadn't had a chance to talk about Damian before the hearing, but Tomi had assumed Iloura knew he was no longer working here.

That little cratter. Why hadn't he handed in his badge and weapons last night?

'He's not here.' She didn't want to waste time explaining when she finally had a proper suspect in custody. She jerked her head for the GO to follow her. 'You can scribe for me.'

She'd explain everything after the interview. First, she was going to get a confession.

Thirty-Four

VERAMINTA LINN PACED THE BACK OF THE ROOM, HER ARMIENE coat swishing behind her. She whirled towards the door as Tomi entered. 'I demand to know what I'm doing here.'

'I'm happy to explain.' Tomi dropped the scroll on the table and sat down. 'Take a seat.'

Veraminta drew herself up to her full height. 'I'd rather stand.'

'Are you sure? We might be here a while.'

'Why? And where's that boy who follows you around like a dopey-eyed zimarool?'

'He's not here. But you should know, it's because of him that we discovered you've been lying to us.'

'I–' Veraminta looked from Tomi to the GO by the door. 'I'm not sure what you mean.'

'Then sit down, and let's go through it together.'

There was a moment where Veraminta seemed like she was about to argue. Then she huffed and bundled herself on the chair opposite.

'Thank you,' Tomi said. 'Now, we normally wouldn't need to check the neighbours' alibis, but Officer Kamara had his suspicions about you and Shiver Whimsy, and I followed up on them. And while *Leya* Whimsy's alibi checked out, yours is looking, shall we say, less stable?'

Veraminta's mouth tightened.

'You said during our initial interview that you spent the night of the murder at the Central Lights Rave. You claimed to have breakfasted the next morning with socialite Evelynn Portio, which turned into lunch. I remember you mentioning the two of you were "closest of friends". Tomi unrolled the report. 'So you can imagine my surprise when I had a GO call Evelynn Portio, only to find she'd never heard of you.'

'That's nonsense!'

'Have you any proof of your relationship with Evelynn Portio?'

'I don't have to prove anything. I don't know why she's lying, but she is.'

'I see.' Tomi tapped her fingers lightly on the report. 'Do you think Shiver Whimsy would lie too?'

'What?'

'When we bumped into you at the ferry terminal yesterday, you claimed to have just been to see Shiver Whimsy. You were playing with her baby minnisks, correct?'

'Yes.'

'But the dress you were wearing was very delicate. A baby minnisk's claws would rip right through it. Not to mention the lack of minnisk fur anywhere on your person. How could you play with an animal that's shedding its coat for the frost without getting a single strand on you?'

'I – what – really! Your accusations are unfounded and ridiculous!'

Tomi turned to the GO taking notes. 'Tell someone to get Shiver Whimsy on the caller. We can ask her right now. Oh, and see if she knows whether Veraminta's acquainted with her grandson Nomik.'

The skin above Veraminta's upper lip started to sweat. She said nothing as the GO left the room.

Tomi waited coolly for the GO to return. The room was deathly silent. The flame of an oil lantern flickered.

When the GO came back, Tomi said, 'Why don't you tell me about Serillia Notch?'

'What about her?' Veraminta was sitting more stiffly than before. Her tone was less high-pitched and more guarded.

'Officer Kamara's notes indicate that your niece Kaya said you were devastated by Serillia's death, not because you cared about her as a person, but because you believed she was your path to wealth. You wanted her to introduce you to potential partners in the Black Ivory District. Her passing was a huge loss for you.' Tomi shifted her chair closer to the desk and lowered her voice. 'You've been having trouble finding other people to help you climb the social ladder, haven't you? Since Serillia's death, you've had to falsify connections to make yourself seem important. It's frustrating, isn't it? A Black Ivory partnership was in your grasp – you were so close to getting out of the Shores. And recently, Kaya started babbling on about Professor Jupel dealing ices. At first you dismissed it. Then you started wondering whether Kaya was onto something. Maybe Professor Jupel *was* dealing ices. In fact, maybe he was the reason Serillia passed. There was no clear cause of death. Maybe the professor had got her addicted to ghost. Now she's gone, and your one chance to find a wealthy partner has vanished. And maybe, just maybe, after failing all year to find someone as useful as Serillia, you decided to punish Professor Jupel for taking her away.'

'Are you listening to yourself?' Veraminta demanded. 'You think I killed Ivan Jupel because he kept me from the Black Ivory District?'

'People have killed for less.'

'You don't have any evidence.'

'How about the salitenine grease found on the handle of the murder weapon? You admitted to visiting the steam spas the days before and after the professor's murder. I happen to know they have a salt bath, where the taps have to be constantly greased to turn properly.'

Veraminta stood. 'I refuse to listen to this any longer. I'm not some common criminal for you to throw fake accusations at.'

An older GO knocked at the door. 'Officer Cardozo? I got Shiver Whimsy on the caller. She says she's had Veraminta over in the past but didn't see her yesterday. And yes, Veraminta and Nomik were partners in the frost of '89.'

'Thank you,' Tomi said, returning her attention to Veraminta. 'Sit back down, *Leya* Linn. Shiver Whimsy has just confirmed you were lying to me about what you were doing at the ferry terminal yesterday. And she's connected you to Nomik Whimsy, who's currently being charged for accessory to murder.'

'What?'

'Were you angry Nomik broke it off with you after the frost three years ago? Another potential connection to the Black Ivory District gone? Did you think this was a fitting way to get your revenge: by forcing him to be involved in your scheme? Are you the witch, *Leya* Linn, or did you hire a witch to do it for you?'

Veraminta's breaths were gasps. 'I don't – I haven't – it isn't–' She burst into tears. 'It's not fair! I didn't do anything wrong. So I lied about knowing Evelynn Portio. So what? I just want to be respected. Is that too much to ask?'

'What were you doing at the terminal yesterday?'

'*Trying* to visit Shiver Whimsy. But her manager said she was too busy to see me.' Her words turned to hiccoughing burbles. 'It's s-so hard. No matter what I do, no one will let me into their inner group. All I want is to find a secure home.'

'Has it ever occurred to you to get a job?'

Veraminta let out an ear-piercing wail. The scribing GO passed over a handkerchief for her to sob into.

'I d-didn't kill Ivan,' Veraminta said. 'I had no idea Kaya was right about him dealing ices, or how Serillia died. Were they really into cutlass?' She blew her nose into the handkerchief then warbled, 'Is that why he smelled so bad?'

'What do you mean?'

'Well, he didn't smell bad *all* the time. But sometimes... ugh.' She continued to dab at her nose. 'It was like curdled milk and urine.'

Something snagged in Tomi's mind. A bad smell connected to the case. She'd heard that before. Where?

She had a vision of a staircase and a corridor.

Eversea Shipping. Georgio Herliz had told her, right before they'd found his dead grandfather, that the smuggled stone had a horrific odour.

Why would a stone stink?

What if, rather than a precious gem, it was something else?

She stood. She needed to talk to Zef.

Veraminta blinked up at her with wet eyelashes. 'Is it over? Can I go?'

'For now, yes.' Tomi turned to the GO. 'You'll be right to take her home?'

He nodded, then grimaced as Veraminta held out his handkerchief.

Tomi stalked back into the main part of the station, but she slowed when she saw two people waiting at the service counter. While the man was bald and bearded, his face was too familiar to mistake. He was standing with an elderly woman dressed as if she were going to the theatre. Their frost coats were old and worn.

'Officer Cardozo,' the man said in relief. He limped forward, and Tomi saw a stub of wood beneath the cuff of his pants. His left hand was heavily bandaged. He pressed his right one to his heart. 'I'm Faeza Kamara, Damian's father. This is Erika Rivers.'

The woman eyed Tomi with distrust. Her lip paint didn't quite sit within the lines of her lips.

Tomi didn't want to deal with these people. They were probably here to argue on behalf of Damian, beg her to take him back. She didn't want to think of Damian ever again.

She headed for the stairs. 'Sorry, I'm not available.'

'Officer Cardozo—'

'Not now.'

'Officer, *please.*'

Tomi turned, a few steps up. Faeza Kamara stood at the base, his right arm looped around the old lady's. Neither of them would be able to climb the staircase.

'Damian didn't come home last night,' Faeza said. Desperation crept into his voice. 'Did you put him on surveillance somewhere?'

A cold, empty sort of dread crept through Tomi's insides. She walked back down the steps.

'No.' She glanced at the bench where she'd left Damian.

The frost had wound its tendrils around him yesterday. She'd let it grip him tighter than she should've, angry as she was at his treachery. But he'd been recovering when she left. And someone would've mentioned if they'd found a corpse here in the morning.

'You probably think he's gone off and enjoyed himself for the settling,' Erika Rivers said. 'But he's a good boy. He was going to come home to look after his Pa.' Her words wavered. 'We went to the collection point, but he wasn't there.'

Tomi let this sink in. She imagined this elderly woman and wounded man hobbling up and down rows of bodies taken by the frost, searching for their boy.

Faeza's eyes were teary. 'Do you have any idea where he could be?'

'Last I saw him—' Tomi swallowed hard '—last I saw him was here, in the station. I don't know where he went after that.'

Both of them stared at her hopelessly.

'Why don't you wait for him at home, see if he shows up?' Tomi said. 'I'll send out some GOs to do a search.'

'Thank you.' Faeza sounded too grateful. Too fond. Tomi didn't deserve his good favour.

She reached gently towards his injured hand. 'That looks recent.'

He recoiled, and she knew at once what had happened.

Vittam.

She thought of her father, his throat and intestines scalded from the bleach. Of her mother, bound and shot in the forehead. She thought of how, if their killers had given Tomi the option, she would've set fire to her own threads to save them from the torture they'd endured.

No wonder Damian had willingly told Vittam everything. He'd had a choice between protecting his father and giving up a secret he didn't think was important. Of course he was going to choose his family.

Clemency help her, what had she done? She could've taken him to her place, sat him down and talked rationally about his debt. She could've just *asked*.

But instead she'd let him freeze to the brink of death then fired him from the one job that was keeping him safe from Vittam. What was wrong with her?

'I–' she started, her voice cracking.

'Any luck with the suspect?' Iloura headed down the stairs to join her.

Tomi turned away from Damian's family, realigning herself with her surroundings. Right – Veraminta and the stone.

'Um, maybe. I was going to make a call–'

'I'm sorry, Tomi, you'll have to get Officer Lorenze to do it. I've already given you more time than I should've.'

Tomi's stomach swooped. How could she have forgotten about her suspension?

'Drop your things on my desk. Officer Lorenze is waiting to be briefed.' Iloura's attention turned to Faeza and Erika.

'This is Damian's family,' Tomi said. 'Damian didn't get home last night. Will you take care of them?'

'The Tassela help us. How awful. He's already a rising star here in the station. Come with me; we'll see about getting a search team out.'

Tomi watched Iloura lead them back to the service counter. She thought of Vittam again. Had he found out that Damian had been caught? What if he'd decided Damian was no longer of use to him? What if Damian's body was frozen under the river?

Tomi headed up the stairwell to hide her growing panic from his family. She needed to get a grip. Dead men didn't pay debts. He had to be alive. And there had to be a way to find him. If only he had some kind of beacon or signal.

She gasped and pulled out her enchanted pendant, ran her thumb across the crystal. Zef might have a potion or spell to help. Witches were supposed to be able to do impossible things, right?

Lorenze was waiting when she reached the next level. He was perched on her desk, grinning. 'I hear you've got a juicy case for me, Cardozo. Can't wait to see the bonus on this one.'

She stalked to Iloura's office and set down her gun, dagger, cuffs and badge. What a senseless choice she'd made, trying to resign when she had the Trio on her side. They would've helped her solve these murders. No one else knew as much about what the killer could do than them.

Cursing, she withdrew the parillion gemstone and two keys from her inner pocket. She examined them in the glow of the boss's oil lanterns. Vittam was definitely connected, cutlass was involved, Notch was hiding something in his terminal.

His terminal.

May the Tassela damn it all. That's exactly where Damian had gone. And if he entered private property without the right permit, he would nullify any evidence he found.

She had to fetch him. Assuming he hadn't been caught by Notch already, she could bring him back before anyone realised they'd potentially ruined the case.

'Oi, Cardozo!' Lorenze called. 'The ledger says you've had evidence taken out. Pass it over.'

She glanced at the two keys in her palm. One of them was the key found in Jupel's apartment, an evidence tag looped through the hole. But Vittam's was technically unaccounted for. No one except Damian knew she had it.

A slow smile spread across her face.

'Just a moment,' she said. 'I'll be right with you.'

Thirty-Five

THERE WERE FOUR OTHER GROUSDU IN THE FERRY TERMINAL'S enclosure as Tomi led Finley inside. She eyed them, wondering who else was here. The terminal was supposed to be closed. And Talcott Notch would have a minnisk-drawn carriage, so none of them belonged to him.

Was one of them Brix? She didn't know Damian's grousdu well enough to recognise it, but the shabby saddle on the furthest one looked familiar.

Finley fluffed his new frost feathers and stalked inside to join the flock. He'd had his gizzard stones and eaten his worm paste, so he wasn't as cranky as before.

'Tomi.'

She almost jumped out of her threads as Zef stepped into the enclosure with his grousdu.

'What are you doing here?' she said, pressing a hand to her heart.

'You rubbed the ettyspar crystal.'

She'd forgotten about that.

'Sorry,' she said. 'I panicked. Damian's missing. I thought you'd be able to help me find him, but I suspect he's sneaked in here. I think that's his grousdu in the yellow grass.'

'Why did he sneak into a ferry terminal?'

'A key I found in Jupel's apartment opens a locker inside, but Notch kicked us out before we could check it.' She glanced in the direction of the terminal. 'I don't know how difficult it's going to be to get in. It's closed, and I'm technically not allowed onto the property without a permit.'

'You said the portmaster was involved in this.'

'I suspect so, yes.'

'Is he the killer?'

'I don't know.' Tomi eyed Zef. 'But you would know if you saw him, right? You could tell from his qoras.'

'You can't use that as evidence in court.'

'No, but it would certainly help.' She hesitated. 'As long as you're comfortable using magic?'

'I'm certainly not as paranoid as other witches in Radaza. And to be honest, I'd be glad for the excuse. I miss it.'

He stepped towards her. Her breath caught as his fingers touched her neck. He gently tugged out her chain and pressed the crystals together to return them to their original colour.

'I should stay with you,' he said. 'If the portmaster is a witch, you might need me.'

'Agreed.' Her voice was wobblier than she'd expected it to be.

Cold air filled the space between them as he moved away. She wondered whether she could tamp down the disappointment in her qoras so he wouldn't notice.

'How long has Damian been missing?' he said, without any indication that something had happened.

She tried to do the same. 'As far as I know, no one's seen him since I left him at the station last night. I don't know whether he came straight here – maybe he hid in the public ablution blocks or something so he would have free rein when the terminal closed. I just hope Notch didn't catch him snooping around.'

They passed through an above-ground corridor made of transparent crested crystal. Sunlight strained to break through – the frost had coated the roof and walls. It was thicker in some places, casting dappled shadows across the floor. When they turned the corner, they found guards standing at either side of the terminal entrance. That accounted for two of the four grousdu. If the third was Brix, who did the fourth belong to?

'We're closed,' one of the guards said.

'I represent the Justice Department. I need access to the terminal.'

'Your badge and access permit, please.'

She tugged her frost coat back to reveal her official tailcoat. 'I'm clearly a JO. Let me through.'

'The boss said no one comes in without a badge and access permit.'

There went that plan. She glanced at Zef, hoping he had something useful to contribute. He only shrugged. She had no choice but apologise to the guards and walk away.

'Is that all the help you can give me?' she asked when they were back in the grousdu enclosure. 'I thought you'd be more useful than that.'

He drew a khar feather out of his coat pocket.

'Oh, of course,' she said. 'Can you make me invisible too?'

'It takes a lot of concentration and energy.'

'But you can do it?'

His gaze remained on the feather as he twirled it in his fingers. 'I can.'

She waited.

There was a long pause before he said, 'You have to be close to me.'

She quashed the emotion trying to spark in her threads. 'I suppose that makes sense.'

But when she started towards him, he shook his head. 'Not yet. Like I said, it takes a lot of energy. We'll have to wait until we're at the corner before the entrance and move along the shadows.'

For some reason, the thought of prolonging it made her nervous. She didn't know why; they'd always been physically close when spending time together. Then again, last night had been... different. That moment between them seemed to have changed things.

She didn't like it. She wanted their relationship to go back to how they had been, when Zef was just a friend and she didn't second-guess every feeling.

They headed back through the corridor and stopped at the corner. There was a breath of hesitation before she stepped against him. He wrapped an arm around her waist. She realised she'd forgotten to ask what being invisible would feel like as he crushed the feather into his hand. She waited. Nothing seemed different. He guided her around the corner, following the shadows cast by the frost. Each step was slow and considered.

The guards stood in the same positions. Their attention didn't waver, their stance didn't change, even as Tomi and Zef passed right by them. Tomi held her breath and nestled closer against Zef's side, certain that at any moment the spell would stop working or the guards would sense the air shift.

Zef drew her into the terminal and against a wall where the guards couldn't see. He released Tomi and pressed a finger to his lips. He looked more drained than he had 20 steps ago.

Together, they stole towards the nearest ferry corridor and jumped the turnstile so they were out of sight.

'Now what?' Zef said quietly, returning the feather to his pocket.

'We need to make sure Notch isn't in his office. It's on the second floor and oversees the terminal. If we can use that invisibility spell to check...'

'I can't do that spell with you again. It takes too much out of me. But I can check myself.' He pulled a fresh khar feather out of his pocket.

'Do you have a whole bird in there?'

'I picked up a few when I felt the ettyspar crystal heat up. I wasn't sure what you needed me for.'

'Turns out, I need you for a lot.'

'Soon you're going to wonder how you ever survived without me. Wait here.' He folded the feather in his hand and vanished.

Tomi crept to the edge of the corridor and peeked at the open space of the terminal. Everything was so quiet. The customer service counter was empty; the turnstiles were still. All lanterns had been extinguished; the only light came from weak sun through the frosted windows.

There was no sign of Zef, which was a good thing. Hopefully, he wouldn't take long. It would be even better if he found Damian, dragged him back and they all got out of here without anyone noticing.

She leaned on the turnstile, trying to see the row of lockers. They were untouched, so at least Damian hadn't tried to break into them.

Any evidence found wouldn't count in court, but if she could just *check* before they left...

Her hand came away greasy. She wiped her face on a nearby rag hanging from the wall, just as a loud clank came from behind her. She spun around. Was that the ferry settling into the frosted river? Or was someone else here?

There was still that fourth grousdu unaccounted for.

'The office is empty.'

She gasped as Zef peeled out of the shadows. 'Don't do that.'

'Sorry.'

'At least you were quick.' She glanced at the lockers and pulled out the key from Jupel's apartment. 'I have a confession to make. I gave the wrong evidence to Jerry Lorenze.'

'Huh?'

'Never mind. Damian will appreciate it. Come on. If the office is empty, we can cross the floor without anyone seeing us.'

She led Zef to the lockers.

'The mysterious 82,' she said, turning the key. 'Let's finally see what's inside.'

She held her breath as she opened it, not sure whether the contents would horrify or thrill her.

'Empty,' she said in disbelief.

All this for nothing? What a complete waste of time.

Zef leaned away. 'It stinks.'

She sniffed and reeled back. There was a sour odour mingled with chemicals that reminded her of embalming fluid. 'This is what Veraminta said Jupel smelt like sometimes – curdled milk and urine. Does that mean this was his locker, after all? I thought it might've belonged to the killer.' She closed the door. 'It must've been a drop point for whatever he was smuggling.'

'It smells like animal organs that have been prepared for a potion.'

'What kind of potion?'

'There are too many to name.'

'But Jupel was smuggling stones, not organs.'

'I don't know about that, but it definitely smells like animal organs.'

Tomi massaged the bridge of her nose. 'We can figure it out later. Let's find Damian and get out of here. Split up? You check the ablution blocks and those two corridors, I'll take the other corridors.'

Before they could move, screams pierced the air. They instinctively ducked behind the lockers. The screams grew louder. Someone was coming. Tomi crept to the edge of the row and risked a glance.

Talcott Notch was striding through the terminal from the direction opposite the entrance. Following him was his purple-haired employee, Katterina Piers. She held what looked like a clay doll with a string around its wrist. With each tug of the string, the screams intensified. Behind them, arm out as if being dragged by an invisible force, was the screamer, poor little Ravern Furling.

'Dear oh dear,' Talcott Notch said, stopping in the middle of the terminal to turn to his captive. 'I'm afraid this is going to be rather unpleasant.'

Thirty-Six

'WE HAVE OUR WITCH,' TOMI WHISPERED, WATCHING KATTERINA wrap the string around the poppet's torso. She was using the binding spell Zef had mentioned – the same one that had been used on Tomi's mother. Poppet craft. 'Notch must've hired her to kill Jupel and Herliz.'

Ravern let out another scream. She struggled to free her arms. They seemed to be stuck to her sides.

Zef moved to see, but Tomi nudged him back. 'Stay down. I don't want to risk exposing you.'

'I won't let you get away with this,' Ravern said to Notch through ragged gasps. 'I know what you've done.'

'Yes, it seems you do. Who else did you tell?'

Ravern didn't answer, still wrenching to free herself.

'Katterina,' Notch said.

Katterina tugged at the poppet, and Ravern fell, landing hard on her rear end.

Notch leaned down so he and Ravern were face to face. 'Perhaps I have to talk into your good ear. *Who else did you tell?*'

Ravern spat on him.

He recoiled. As he took out a handkerchief to wipe off the mess, Katterina pulled on a pair of gloves and withdrew a pouch from her pocket.

226

'Who else did you tell?' he said a third time as Katterina sprinkled the contents of the powder over Ravern.

Ravern's screams started again.

Tomi moved to help, but Zef gripped her. 'No. I know you can hold your own but not against a witch.'

'Then tell me you have something besides feathers in your pocket. A potion, a gun, that itching powder you used on Vittam's men in the alley.'

'I have moulash powder.'

'What does that do?'

'It can start a fire, but the flames burn different colours. They'll know it's magic.'

'That could work in our favour.' Tomi crawled to the other end of the lockers to see the passage leading to the grousdu enclosure. The guards were still stationed by the entrance. They kept their backs to the terminal, apparently determined not to witness what was happening inside. 'Open the enclosure and set fire to the grass. That'll cause enough of a distraction. Meet me with Finley outside the frost doors.'

'They'd be locked for the season.'

'I should be able to open them from the inside.'

'Are you sure–' Zef started, but cut off when Ravern's screams turned into an agonised wail. He grimaced and took out another feather. Tomi waited until he'd disappeared before crawling back to see what was happening.

'You,' Ravern said, chest heaving, 'are a monster. We're going to stop you.'

'And who is "we"?'

Tomi sat back on her heels. By the Tassela, Ravern hadn't roped Damian into this, had she? They seemed to be friends, and if Ravern were going to trust someone with snooping around Notch's property, it would be an attending officer.

Tomi willed Zef to move fast. If Ravern gave up Damian's name, who knew what Notch would do?

She winced as Ravern screamed again. This was unbearable. How difficult would it be to fight a witch, really? She couldn't sit here doing nothing for much longer.

'All right,' Ravern said, gasping. 'Stop, stop! It's the *Kari Shakari*.'

Tomi didn't recognise the name, but Notch's lip curled. 'Nice try. They're long gone.'

'No.' Ravern wriggled back as Katterina dug into her pouch for more powder. 'No, they'll always be around. They'll stop you. They'll–'

'*Seno* Notch!' One of the guards ran in. 'Fire – a witch's fire, in the grousdu enclosure!'

Notch swore. He and Katterina raced into the passage with the guard. The moment they were out of sight, Tomi sprinted to Ravern.

'What?' Ravern said, snivelling. Her skin was bubbling, just like Park Herliz's corpse had.

Tomi hauled her to her feet. 'I don't know how to undo–'

Ravern's arms fell free before Tomi could finish the sentence. Maybe the poppet had to be a certain distance for a binding spell? It didn't matter; she could ask Zef later.

'Frost doors, come on.'

She and Ravern ran.

'They're deadbolted,' Tomi said as she tugged at them. 'Ravern, where's the key?'

Ravern was shivering violently. She stared towards the passage to the grousdu enclosure where Notch had gone.

'Ravern! The key!'

'Oh – the customer service desk.'

Tomi raced to the counter and found a keychain hanging behind it. It was a large loop with at least 10 big metal keys. They would have to fumble around to find the one that opened the door.

She'd almost reached Ravern again when the key from Jupel's apartment slipped from her grasp. She skidded to a halt as it clinked on the tiles. A memory flashed through her of a similar sound. The crime scene, Damian nervous and keen to make a good impression, the key slipping between their fingers...

Tink.

Tink.

Tink.

She spun to scoop it up. As she straightened, she noticed Ravern was still staring at the passage to the grousdu enclosure. She hadn't turned at the sound. She might not have heard it, being partially deaf.

Tomi took a step, then stopped again.

Ravern hadn't turned at the sound.

She hadn't turned at the sound.

The big keychain fell out of Tomi's hand. This time, the clatter was enough to catch Ravern's attention. 'Officer Cardozo?'

Tomi's mind worked overtime. She stared at her palm, recalling the greasy smear from the turnstile. Gearwheels were clicking into place before she could properly understand what they meant.

The connection to Nomik. The empty locker. The menagerie.

And the stone.

Of course.

Of course.

'Bless'd shit, Ravern,' she said, voice strained. 'The killer isn't Katterina. It's you.'

Thirty-Seven

'No.' Ravern ran for the keychain. Tomi stamped her boot on it before Ravern reached her. 'No!'

'You dropped the key in Jupel's apartment,' Tomi said. 'But you didn't hear it clink on the stone floor.'

Ravern glanced desperately at the passageway to the grousdu enclosure. 'We have to go. Notch will be back–'

'Notch isn't my problem right now. Ravern, you left salitenine grease on the handle of the murder weapon. That comes from the rags you use to wipe down the turnstiles.'

'Wait–'

'Ivan Jupel wasn't smuggling gemstones. Or animal organs – not exactly. It was gizzard stones. The stones in the pouch were too big for an ordinary bird, but a volfe? The creature who's poached to near extinction in the wild? They'd have a gizzard stone that size. You would've known that. You used to work at the menagerie. You were my damn witness against Nomik Whimsy, proving he would sneak away from the island at night to go to the gambling dens.'

'But I–'

'You knew Nomik was in debt. You told Bunter Vittam to use him to get the halicort horn shavings from the menagerie.'

230

'I–'

'You're a witch, aren't you?'

'Please!' Ravern said. 'Notch will kill me. I thought it was safe. I thought Katterina had gone home for the season. There's so much more that you don't understand. We have to get out of here.'

'Yes, we do. I'm taking you straight to the station.'

'You can't!'

'Watch me.' Tomi had surrendered her handcuffs and weapons, but she was perfectly capable of taking down a woman half her size. She kicked the keychain across the floor and started forward.

Ravern backed against the frost doors, blistered hands raised. 'Wait, wait – what about Damian?'

Tomi paused. 'What about him?'

'He's here. Don't you want to get him out?'

'Where?'

'I'll show you.' Ravern's breaths were choppy. She kept glancing towards the passage to the grousdu enclosure. Smoke was drifting out.

This could very well be a trap, but Tomi couldn't leave if Damian was still here. She stepped back to let Ravern pass, certain she could run her down if she tried to escape. 'Show me.'

Ravern edged around Tomi, then started for the same corridor Tomi and Zef had first hidden in. Tomi thought of the clanking sound she'd heard and wondered whether it had been Damian.

'Take me through what happened with Jupel,' Tomi said as they jumped the turnstile. 'What made you go to his apartment that night?'

'I could smell the stone on him,' Ravern said. 'The second-last day of every month, he'd catch the ferry from the University, and he would stink of it. I didn't know for sure that it was a volfe stone, but I had my suspicions he was up to something terrible. I wanted to check. I planned to break into his apartment the night before his next due appearance to see whether I could find what he was carrying.'

'Why did you get Bunter Vittam involved? He's the most dangerous person in the city.'

'Exactly. He deserved to be terrorised. Nomik would've recognised my voice, and I'm not afraid of Vittam. I've come up against much scarier people before.' Ravern glanced over her shoulder, looking past Tomi. There was still no sound from Notch or Katterina.

'What did Nomik have to do with it, though?' Tomi said.

'He's a selfish brat. Years ago, he was in so much debt he started stealing from his grandmother. And do you know what he did? He blamed *me*. I kept his gambling habit a secret, and he got me fired from the menagerie. I wanted to return the favour. When Jupel woke up the next morning, knowing Nomik had sedated him with a potion, I knew he'd expel him.'

'But Jupel never woke up, Ravern. You killed him.'

They reached the second turnstile. The frost doors were closed. The entire ferry was encased in a container of coruscat glass, impossible to see through from the outside.

'That wasn't the plan,' Ravern said. 'I only wanted to search his apartment. But then I found it – I found the stone in a pouch in his work satchel. I lost my head. He lived in his fancy apartment, without a care for anyone or anything else, and I just–' angry tears filled her eyes '–I stabbed him while he lay sleeping, and I pulled out his guts, and I screamed into his face *how does it feel?* because he was a monster. A *monster*, Tomi. Those poor, beautiful creatures are getting slaughtered every month.'

She pushed open the doors to the ferry container. Tomi staggered back from the heat. The interior was filled with clouds of steam. Water dripped from the coruscat glass, the ferry, the jetty railing. Even the frozen river was sweating. Steam billowed from the ferry's funnel. It was the biggest ferry in the terminal, the only one designed to go out to sea, all the way south to Deep Water Bay.

'What is this?' Tomi said, gasping in the humidity.

'I ran the engine fire to keep the dock warm. Damian didn't have a frost coat, and I didn't want him to freeze to death.'

'Why is he in here in the first place?'

'He came to me last night, asking for my help to get into the terminal. He wanted to look in Jupel's locker and snoop around Notch's office. I had to trap him in here to keep him safe while I dealt with Notch myself.'

Tomi glanced at the giant paddle wheel at the back of the boat. 'That wheel can't move in the frost. You're going to explode the boiler if you keep the engine running.'

'Don't worry, I used moulash powder. It's magic.' Ravern sounded unconcerned as she headed down the jetty.

Tomi was less sure. She didn't understand magic, but she understood the basics of machinery.

'You shouldn't have given away that you were a witch,' she said. 'Why would you turn Jupel's blood into powder?'

'Like I said, I lost my head. When his blood got all over me, I panicked and whipped up a quick potion with ingredients from his kitchen. It didn't work properly, though. It was supposed to turn to water, but it turned to dust. It was the best I could do with what I had.'

'What about what you did to Park Herliz?'

'I realised Jupel was getting the stone from his neighbour working at Eversea Shipping. I followed the neighbour and found out his grandfather was doing all the smuggling. I tried to make Park Herliz talk.'

'By taking his eyes and tongue?'

'I had to. He wasn't giving me the information I needed, so I used them for a spell to tell me who he was working with. He was part of a group, years ago, that sold cutlass. Him and Talcott Notch. I couldn't go after Notch because Katterina's been acting as his bodyguard. I thought she'd gone home for the season. I thought now was the time to attack.'

'Notch is involved in cutlass?'

'It was his and Park Herliz's job to bring in rare ingredients needed to make the brew. They worked for – Have you heard of Oclavida?'

'Yes,' Tomi said warily. 'He's back?'

'Not back. Reborn. We took the last one down. Someone else must've inherited the name.'

'You took the last one *down*?'

'What do you expect? ISEF doesn't know how to handle cutlass – it's a potion. And people were dying. A few witches banded together to stop the manufacturers. They called themselves *Kari Shakari*. I was only a teenager; I helped where I could. It took us years to figure out who was involved, to infiltrate their business, to finish them. We saved Radaza, at least, we thought we had. I had no idea ghost was back on the streets until I found the stone. A volfe stone is used to make the brew,' she added miserably. 'Only the most depraved, malicious potions can be made by defiling a creature like the volfe.'

Tomi couldn't believe it. Ravern was the key to everything. She knew about cutlass, she knew the people manufacturing and distributing it, she knew how to stop them. Commander Parsons wouldn't have anything to say once she heard Ravern's confession.

Ravern needed to be protected. They had to get out of this terminal, now.

'Where's Damian?'

Ravern hesitated.

Dread crept through Tomi. 'Ravern,' she said slowly. 'Where's Damian?'

'Here's the thing,' Ravern said, and it occurred to Tomi, too late, that if Ravern had come here to kill Talcott Notch, she was prepared for a fight.

Tomi rubbed her enchanted pendant through her blouse as Ravern yanked a brass button from her coat and threw it on the jetty by Tomi's feet. There was a *crack* and a blinding flash. Tomi flew backwards from the force of the explosion. She landed hard on the wet boards, stared dazedly up at the coruscat ceiling.

'Ravern,' she croaked. Her throat hurt from the smoke of the mini bomb.

'I'm sorry.' Ravern stood over her with Katterina's clay poppet in her hand.

'How?'

'This is mine,' Ravern said. 'It can't stray far from me.' She plucked a hair from Tomi's head and pressed it into the clay. 'They used my spells and potions against me. Their mistake.'

Tomi kicked out, but Ravern jumped back.

'I have a family,' Ravern continued. 'A son, a mother, a brother, an aunt. If you bring me in, TADOW will kill them.'

'No.'

'No? You think TADOW exile witches? Try again. They take us to the border and shoot us dead.'

Tomi staggered to her feet. 'That's not true.'

'Don't be so naïve. You've worked with them before. You must've seen the way they hunt us like they're hungry for blood.'

Tomi swallowed, trying to wet her parched throat. Ravern was lying to save herself, she had to be.

And yet, it wasn't a stretch to believe what she was saying. Tomi thought of the TADOW officers she'd dealt with in the past, of their reputation, of how gleeful they were in their violence.

'I know I killed people.' Pain leaked through Ravern's voice. 'I know I deserve punishment. But if you take me in, my family will suffer too.' She pulled out a piece of string. 'I have to protect them.'

Tomi lurched forward, but Ravern wrapped the string around the clay doll, pinning its arms. Something pressed against Tomi's skin in the identical place. She strained to move and found she couldn't. It was like she was bound with wire.

'Ravern, wait!'

Ravern tossed the doll up. Tomi jerked as she was thrown over the jetty railing. There was a heart-stopping moment when she was falling, then she swung upwards as an invisible rope stopped her descent. She was lowered gently to the frozen river next to the ferry's paddle wheel. Her arms came free as she fell to her knees.

'Tomi?'

She spun around. 'Damian?'

There he was, on the ice under the wheel. He crawled to her, slipping and sliding. His curls hung low, heavy with moisture. One side of his body was covered in blood. He had a gash through his shirt, across his ribs.

'What happened?'

'She stabbed me with my own dagger,' Damian said. 'She tried to stitch me up, but I don't think sewing is one of her strong points.'

'I'm sorry.' Ravern leaned against the railing to call down to them. 'I have to take down Notch now, while I have the chance.'

Tomi climbed to her feet. She used the lowest spoke from the paddle wheel for support. 'Stop this, Ravern. I promise I won't tell TADOW about you or your family, but the Justice Department can take over the cutlass case now.'

'I don't trust them. Witches are the only ones who can find the new Oclavida. I should know – it took the *Kari Shakari* so long to take down the Glisks.'

Tomi's heart slammed to a stop.

'The Glisks?'

Her voice didn't reach above a whisper. She gathered her breath and forced the words out again, louder.

'What do the Glisks have to do with it? Ravern!'

But Ravern's attention was elsewhere. 'What are you doing here?' she asked.

Someone was at the entrance of the dock, out of Tomi's view. A shot echoed across the steamy space. There was an awful thud before blood dripped between the boards of the jetty, landing on the ice in red rivulets.

'Ravern!' Tomi shouted.

The boat shed door slammed closed.

Tomi stumbled forward, but as she moved, there was an ominous cracking noise. She stared down as thin lines webbed across the ice beneath her boots.

'Oh,' she said. 'Shit.'

Thirty-Eight

TOMI PULLED OFF HER FROST COAT. SHE WAS SOAKED IN SWEAT. The jetty and the paddle wheel were at least four times higher than her. It wasn't an easy climb, but it wouldn't be impossible.

'We have to climb up the wheel,' she said.

Damian, on his knees, clutched his injury as he stared at her in disbelief.

'I know.' She held a hand out for him. 'You're going to have to deal with some pain.'

He winced as he reached towards her. Another, louder cracking noise echoed through the dock. The paddle wheel shifted slightly.

'I knew it,' Tomi said grimly. 'Magic isn't going to make a difference here. Either that wheel is going to break the ice, or the boiler is going to explode.' She put tentative pressure on the nearest spoke. It seemed to hold. For now. 'We need to move.'

She grabbed Damian beneath the arms and hauled him to his feet. He choked in pain. More cracks skittered across the ice.

'Come on, fight through it.' She positioned his hands on the wheel, then used her strength to help as he strained to pull himself to the top of the lowest spoke. It took a long time for him to finally get there. Too long. The spokes dripped with condensation.

She climbed up after him. The wheel felt precarious; as soon as the ice was weak enough, they were going to plunge into the river.

Damian clung to the edge of the spoke, panting. Blood dripped down his side. He must've torn his stitches.

Tomi wrenched him to his feet again. 'You shouldn't have come here.'

'I'm sorry. I thought if I found evidence to prove Talcott Notch was involved, you'd take me back.'

'Your plan involved informing a civilian about our active case. A civilian, I might add, who ended up being the killer.'

He wavered, his eyes fully closing. 'At least I'll die here. It's better than getting a reprimand from the Justice Department.'

'Oh, no you don't. I'm going to save you so I can reprimand you myself.'

Tomi grabbed him around the waist to lift him to the next spoke. The wheel shifted. She almost lost her balance, jolting against Damian. He cried out. She winced as she imagined how she must be ripping at his wound.

'Sorry!'

He hung where he was. His breaths were wheezes. She released him to hold the next spoke. It was just in time – the wheel dropped again.

Tomi swore loudly.

'We have to go, Damian. Forget the pain. You can worry about bleeding and dying when we're back on the jetty. Move it, move it.'

She swung onto the next spoke and helped pull him up. His face twisted in agony. Beneath him, the ice began to crack into separate sheets.

Tomi sucked in the heavy, hot air. 'Come on, Damian.' Emotion clogged her voice. 'You can't die here. I refuse to be the only JO who gets her apprentice killed.'

He didn't answer. There was no blood flush to his cheeks. Most of his blood was dripping down the spokes onto the ice.

She wrenched him to his feet for the third climb. 'Two more to go.'

He reached for the next spoke, wavered and almost toppled.

'No!'

Tomi grabbed the back of his shirt to keep him from falling. His eyes were half closed. She choked down a scream of frustration.

'Wake up, you useless soff!'

She bent down, wrapped her arms around his legs and heaved him to the next spoke. He pulled himself forward with excruciating slowness. Then she swung up and did the same thing for the top spoke. The ferry shuddered as they both made it to the peak of the wheel.

'I'm sorry,' Damian murmured. 'You're right. I should've just left it alone.'

Tomi's groan turned into a pained laugh. 'You want to know why I accepted your application?'

'Huh?'

'Your mentorship application. The reason I accepted you was because you were the first cadet who came with a warning.'

He opened his eyes to give her a puzzled look.

'Your training officer told me not to pick you, even though you were one of the top graduates. He said you took risks, you were a rule-breaker, you made unconventional decisions – and you claimed every reckless act was because you knew it was the right thing to do. The only time I'd properly broken the rules was 10 years ago, when I let a witch walk away. I'm paying for that mistake over and over, and yet no matter what I tell myself, I've never been able to shake the feeling that I made the right choice. I accepted your application, Damian, because I want to be more like you.'

The confession earned her a small smile before his eyes drifted closed again.

'So no,' she said desperately, 'you *cannot* give up.'

The wheel started to turn. She glanced down. Turquoise water from the river spilled over the ice sheets.

'Move. Move, Damian!'

Damian leaned heavily against her as she lurched along the spoke towards the jetty. The spoke was getting lower with each step.

'We need to jump. It's not far. But we need to do it now.'

He moaned.

'You can do this.' She unhooked his arm from her so he could use both hands to catch the jetty. When she was sure he was conscious enough to take the jump, she said, 'One, two, three!'

The wheel shuddered downwards as together they flew forward, catching the edge of the jetty. Tomi hauled herself up, but Damian had no strength to climb. She turned to pull him.

His fingers, slick with blood and water, slipped.

She cried out and grabbed his arms. He dangled beneath the jetty, semi-conscious. The paddle wheel was turning. Ice cracked. Water gushed below.

'Clemency help me.' She couldn't get a grip on him. He was sliding through her hands. 'Damian. Damian!'

She was sliding too. He was heavy and the jetty was slimy. She tried to latch her knee against the railing post. It wasn't enough. She felt the moment her body reached the tipping point.

She was going over.

She stared down at the cold water, resigned to her fate.

Someone strong snatched her waist in the last breath and hauled her backwards. Just as she lost her grip on Damian, the hands released her and caught him instead, wrenched him up. She rolled over to see their saviour.

Zef.

May the Tassela bless his every thread.

Her head flopped back on the jetty as she fought to catch her breath.

'Took you... long enough,' she said.

'You're welcome?'

She had no energy to do anything but reach out and pat his knee.

Damian groaned. He was slipping in and out of consciousness.

'We need to get him to a hospital,' Tomi said.

She rolled over to find Ravern lying further away, a ragged hole through her throat. Her eyes were frozen open in surprise.

There would be no hospital for Ravern. Only a morgue dais and a funeral pyre.

The information about cutlass, the smuggling, the group who took down Oclavida last time... it was all lost.

And the Glisks. Tomi would never find out what Ravern had been saying about her parents.

She had an inkling, though. A terrible, unspeakable suspicion.

And for the first time in her life, she wondered if maybe the truth about her parents' murder wouldn't bring her the peace she craved after all.

Thirty-Nine

DAMIAN DIDN'T KNOW WHAT TO SAY WHEN TOMI WALKED INTO the hospital room. She crossed the floor, passing rows of beds before reaching his at the end. Though she was dressed in an elegant red coat, with her hair pinned in its usual perfect style, she looked exhausted.

'You're here,' Damian said when she reached the foot of his bed. He couldn't hide his surprise. He thought he'd never see her again.

Was she visiting to yell at him?

Or was she going to arrest him? She had reason to. He'd lied on his academy admission form. He'd given confidential information to Vittam. He'd told Ravern details about the case when she was the Tassela-damned killer.

'How are you feeling?' Tomi said.

Damian's chest gave a throb, as if reminding him of the gash. 'The pain easers help.'

Her gaze flicked to Pa, who was sitting beside him. 'May we have a moment?'

'Of course,' Pa said. 'I'll find out when Damian will be discharged.'

Tomi smiled at Pa as he passed.

That had to be a good sign, right? She wouldn't be smiling at his father if she were planning to arrest him.

'So how are you really feeling?' she said, taking the chair Pa had just vacated. Something jingled in her coat as she settled.

'Running like a river.'

'It's time to stop lying, Damian.'

He met her steady, unimpressed gaze. Then he said, 'I hurt. I hurt all over. My side feels like it's burning, but my bones are cold. Can the frost get into your bones? Because I think the frost got into my bones.'

She patted his arm.

'I can't believe how much I screwed up,' he said. 'Between lying to you about Vittam and letting the killer in on the case, I deserve to be fired. Into the sun, probably.' He scrunched his face. 'And there's this awful taste in my–'

'That's enough now.'

'Sorry.' He hesitated. 'So what happened?'

'Ravern's dead. I'm not sure who killed her, but I could guess. She knew too much about cutlass. About Talcott Notch.'

'Can you bring him in?'

'No. We trespassed on his property, which already looks bad for us. Plus, I'm suspended, so I wasn't supposed to be investigating the case anyway.' She let out a sigh. 'And the councillors have provided Notch with an alibi. According to reports, Talcott Notch and his assistant Katterina were at her house all day yesterday.'

'But that's a lie. He was in the terminal.'

'Yes.'

'The councillors *lied*?'

'At least one of them did, yes.'

'Can they do that?'

'Apparently. Iloura told me to keep my head down and be glad we're not in more trouble. My story was already sketchy, considering what happened. I had to say we chased Ravern into the terminal after she confessed to you.'

Damian's memory of the entire incident was blurry. Mostly, he remembered going to the terminal with Ravern, getting thrown back by an exploding button, taking out his dagger to protect himself, then being stabbed in the side. Ravern had sedated him during the night – he'd woken up on the ice beneath the ferry with a poor stitch job on his wound.

She had claimed the ice would slow the bleeding, that he would be safe there until she sorted things out. She must've had a plan when it came to Notch, but when it came to Damian, she'd clearly panicked and made poor decisions.

'The stone we were looking for was a gizzard stone,' Tomi continued. 'TADOW found it after they searched Ravern's apartment yesterday afternoon. I've talked to Shiver Whimsy and Border Control – they'll be able to inform the people enforcing the Volfe Protection Act in Elumina about the smuggling.'

'Wait, a *volfe* gizzard stone?' Damian thought of the beautiful animals swooping and soaring above him in the menagerie. 'Who would kill a volfe?'

'Someone who cares more about coin than the cleanliness of their threads. I've put forward a report explaining how it's used in cutlass, but I don't know whether anyone will do anything about it. Considering the only proof I have is what Ravern told me, they're probably going to disregard it. They're desperate to find any reason to ignore the fact cutlass is back.'

'But people will die. We need to put a team together, bring Notch down, find who's behind the manufacturing, the distributing–'

'I know, Damian. Don't worry about it for now.'

He turned his gaze towards the ceiling, which was painted with the constellations. 'Ravern was trying to do all that.'

'I know.'

'She was chasing something bigger than her.'

'I know, Damian.'

He blinked rapidly. Back when he was Vittam's runner and his life was a waking nightmare, Ravern was one of the few people he could rely on. Yes, she'd betrayed and attacked him, but she'd stitched him up, too. She'd tried to make things right. If anyone knew how hard it was to make things right, it was him.

'You told TADOW about her,' he said quietly.

'Yes.'

'On the river... you promised you weren't going to.'

'She was dead. And she was our killer. There was no story I could've come up with to explain everything.'

'She had a family.'

There was a pause before Tomi answered. 'Yes.'

'Ravern told me TADOW kill witches at the border.'

'It might not be true.'

'And what if it is?'

Tomi sank her face in her hands.

'Tomi,' Damian said. 'What if they kill her family?'

'They won't.'

'How can you–'

'TADOW couldn't find anyone in Ravern's bloodline.' Tomi lifted her face. 'Someone must've tipped them off early; they'd cleared out before authorities arrived.'

'Who–'

Tomi.

Tomi had tipped them off.

She'd narrowly avoided losing her job only yesterday because she'd let a witch go. Now she'd helped more escape.

She met Damian's gaze, as if daring him to accuse her.

'Huh,' he said casually. 'Terrible shame.' He shrugged. 'So did you find out about the bones and teeth being shipped from Eversea? Where were they going, and why? Are they part of cutlass too?'

Her entire body seemed to relax. She sank more comfortably into the chair and said, 'No, they're for a different potion. We'll talk about it when you get come back to work.'

Damian moved to sit up, but his injuries objected angrily. 'Back to work?'

'I didn't tell Iloura about your debt, and from now on, it won't be a problem anyway.'

'Why not?'

She dug into her coat pocket and withdrew a bulging pouch. It jangled as she dropped it onto the mattress beside him. 'This is just a representation. I didn't want to walk around with 720 pieces of gold.'

Damian opened his mouth. Nothing came out.

'You're going to use my coin to pay your debt,' Tomi said. 'Your contract with Vittam will be over. You owe him nothing, and he's not allowed to do anything about it.'

She couldn't be serious. Who had 720 gold pieces to throw about?

'I can't–'

She held up a hand to stop him. 'This coin doesn't come for free. You need to give me something in exchange.'

He eyed her warily. What could he possibly offer Tomi Cardozo?

'You worked as his runner, right?' Tomi said. 'I want you to give me everything you know about those days. Who you sent messages to, where all his secret drop points are, what routes you took. I want to know who else is in Vittam's pocket.'

Damian swallowed. He wasn't lying about the taste in his mouth. The back of his throat was bitter from the many elixirs the medica mavens had given him. And maybe they were making his head muddled, because he was fairly certain Tomi Cardozo was giving him coin to incriminate Bunter Vittam.

'I think,' he croaked, 'I think you need to be careful of Zeffir. He knew about me, and the only way he could've is if he works for Vittam.'

'That's not the only way. Don't worry. I'll explain later.' She patted his knee over the blanket. 'Zef's on our side. With his help, we're going to take Bunter Vittam down.'

Damian's chest loosened. He hadn't realised how tight it had been for the past seven years. It was as if an iron band around his lungs had fallen off.

An intergenerational debt wiped clean. The monster gone from his door. He might've suspected magic if he didn't know any better.

'Tomi?' he whispered. 'Are you a Tassela in disguise?'

'No, Damian. I'm just your mentor.'

Then she politely averted her eyes, which was probably good, because no mentor needed to see their apprentice crying.

Forty

TOMI LEFT FINLEY IN HIS ENCLOSURE, GRABBED HER OVERFLOWING mail from the atrium's letterbox – she always forgot to check it while on an active case – then turned for her apartment. She needed to sleep until at least the half moon.

'Where are you off to so quickly? We've been waiting for hours.'

Mia, Payana and Zef were in the communal dining area among her neighbours. They were partaking in the supper that had been cooked by the oldies, which Tomi knew from experience to be all mush and no flavour. Not that she could complain. She was never around to help with the cooking. She contributed to the group meals by providing more coin than anyone else – her bonuses for solving cases were a great cover for her true wealth. Even after giving Damian enough jingle to purchase a home in the Shores, she still had access to more than she would ever be able to use. Her *ama sector* had seen to that, having arranged a vault for Tomi before disappearing forever along with the rest of Tomi's family.

Payana scooped a bowl's serve from the large pot on the fire and brought it over. Zef and Mia followed.

'How's Damian?' Mia said.

'Looking better than he did at the ferry terminal, thank the Tassela.' The four of them started up the curving balcony. 'I think he'll be out of action until my suspension is lifted, though.'

'How will you survive not working for a whole season?' Mia said.

'I'll still be working. I'll use the time to gather information on cutlass. With Zef's help, of course.'

'I don't think you should get Zef involved,' Payana said.

'I want to be involved,' Zef said.

Tomi smiled. 'Good, because I can't do it without you. If your theory is right about what cutlass does to qoras, you're the only one who can see whether someone's using it. We should start at that Weavers' sanctuary, find a recovering addict who'll give us information on their dealer.'

'Not with Notch?' Mia said.

'With a city councillor on his side, Notch is untouchable. And I've sort of been given an official warning not to go near him again. It's fine; I'll figure out another way to take him down.'

Zef, Payana and Mia exchanged glances.

'What?' Tomi said.

'There's something we want to discuss with you,' Payana said. 'But let's wait until we get inside.'

'That sounds ominous.'

'It's not,' Mia assured her as they continued up the spiral. She smiled at a mural. 'I love this place. Are you going to miss it when you move to Brackenlong Manor?'

'No,' Tomi said. 'Because I'm not moving.'

'What?'

'I'm sorry, Mia. I know how hard you fought to get it for me. But it hurts to be there. I don't think it's the best place for me.'

'You're just going to let it fall to ruin?' Payana said.

'I never said that.' Tomi smirked. 'Bunter Vittam thinks he's hurt me by ruining Bleakhouse, but in reality he's given us a beautiful opportunity. When the frost thaws, I'll have Brackenlong cleaned out, and my sister and all the other residents will move there. That way, they won't be out in the middle of the sea, they won't have to pay exorbitant fees for upkeep *and* relatives can visit them during the frost.'

'That's a brilliant idea,' Mia said. 'I heartily approve.'

'I'll close the study, though. No one, especially my sister, needs to go into that room again.'

'And you'll have to let us cleanse the place,' Mia said. 'It has the worst energies.'

Tomi glanced at her sideways. She didn't know much about how witches used and harnessed energy, yet it was in her blood. Just because she didn't have the magic thread, didn't mean she had to be ignorant. She would have to ask how it worked. Not today. But one day.

They reached Tomi's apartment. Home carried the comforting fragrance of floral candles and oil-soaked reeds. For the first time, she wondered whether her penchant for house plants and candles came from her parents.

She tossed her mail on the low lounge table and settled cross-legged on her couch with her bowl of soup. 'All right. Out with it.'

Zef closed the door. He and Payana sat down. Mia tried to, but she jumped right up again and clasped her hands. 'I'm sorry. I'm too excited.'

'Is this supposed to be exciting?' Tomi said. Both Zef and Payana looked too solemn for her to believe it.

'Yes,' Mia said firmly. 'I've been wanting to involve you in this for years. I think it's going to be good for us. Good for the city.'

Now Tomi was *really* nervous. She put her bowl on the table.

'We have a proposition for you,' Zef said. 'And you're allowed to say no.'

Mia said, 'She's not going to say no.'

'She might.' Zef watched Tomi closely, and she found herself instantly defensive against his scrutiny. Would she ever be used to knowing he could read her every thought and emotion?

'We understand why you considered quitting your job,' Payana said. 'We know it must be difficult for you to hide our identities while still calling yourself a justice official. And–' she struggled to continue '–and we truly appreciate you protecting us.'

Tomi squirmed. She didn't like to think about it. Picking and choosing what laws to follow still felt wrong. Like an abuse of power.

Mia spoke up. 'The problem is, witches need help: Justice Department help. We know things, but we can't go to the authorities about it. Especially if what Ravern told you about TADOW is true.' She shuddered. 'I knew I should be scared of them, but not *that* scared.'

'Unfortunately, if we can't go to the authorities, you end up with groups like this *Kari Shakari* you mentioned,' Zef said. 'Or someone like Ravern, running around trying to take on criminal organisations on their own.'

'Ravern is a perfect example of how messy things get if untrained witches take the law into their own hands,' Payana said.

Tomi had a flash of her parents. Her father bleeding on the floor. Her mother slumped in her chair.

Had that been the result of witches taking the law into their own hands?

'We want someone on the inside to represent us,' Mia said. 'Someone witches can go to if they have information on cutlass. We'll spread the word, let them know you can be trus–'

'Wait.' The word came out panicked and breathy. Tomi's heartstep was at a sprint. 'You're asking me to go directly against Radazan law here.'

'You're already doing that,' Mia said, gesturing to the three of them. 'And you did it for Ravern's family, too.'

'Standing for the law isn't always the same thing as standing for justice,' Zef said.

Payana squeezed Tomi's hand. 'I was angry at first that we told you the truth. But I think we need you. I think a lot of people need you.'

Don't give up your position, Tomi. I need you on this.

Iloura had asked Tomi to stay on as a justice official because she suspected an internal cover-up. The Radazan commander was possibly involved with Bunter Vittam. A *city councillor* was providing cover for Talcott Notch's dirty secrets. Then there was cutlass, the smuggling of volfe stones, Ravern's murder, the shadowy figure known as Oclavida... and her parents, who might've been involved in this mess all along.

She needed answers. If she could find out more about *Kari Shakari*, she might be able to learn what Ravern had been about to reveal. And the only way she was going to do that was by staying in the Justice Department and working with witches.

'Maybe,' she said slowly. 'Maybe I could do *some* things. I suppose I'd at least be willing to look the other way when witches approach me with information.'

Mia gave a delighted giggle. 'I told you she wouldn't say no!'

It was still a terrifying idea. If Tomi got caught, she'd be caged for life.

She picked up her mail and flicked through it restlessly, trying not to let panic overwhelm her. Wasn't this why she'd taken on Damian? To learn how to listen to her threads when they were telling her to do the right thing? She had to at least give it a try. Especially if TADOW were actually killing witches.

Her careless sorting paused when she found an unstamped letter in the pile. It had no address, simply the letters *MG* written on the front.

'What's wrong?' Zef said.

She stared, unable to believe what she was seeing. It had to be a mistake.

'Tomi,' Mia said. 'What is it?'

'"MG",' she said. Her hand shook as she showed the Trio. 'Maribelle Glisk.'

Her real name.

'Clemency help us,' Payana whispered.

With shaking fingers, Tomi opened the wax seal. Had Bunter Vittam discovered her real identity? Was it her parents' killers, closing in at last?

A familiar scent touched her nostrils. Her eyes blurred as she tried to read the message. She drew a deep breath and forced her panic down. The jumbled words slowly rearranged themselves into letters she understood.

Stay away from the case. Your life depends on it.

The bile rose, unbidden, in her throat. The letter smelled of bitter pinjora.

And at the top, an insignia on the parchment – the face of a raizelet beneath an arched motto: *Lussisco Harldah Buhkasa.*

Light Flares Eternal.

Acknowledgements

Firstly, I want to give a huge thank you to Lindy Cameron, who read this book and said YES! I'm so proud of this story and this world, and I'm incredibly grateful that you've given it a chance to see the light of day.

Thank you to Narrelle Harris and Atlin Merrick. This book wouldn't have landed in Lindy's inbox without you.

Thank you to Jason Nahrung for your thoughtful and comprehensive line edits.

Thank you to Dimi Stathopoulos for the beautiful book layout.

Thank you to Beauregard C. Furu for proofreading and saying such nice things about the book.

Thank you to Willsin Rowe for that gorgeous cover. It's exactly how I dreamed it would be.

Massive shout out to my beta reader Marissa Meyer, who sent me a very gushy critique, which is always a lovely thing to receive.

My darling Scout, who has been an excellent baby and toddler, thank you for allowing me to get edits done in great time.

And thank you to my husband Chris, who read every single draft of this book and acted with the same enthusiasm each time. I don't know how you do it, but I'm so lucky to have you. Thank you for being my first reader, for taking care of house and baby things when I need it, and for your constant encouragement. I love you.

About the Author

Tamara M Bailey is a West Australian author of adult and children's books. Her first book for Clan Destine is the fantasy-crime, *Blood and Stone*, but with our imprint, Improbable Press, she has the riveting techno-thriller *The Other Olivia*.

Tamara also has short stories in our anthologies: *Dark Cheer: Cryptids Rising Vol Blue*; and *Clamour and Mischief*.

As Tamara Moss, she's the author of the middle-grade Lintang series, including the award-winning *Lintang and the Pirate Queen*.

www.ingramcontent.com/pod-product-compliance
Lightning Source LLC
Chambersburg PA
CBHW060349030726
47497CB00003B/655